CLARICE

CLARICE

Imogen Radwan

The Book Guild Ltd

First published in Great Britain in 2018 by
The Book Guild Ltd
9 Priory Business Park
Wistow Road, Kibworth
Leicestershire, LE8 0RX
Freephone: 0800 999 2982
www.bookguild.co.uk
Email: info@bookguild.co.uk
Twitter: @bookguild

This work is entirely fictitious and bears no resemblance to any persons living or dead.

Typeset in Aldine 401BT

Printed and bound in Great Britain by CPI Group (UK) Ltd, Croydon, CR0 4YY

ISBN 978 1912083 275

British Library Cataloguing in Publication Data.
A catalogue record for this book is available from the British Library.

To Papa

We have lingered in the chambers of the sea
By sea-girls wreathed with seaweed red and brown
Till human voices wake us, and we drown.

— T.S. Eliot, *The Love Song of J. Alfred Prufrock*

PART I
1940 – 1957

I

On the twentieth of July, 1940, I was born to the sound of Billie Holiday on our record player. The song was *Summertime*, trickling through the speaker like honey, as my mother once described it. She loved her jazz. She loved to dance to those syncopated rhythms, to the toe-tapping soul-expansions of vibrant trumpet solos, to the dark blue notes that propelled it all forward. She had the voice for it too, and would often sing around the house. So haunting and etheric were those tones, they induced a kind of homesickness, even as they lulled me to sleep.

My father preferred classical music. His collection was extensive, our attic filled with countless boxes of records, with everything from fugues to nocturnes. He would often find me pretending to conduct an orchestra, waving my arms about to the imaginary ensemble, or sometimes singing along to an aria, replacing Italian with my own private language.

My parents' love of music was so great that I was named 'Clarice' after Debussy's *Clair de Lune*. Naturally, my parents encouraged my musical endeavours; I began singing at four, the violin at five, and the piano at six. Imaginably, all of this took a great toll on my early social life: I was the child who missed birthdays for choir practice, forfeited tea parties for string ensemble. Soon enough, my classmates learnt not to be too concerned with inviting me.

Indeed, I was the outsider at school. I shall never forget the Christmas of 1946, when my mother told me to write cards to everybody in the class. Having carefully inscribed a message to each of my classmates, I did wonder why I had, for it was not as if anyone would care whether I wrote them a card or not, but, essentially a thoughtful gesture, I saw no harm in it. However, this simple act somehow managed to backfire to my utmost humiliation. As I sat in a corner of the class learning my sums, I was suddenly confronted with the looming figure of Gerald Huneycutt. Gerald was one of the more outspoken members of the class, now towering before me, backed by two or three allies. Holding the cards I had written they proceeded to tear each one in half, as I stared back in horror. How do I begin to describe the sheer embarrassment, the all-consuming dread that came with those impending sobs? I was too afraid to speak, and yet as the silence extended itself, I finally burst into tears. The whole class began to gossip as Gerald and his friends jeered and laughed, and it did not take long for Miss Valance to notice. She hushed the class, her piercing gaze scouring the room, her voice soft, almost lilting, achingly patronising.

"Gerald, would you like to tell me why Clarice is crying right now?"

"I don't know," he mumbled.

Laughter rippled across the room. She glowered at Gerald before continuing.

"Oh, I think you very well do. Reducing our classmates to tears is unacceptable behaviour…"

And so the lecture was given, not that it made much difference. The taunting continued, for reasons I will never understand. Nonetheless, I took my mother's advice and carried on doing what I loved in spite of what others thought.

Eventually, my perseverance somewhat paid off. My solo voice – mostly ignored up until the age of nine – was one day put on show. Snatched from my piano stool and placed centre stage, I was to perform *Over The Rainbow* at our annual school concert. By then, I was at the local preparatory school, St Agnes' House, *where girls become ladies*, or so it claimed in the archaic brochure.

The school hall was stuffed full with gushing parents and envious siblings. My shoulders hunched, I stepped onto the stage like a lamb facing slaughter. The tiny piano stool creaked as Mrs Dubrovsky lowered herself down upon, as if easing herself into an ice bath. The hall went silent; the stillness of the room ran through my hair, goosebumps forming upon my skin; and that first chord – it played with such resonance that it stole the very air from my lungs. I regained one long, deep breath before my cue, taking in all that I could, to be so full of oxygen that I dissolved into it. And I sang; I sang wonderfully, marvellously, perhaps even beautifully. I was no longer a reticent child, but an ardent performer with stories to tell, and people were listening.

The song came to a close; I forced a smile. To my surprise, the audience were applauding. Whole-heartedly they clapped and cheered, confirming once and for all that I could sing. I have always believed that the voice is the most revealing instrument. With the piano, one can express their deepest emotions by putting pressure on certain keys, sustaining the note, speeding up or slowing down; techniques such as these can provide portholes into the soul of the player. Nevertheless, the piano is a curtain, behind which the pianist can hide; guarded against judgmental eyes, the piano acts as a shield, projecting the passion of the piece unto the audience. With singing there is no such curtain. All is laid bare, unadorned, like having one's clothes disintegrate in the middle of the street. It is harder to discount a wrong note, no matter how benevolent the audience may be; they will hear the element of surprise in your inflection. Using one's voice to convey emotion requires a great exposure of the self; singing alone is essentially a monologue with a melody. So when my peers heard me sing, I wondered whether they had gained some kind of insight into my soul. Remarkably, after my performance, they did seem to treat me with a little more respect; it was as if I had proved myself in some way, now that I had sung. This newfound recognition from my classmates meant that by the time I left St Agnes' House, I had made quite a few friends.

★★★

At eleven I was sent to boarding school. It was here that I would meet *those* friends, the two or three that remain in your life forever. At first, all I could think of at that school was how much I wished to go home. The idea of boarding school had conjured up images of beatings, gruel, and hours of homework, and upon arrival, the gloomy place certainly matched my preconceptions. The tall, brick building loomed, leaning over against the grey sky, as if always on the point of falling. To remain there for the next seven years of my life, I would have to "learn to like it", as my mother had suggested.

The influx of glum-faced newcomers, fresh from the train station and their parents' motor cars, were greeted by a sixth former named Joy. She walked briskly ahead with an innocuous smile that looked to be pasted onto her face, a petite girl with a high-pitched voice, and a suspiciously prim demeanour.

"Hello girls!" she chirped, the grin still fixed. It remained fixed as she lead us on a tour of the school, an enormous place with three different playing fields, a chapel and a large, brooding forest surrounding the north and west borders. At intervals she would often stop to survey the group, her eyes darting towards certain individuals, sweeping over others entirely, as if she were scouting for someone she could perhaps take under her wing. We were led to the oldest house within the grounds, where we were met by the matron, a short, stocky woman, somewhat resembling a pit bull terrier. She barely mumbled "hello" as we filed through the narrow door into the hallway, where old school photographs hung; they had faded over the years so much that the subjects' features were hardly perceptible anymore.

"Welcome, girls," came a sharp voice from somewhere above. Everyone looked up to see the tall, lean figure of our housemistress, leant against the twisted iron banister of the staircase. If these sound like the beginnings of a ghost story, that is merely a coincidence. It just so happened that Willow Hill had this aura, I can feel it when I close my eyes now, that poised one always on the edge of this dimension, that allowed one to feel there was always something beyond. Mrs Bristow was a frightening woman; she went about her business in a placid manner, betraying no trace of emotion at any time. She patrolled the corridors as though in a trance, her eyes slowly glancing this way and that, seeking out bad behaviour. When locked onto a likely culprit, she would apprehend the offender and ask, in her calmly unnerving fashion, *what on earth* they thought they were doing. It was often this question alone that served as the greatest deterrent to misconduct.

Perhaps the only thing I found more daunting than Miss Bristow's frosted gaze was the task of making friends. The very prospect stirred up a mixture of anxiety and longing. I had no idea how to go about speaking to new people, how to do 'small talk', how to strike up a conversation; social prowess was something which had always eluded me. I was designated to dormitory five, with three other girls called Hannah, Polly, and Doris.

Polly was the easiest to talk to. An approachable girl with round, inquisitive eyes and large dimples, she had perhaps the least threatening face imaginable.

"I'm Polly," she said, with a broad smile. She had an almost doll-like prettiness, with her bouncing, blonde curls and delicate features, I thought. Polly asked a lot of questions. She was curious, for example, to know why I had been sent to boarding school when my family lived in the area – a reasonable enquiry, I thought, but one that I didn't know the answer to. I supposed that it had something to do with the fact that my mother had once attended the same school. I was also curious to know about her – what she wanted to be when she grew up, what she thought of Doris Day and Patti Page, what it was like to live in London. Little did I suspect that by the time we left school, I would know her better than anyone else did.

I remember seeing Hannah for the first time, when we passed each other in the corridor; her alarmingly pale skin had caught my eye. It was so white, almost translucent. She was far less talkative at first, and paired with my own reserve, the conversation began as an effort. There was no reeling off each other's last words, no thread to which questions attached themselves, but long pauses and awkward laughter. She was actually far more convivial than she initially let on, and once we started talking, we didn't stop for a long time. Hannah told me that she lived on a farm in Suffolk, with three siblings and so many animals that her home verged on a menagerie. Her complexion had startled me at first, as did the amount of medication that she had to take; I soon discovered that everything remotely unearthly about her could be put down to the simple fact that she was anaemic. The mystery was removed, the veil drawn up, to reveal the underlying truth.

8

Over that first year, Hannah, Polly and I shared many experiences together that would affirm our friendship; in the autumn term we would get woken up by Matron at a ridiculous hour – far too early to register fear. We would pull our duvets up over our heads while mumbling protestations under our breath – some of them even blasphemous, *Jesus Christ!* or, *For God's sake!* being among our favourites. If Matron had heard us, we would certainly have been reported to Miss Bristow. Only when she grew irritable would we sleepily stumble out of bed, pull on our woollen tights, shivering as we did, with the consoling thought that there was hot porridge and jam awaiting us in the dining hall.

It was during this term that our first big argument ensued. It was a cold, November day, and we were flicking through Hannah's astronomy book. Hannah was an aspiring astrophysicist, a rare ambition, I had always thought, for a girl. She constantly informed us that within the next twenty years, man would walk on the moon – the US were planning it, apparently, and so too were the Soviet Union. An astronomy book may sound dull for some, but this one was different; a myriad of exquisitely painted planets and galaxies filled each page. One picture which stood out for me was of a red galaxy full of fiery colours; coppers, corals and rubies lit up the surrounding darkness; passion erupting through an empty void.

On one of the pages is Botticelli's Venus, "*Of august gold-wreathed and beautiful*". When the three of us found this page, the subject of romance was quickly brought up, which soon led to questions about which males we found attractive in the school. Of course, we were strictly limited to talking about teachers, being in an all-girls' institution; nonetheless, these were important matters. Polly and I knew that it would be too much of a risk, for example, only two months into our friendship, to confess that Mr Abney was by far the most attractive teacher at the school, being around thirty years younger than any of the others. Gossip is the most prevalent form of conversation at boarding school, and to reveal even something as trivial as which teachers one finds attractive has its ramifications.

"Mr Abney is so handsome!" Hannah marvelled. "I was just staring into his eyes during Latin on Thursday – they're like these perfect blue marbles…"

Polly and I sniggered at the comparison.

"You didn't tell him that, did you?" I joked. "*Tu pulcher oculos.*"

"What?" said Hannah, raising a quizzical eyebrow.

"*Latin*," Polly laughed, and I couldn't help but join in.

It was in our next Latin lesson that Doris, who now also knew about Hannah's crush, decided to share it with the class. Doris seemed to revel in others' humiliation, often dragging her peers into the harsh glare of the spotlight. This was just one of the reasons that I was closer with my other two roommates in the first year; the primary reason, however, was that Doris wanted little to do with us. She preferred to spend her time around girls that acted far above their age, who seemed concerned chiefly with their external appearance and little else – these were the girls who were sent to remove their makeup at roll call, to roll down their skirts, to button up their blouses – and it was the appearance of other girls which they talked about the most. Moreover, Doris was also captivated by scandal and rumour, and it was while Mr Abney was out of the room that she began drumming her pencil against the table, attracting attention to herself and her impending announcement. Luckily, Hannah was in the other Latin class, at least avoiding what I imagine would be complete mortification.

"Everyone shush!" Doris commanded, as the whole class turned their heads obediently towards her. "Hannah fancies

Mr Abney!" she declared. I doubt that anyone could truly have cared less; regardless, they all burst into laughter, and it was not long before the word spread and finally came back around to Hannah.

"I told you that confidentially!" she snapped, evidently furious. "You're the only people I trusted here – why would you tell this to Doris? Now everyone's going to make fun of me! And I bet Mr Abney knows too. Thanks a lot, *friends*," she slurred, a contemptuous glare shot in our direction. A grand betrayal of trust had taken place, and only time would heal the damaged bonds of our friendship. Hannah would dread Latin lessons for the rest of the year, and would use our crime against us in the coming months; but once an initial period shouting, sulking and ignoring each other had passed, apologies were eventually made, and Hannah slowly regained her trust in us.

From what I can remember of my first term at Willow Hill, it was certainly turbulent; each day presented a new drama, in which each of us played some part. Boarding school soon proved itself to be an intimate bubble, in which our trivial concerns rotated around each other. The outside world was of little relevance – what difference did it really make that Churchill was Prime Minister again? What was a nuclear war to us, if it was not actually happening? Whatever happened in the world outside, to us it was just knowledge; if the rest of the world was Rome, we were in Middlemarch.

The next eighteen months or so passed us by as swiftly as the breeze ripples through the rye. Our first two years ended with a nervous smile and a speech day reception, and I felt the waning of my childhood days. That summer Polly and I went to visit Hannah in Suffolk; I remember going down to the lake near her house, and jumping into it from the old tyre tied to the sycamore tree, oblivious to the future, indifferent to the vain concerns of adulthood. I also remember how uneasy I had felt visiting Hannah at the time, for earlier in the year there had been a storm surge in the surrounding villages, in which many had lost their lives. I had half-expected to see some sort of sunken Atlantis, with abandoned houses submerged beneath the sea, inhabited by fish who gaped at the photographs on the mantelpiece. I did not know that these extravagant fears were soon to cease, making way for the stark realism that paves mature thought.

I loved to visit the lake near Hannah's farm. I loved swinging into it, the shadows of the trees making shapes on our faces as we flew through the air, but the real reason I loved being at the water's edge was because there we talked of things that could not be mentioned elsewhere, even in the dormitory at school; it was a kind of unspoken rite between us. Perhaps if the incident with Doris had not occurred, our conversations might have been more open.

One particularly sweltering day, as we dangled our toes in the cold water, Polly broached a question that strikes us all at one point, if not all the time: "Have you ever thought that you were mad?" she conjectured, squinting at the sun, as if talking to its vast glowing face.

"What do you mean?" I replied, in tune with the lethargy of the summer's afternoon.

"Well, I don't know how to explain it – it's sort of like, don't you ever think that everybody else seems so normal – they go about their daily lives and have normal conversations and everything, and it just makes me wonder – all the things that I think about, do they think about them too?"

"Like what?" I asked, now intensely curious to know what exactly it was that she thought about.

"Like what happens when we die, and whether there's really a God." She paused for a moment, searching for the right words, as she noticed Hannah and I exchanging glances. "It just seems like everyone is so happy to get on with their lives without questioning it."

"I don't think that makes you mad," I replied. "I think everybody thinks about stuff like that; how could you not?"

"Maybe you're right, but I don't know, I always end up questioning everything to the point where I end up thinking that maybe – and this is even sillier – that my whole life is just one huge setup, and everyone else is programmed to act just like me. Sometimes I think that everybody in the world, even you," she paused for a moment and laughed inwardly, "even you, are not real... I can't really explain."

And although she could not further elaborate, I believed I had grasped the essence of what she meant; I too was no stranger to questioning the contents of my own mind for the simple reason that I could not gauge anyone else's. The three of us often had this type of conversation, unknowingly discussing the age-old topics that were already heavily traversed by the world's greatest minds; as the late afternoon sky dulled from light blue to blue-grey, we stayed talking by the lake, basking in the last of the sunlight, until it began to fade into darkness.

We would then be summoned by one of Hannah's siblings in to supper. I still recall how painfully anxious I would get over my table manners when eating at someone else's house; if there was one value that my parents ever enforced, it was impeccable etiquette. At home, we would always sit at the table together, and never start eating until everyone was seated. Conversation was polite and trivial, and Father would give a tedious lecture to my brothers if they ate with their fingers. To find that Hannah's family were so relaxed around the table should therefore have been a source of comfort, but their insouciant, uncritical attitude only somehow heightened my anxiety. This might in part have been because the entire experience was a manic rush; her three siblings, all younger than herself, pushed and shoved each other in an attempt to get to the food first, and it was not uncommon for a quarrel to break out. And it was no less frenzied at the table – bread was thrown, fingers were used, and children stood on chairs to sing. I wondered how Hannah could withstand the noise of living in such an unruly household, being unable to imagine my brothers behaving in the same way.

During dinner, I got to know each of Hannah's siblings individually. Olly was eight years old and liked to make conversation with Polly and I, telling us all about the woman he loved – apparently Miss Day, his English teacher, had the most beautiful smile. Then there was Stanley, aged five – a small boy with angelic, curly blond hair and a devilish vocabulary, gaining amusement from cursing loudly for the sake of it. Little Pam, however, was the most monstrous and melodramatic of them all; at just three years old she had acquired the skills of swearing, answering back, crying on cue and bringing Stanley to the end of his tether. Over time it became apparent why we spent so many hours over at the lake, and not nearer to the house.

I spent the remainder of the summer striving to enjoy the peace and solitude down at another favoured waterfront at mine. There happened to be a lake near my own house, and when the weather was nice it was an idyllic spot; the only issue was that the weather got progressively worse as that summer wore on. On the train back from Hannah's, I had envisaged myself happily reclining in the old tethered boat, gazing at clear blue skies with white clouds scudding this way and that, the gentle hum of bees, the sweet smell of pollen. Inevitably, I found myself instead scowling at an off-grey sky, thinking far too much, and feeling a little cold. However, refusing to accept defeat so easily, I decided that this would be the time to begin my long-awaited career as a poet. Writing poetry was something I had always wanted to do, but had somewhat lacked the motivation; this was not helped by my creative writing experiences at school. I used to spend hours perfecting my neatly hand-written stories, whilst my friends simply scrawled something down in half an hour, and yet my efforts led to very little. *Some imagery needed; be certain of the plot; not up to standard* – these were the kind of comments I was presented with after spending days poring over my work, trying to write a story that was truly interesting. The best I could hope for was a *good effort*, which is no more a compliment than it is a simple observation. Now, however, I was alone on the lake, with no teachers or classmates, and a pure urge to create something; it was that all-consuming need to scratch one's mark onto the surface of time and breathe life into a wealth of ideas.

As I began to write my poem, a woman's face entered my imagination. She looked oddly familiar, and yet I could not quite place her. What I did know was that I was compelled to tell her story, and it soon became apparent that her character was an archetype delineated by writers, artists and composers for centuries: the whimsical, romantic, free spirit of a woman, the nonconformist – so different, I thought, to the women I knew, endlessly led by trends and fashion.

Stanza upon stanza, I replicated in words the intricate paint designs on her face, her long golden locks of hair. I described the smell of incense in the air, the tinkling sounds of the bells on her bracelets. Where the inspiration came from, and why I was driven to write about this figure eluded me at the time, but perhaps sitting by the water had conjured the image of a siren's golden tresses. Over the years, however, the image has come to bear more significance than I ever could have anticipated.

"Where have you been all day?" asked my mother, as I returned from the old boat.

"Just the lake."

"The lake? What were you doing all that time? You've been down there since lunch!" she said, bemused.

"If you must know, I was drawing – and before you ask, no, I won't show you what I've done – I'm not finished yet," I retorted, irritated by the mere fact of her asking. I had absolutely no desire to tell her that I had been doing something so introspective, so useless, as writing poetry. I also knew what she would think, that I was a thirteen-year-old girl, living a comfortable life – what experiences could I possibly have to write about? Of course, I knew I could never compare to the great Romantics – I was not deluding myself – but I didn't want her, or worse still, my father, to find out that I had been putting the lyrical pen to paper.

As my mother stirred a saucepan of gravy, she turned to face me.

"Clarice, I've been meaning to talk to you about something." I rolled my eyes emphatically, wondering what she the topic of her lecture would be.

"What is it?" I sighed.

"Well, you see, now that you've… *become a woman,*" I could feel my cheeks flush as she referred to my recent introduction to menstruation, and fumbled for the right words. It was going to be another of her embarrassing mother-daughter *tête-à-têtes.* "You're probably going to start viewing boys in a different way. Sooner or later – preferably much later – you're no doubt going to fall in love with someone, and I want to warn you that there is danger in love."

My mother's eyes darted around the room nervously before she turned to stir the gravy again.

"The thing is, Clarice, you must remember, you needn't rush things. Often when a girl falls in love for the first time, she thinks it will last forever, when in reality, it seldom does. More importantly, the chances of a relationship failing are increased ten-fold if you…" She squinted.

"If I what?"

"If you – fall for someone who is… the wrong type."

I knew exactly what she meant. I had received the warning more than once – but for the sake of the conversation, I feigned ignorance.

"The wrong type?"

"You know… how can I put this?" For a moment she looked as embarrassed as I did. "When, *if*, I was to ever hear that you were stepping out with…"

"The wrong sort?" I offered, trying not to look sarcastic.

"Yes, exactly – if something like that ever happened – if you were involved with some troublesome, or let's say, disrespectful young man, I want you to know that it could end in heartbreak. I know it sounds depressing, but I wanted to warn you before you became wrapped up in these things." She studied the expression on my face, looking for signs of recognition, as she picked her way through this minefield of a topic.

"I'm only telling you this because I've been there before, Clarice, and there are a number of dangers when it comes to the subject of love. I just want to see you making the right choices, that's all. Look for someone respectable, someone from a good home – that much should be obvious – after all, marriage is forever – you really should try to get everything right first time."

It was obvious to me what she was alluding to. Her own marriage to Father had not been without its problems.

"I married your father because I wasn't looking ahead," she continued, confirming my suspicions. "He was very attracted to me, and in all honesty, as much as I loved your father, I was also rather attracted to his success, and so we decided this was a perfectly reasonable foundation for marriage." I supposed they had even managed to convince themselves that they had this profound emotional bond, but really, they had never had too much in common.

"That's not to say we didn't love each other, of course we did – we do, very much. It's just that we've learnt to share our different interests, to compromise." She hesitated for a moment, before speaking her next words. "But he is not, and never has been, the *one*, so to speak."

Noticing the look of astonishment on my face, she paused for a moment, then decided to elaborate further.

"Oh darling, don't look so tragic – let me explain! When I was sixteen, I met a boy called Robbie. We had a brief relationship, until he went off to study in Edinburgh. I assumed the distance would damage things – I'd been warned about long-distance relationships, and so I ended it with him. The thing is, Clare, the time I spent with Robbie, although it was not very a long time, was one of the happiest times of my life, because that was true love. We loved each other, regardless of our flaws and differences – it was unconditional." My mother gazed at me wistfully before continuing. "You know when you fall in love with someone, because suddenly you find yourself looking forward to the next day like never before when you're near them. Everything else becomes so insignificant, and all you can do with yourself is romanticise about life together, and deep down, despite the pain you know it would bring, if you ever lost that person, there would always be a place in your heart devoted solely to them."

Although I had never experienced love in the romantic sense, I felt I knew what she meant.

"Robbie's probably married with children now," she mused, the tiniest flicker of distaste dancing across her eyes as she spoke. Thinking of Robbie and what could have been, I realised, was where my mother must have taken refuge when life was cruel – and I could not blame her for it.

"And then I met your father," she continued, "a few days after my twentieth birthday. It was in the June of 1931, it must have been, and I'd been invited to attend a dinner party at some family friends'. My parents and his were already acquainted, but it was the first time I had ever met him. To be honest, I only went along because I had nothing better to do, but when I saw this beautiful, big house – the very one you are now standing in, I might add – and when I saw how good-looking your father was," she paused, smiling in reminiscence, "I realised that this was an opportunity I should, at the very least, explore." A look of instant regret flitted across her lips as she spoke those words and noticed my eyes widening even more in response.

"I know it sounds mercenary," she fretted, "but as long as he was not insane, or a criminal, or disagreeable in any other way, shape or form, I would have been foolish to pass it by! And he seemed to take a liking to me too – he was paying me compliment after compliment, even going so far as to laugh at my awful jokes, he was such a darling, your father. Over time we grew closer, and one day, just like that, he proposed marriage. There was no way that I could refuse. Robbie was long gone by then, and your father was such a sweet, kind gentleman – it would have been churlish for me to have turned him down. And although I often wonder how things might have turned out if I'd stayed with Robbie, I don't regret a single thing, my dear. If things had not turned out the way they did, well, you or your brothers wouldn't exist, for a start – and the world would have been a far poorer place as a result!"

Her last words had sounded slightly rehearsed to my ears, as though she was still trying to come to terms with a life without the man she truly loved. It is only in retrospect that I can truly comprehend how emotionally distressing this speech had been.

"I suppose what I'm trying to say is – focus on what you have in common, rather than on the differences – and never make decisions based on what's happening at any one point in time – use foresight to picture what kind of life you might be entering into."

Noticing the anxious look on my face, she added, "Look, I just don't want you ending up miserable, Clarice, that's all; there's a tendency for that in our family, you know."

I nodded in agreement. On the one hand, I appreciated her wisdom, but I also felt that she had underestimated my ability to make decisions; for I was not about to marry someone that I barely knew. Perhaps my mother already knew that; I could hardly resent her for wanting to make sure. Yes, she claimed they were in love – although I could not see it myself. All I could see was the way that they looked at each other. Familiarity, they say, breeds contempt, and perhaps that was all it was – contemptible familiarity – not an accumulation of longing and despair over Robbie. But the emptiness between my mother and father seemed to say everything; empty exchanges, empty words and empty gestures, better suited to acquaintances than lovers. In fact, it was conceivable that they had never loved each other at all.

After further contemplating my mother's words that night, I came to a realisation that her advice was in fact golden. She had been trapped in hollow matrimony since she was twenty years old, but I was free, and decided I would not love until I knew it was true. Although it strikes me now, that for all her knowledge on Love, and her emphasis on loving others, my mother had never taught me to love myself.

▮▮

As Hannah and Polly sat on my bed, preening and pouting, I stood in front of the mirror, marvelling at the transformation that only make-up can provide. It was hard to believe that it was my plain face lurking beneath the painted apparition who gazed back at me. My neatly curled hair pleasantly framed my features, and my eyes, their boldness emphasised by mascara, beckoned, drawing in all that was before them; my lips were full, accentuated by red lipstick. The white dress that I wore, with its blue and green floral print, seemed to enhance the new Dior fragrance that I had liberally dabbed on. I wondered if it really was me, this vision in the looking-glass. It seems a kind of deception to say that it was, for I had always been a plain girl – pretty, perhaps – but no exotic or celestial beauty, but at that moment, I was no longer simply an available, amiable female; I now felt invincible. It was a timely discovery, with my sixteenth birthday fast approaching.

My mother had been planning a birthday party for me; at least, that is what she had said. In reality, it was more a summer garden party, with my birthday being the backdrop for it. Whatever the case, because of this joint theme, many people were expected. Not only would there be her friends and the usual relatives, but I had also been allowed to invite whomever I wanted. The age range would therefore certainly be interesting.

The planning of the party was rigorous, if a little overwrought. Not only was there to be a marquee, caterers, and a dress code, but due to all the teenagers expected, a specially prepared dance floor was laid down, and a stage erected. No expense had been spared; my mother had even hired one of the leading dance bands of the day.

Admittedly, at first, the idea of celebrating my sixteenth birthday in such an ostentatious manner did not appeal to my modest tastes; I would have been content with a trip to the beach with a handful of friends, but my mother was in no mood for discussion, despite my protestations.

"Isn't it a bit early to be planning my birthday?" I suggested, knowing full well how much she loved jotting down dates in her diary. "It's not until July."

"Clarice, it takes an awful lot of organisation to plan a big party, you know, and I thought you might want to do something special – after all, you're only sixteen once," she replied, ignoring my concern. I was amazed that my mother, of all people, could have fallen for such an Americanised ideal as the 'sweet sixteenth'. Considering that she had always held a very British grudge against the dominance of American culture, I was left wondering what her real motivation might have been. Perhaps my cynicism had been misplaced – perhaps she really was just thinking of me.

"You would actually let me have a big party?" I asked flatly, almost certain of a catch.

"Just an idea," came the rather unconvincing reply, forcing me to consider the possibility that she had already organised the entire affair. I knew her too well; she had probably already booked and paid for everything too. All she was truly seeking now was my consent, however poorly informed. I should have known better; after all, I had had my whole life to get used to my mother's unassailable plans. In this instance, sensing a legitimate excuse to perhaps hoard copious amounts of alcohol with my friends, I did not complain too much.

And so there I stood, in front of the mirror, marvelling at my own features, enjoying an unusual sense of self-importance, as Hannah and Polly sang along to Doris Day.

"When Jim sees you in that dress he's going to pass out!" Polly giggled.

"Yeah!" chirped Hannah. "Do you think there'll be any kissing tonight? Or are you just going to leap straight to the finish line?" she smirked slyly.

"What? Since when— I don't think he sees me in that way," I protested, my cheeks reddening in embarrassment.

I had met Jim Pray a few months before, during one of our regular jaunts to the café, where Polly, Hannah and I would go after Sunday's chapel. It served as a reward for sitting through monotonous sermons that exalted chastity, prudence, and other such virtues. One Sunday, after we had been walking around town for some time, we found that the café was closed for the day, which was certainly unusual. It was not until we overheard a woman talking in the bookshop next door that we discovered why.

"I think I'm going to have to sell the café," she sighed, addressing the shopkeeper. "I don't know what I'm going to do now," she added, fixing her eyes on a solitary copy of *The Myth of Sisyphus*.

"I'm so sorry for your loss; he was such a good man," replied the owner, before turning to us.

"Can I help you, ladies?" he offered, as we eavesdropped.

"You used to frequent the café, didn't you?" the woman interjected, recognising us almost instantaneously, despite my having no recognition of her.

We nodded in the affirmative.

"John's passed away, I'm afraid," she said. "It was a heart attack last Thursday. A shocking... experience."

John had been the owner of the café, a friendly man who always beamed whenever he saw us, addressing us as 'mademoiselles' in an overstated French accent. As teenagers, we were unaccustomed to death; the concept of someone being there one minute and gone the next was too large for us to fully comprehend. For the next two or three weeks, we avoided the café; handling loss was not something any of us were used to.

Walking in town a few weeks later, and finding that the café had miraculously reopened, we decided to go in. It was surprisingly quiet for the time of day. A well-dressed woman with platinum blonde hair, scarlet lips, a cigarette and an espresso, the epitome of glamour, sat at one table reading a copy of *Vogue*. A young couple laughed between themselves at something amusing. In a corner sat an elderly man, reading a novel with a steaming bowl of soup before him. The interior had remained unchanged; the old wooden chairs, the checkered table cloths, the photograph of New York City – but, naturally, there was a different atmosphere in John's absence.

The new waiter, a young man who could not have been more than a couple of years older than me, showed us to a table by the window. This was an excellent vantage point for watching the world go by, a favourite pastime of ours. We watched the rain-drenched shoppers, judging each one brutally. Watching people, I find, is one of life's smallest and greatest pleasures. The whole process in itself confirms the curiosity of the human mind, for there is something so simplistically wonderful about sitting in a café window, or at a bus stop, or on a park bench, and watching the motions of our fellow beings, scuttling about with their individual lives. On this particular day, we observed a middle-aged woman in

24

weathered clothes, and a face to match, a pink-skinned man with an angry expression, and a scathing force to his stride, and as usual, we learnt a little more about humanity than we had known before. However, we soon tired of watching the passers-by, shifting our attention to the attractive new waiter, whom we would soon come to know as Jim.

"Wow, I could swim in his eyes, they're so blue... and his accent, it's like in the movies!" Hannah marvelled. Polly and I shrank into our seats – we were sure that he had overheard everything – but Hannah wasn't wrong, he was very good-looking indeed. In fact, there was something so ridiculously attractive about this boy with the American accent, that I felt my cheeks flush a little when he came back with our order.

How strange, I considered, those changes of feeling that come into play, exposing the law of attraction for what it is – lust! Since time began, we have been paralysed by it. When caught up in the moment, we are blinded to everything else, as though none of it matters. The power it holds has been prominent and recorded throughout history; Keats, for example, devoted volumes of his poetry to the subject – *The Eve of St.Agnes, La Belle Dame Sans Merci, Lamia* – Porphyro did not feel love, but lust! It takes but a matter of seconds to form that first impression, and yet it is like buying a record based on the artist's physical appearance. My initial attraction to this young man, I supposed, was just as superficial; yet, as I got to know him, I realised that his character actually matched his surface qualities, which I find to be a rarity in itself. I had never met anyone so peaceful and considerate, and yet so driven in his ambitions.

"What I really want to do with my life," he explained that rainy, Sunday afternoon, "is write screenplays for the movies, you know, or something 'behind the scenes', to do with writing." If anyone had the stamina to survive in such a competitive industry, I decided arbitrarily, it was him.

"I want to redefine the world of film," he continued. "You know, draw away from the traditional, chronological way of doing things, go down a more exploratory route – multiple plots, shared messages, you know, that kind of thing."

Hannah, Polly and I nodded, pretending that we understood. I felt Hannah playfully kick me from under the table, and her subtle teasing continued on the way back to school, and for the rest of the afternoon.

We began to visit the café more regularly after that day; we were really beginning to enjoy Jim's company. He was the only boy that had ever taken any interest in me, and this had a strange effect, my mother's words on love now often returning to me. It did, however, occur to me that had Jim been plainer looking, I might not have taken the time to get to know him, and each time it did, I would flinch at my own shallow disposition.

"I'm only working for the extra cash," he said one afternoon, flashing that brilliant smile he had; he could have starred in any film he wrote, I thought to myself.

"So you've only just moved over from America?" Hannah asked.

"Yeah, a couple of months back – my father's a lawyer, and he was transferred to London. But he actually grew up in England. And then we've got this café going on the side, which was my mother's idea."

"That's quite a big change," Hannah said, flashing him a flirtatious smile.

"It definitely is. How about I get you all some real drinks on the house? My dad keeps too much beer for one man in the cellar," he hesitated for a moment, before adding, "but only if you want them?"

"What do you think?" Hannah replied dryly, holding him in her gaze.

After a couple of beers and a rambling conversation, it felt as though this was the only way to go about making friends. Alcohol, I was discovering, seemed to be the key that unlocked my inhibitions, revealing the person that I wished to be more like. Certainly, it was helping me further my acquaintance with Jim. I'd had little drinking experience before, and it did only take a couple of beers before I was fooling around, laughing and feeling everything. But before long, we had to be back at school, and I dragged myself away from that table with a newfound bliss, a sort of inner-contentedness that I had never before experienced.

Before the party had got into full swing, a few of the guests were milling around in the garden. My Aunt Grace was looking lost and mildly drunk, and Granny Beamish was wandering around taking pictures for the family photo album. Mother was fussing over Granny Stratford's dogs, huskies – she had always gone for difficult breeds – who were yapping noisily, while Father and Uncle Alexander were sitting on a bench smoking pipes, and discussing, I presume, one of their three favourite topics: politics, golf, or bridge.

As the party got underway, the sky dimmed, the music got faster, and the dancing got wilder; *Rock Around the Clock* was playing and the floor was filled. Moving from partner to partner, doing elaborate twists which most likely looked awful, I lost myself completely; how thrilling it was to be young and drunk! I was so captivated by the atmosphere, that when I found myself dancing with Jim I was not even slightly nervous; that is, until Pat Boone's *I'll Be Home* began to play. Yes, that lazy love song filled the air as I danced with the boy that I longed to kiss more than anything else; thinking of it now, I don't know whether to laugh or cry; it was a tragic comedy of mixed feelings, so distinctively adolescent.

As we danced, movements that had been lively and fluid

became stiff and awkward on my part; Jim had pulled me closer, and it was becoming fast apparent that he felt the same way as I did. Knowing this effected a strange sensation; I was partially euphoric, and part filled with dread – for it was my sixteenth birthday and I had never danced so intimately with anyone in my life; and now there I was, up close with a boy that made me stutter when I spoke. Almost my entire circle of friends and family surrounded us, and this only heightened a growing sense of panic; our dance was bound to cause speculation. When I closed my eyes I felt the goosebumps on my arms, and when I opened them, I was confronted with the face that had managed to stir my heart into avid turmoil. The music soon became a distant background noise, drowned out by the sound of my own heart beating, as Jim leaned in and spoke.

"Do you feel the same way as I feel about you?"

In a word, I was stunned. For all the signs he had been communicating, I had never imagined for a moment that it would actually come to this. He was the person that mingled with everyone, but showed no particular attachment to any one individual. When it came to girls, he was affable, but he never seemed to get overly enthusiastic about anyone in particular. For so long I had fantasised about this moment; that it was actually happening – in reality – gave me the opportunity to respond the way I had always wanted to.

"I really like you too," I responded, amazed that my words had come out in an orderly fashion. And then something unusual happened; I found that I was biting my bottom lip, almost involuntarily, as if to say *kiss me*. This wasn't an attempt at flirtation, since the act seemed to come entirely from the unconscious. Nonetheless, it was not long before we had kissed under the willow tree.

Our departure from the marquee had been so hasty, that I failed to realise we were being watched by those who had caught sight of our escape. This, however, did not bother me, for perhaps rather naïvely, I felt that all my personal misfortunes were being compensated for by this very moment.

Hannah and Polly were standing in the marquee, clearly gossiping. Noticing that I had noticed them, they quickly turned away. We decided to return to the marquee, to eliminate any further suspicion, changing partners. I went straight for Polly, who looked eager for me to tell her about what had just happened.

"Nicely done!" she said with a wide grin, before we both burst into laughter.

"I was right! I knew it!" Hannah chimed, as she, Doris and some other girls joined us.

In the midst of our innocent and light-hearted dancing, we were soon approached by a group of boys – Jim being one of them.

"Hey, we've got booze and cigarettes if you want to join," said my cousin, George.

"Sure," replied Hannah, nudging me in the ribs. I smiled back at her, wishing I could have been as carefree as she was.

"We can all go the hermitage," I suggested, the others nodding in agreement.

The family that had lived in the property decades before us had constructed the hermitage in the early nineteenth century. There were three old sofas, an armchair, and a bare lightbulb hanging from the ceiling. The only original fixture that remained was a small round table and the Argand lamp which sat on it. At the time, it was fashionable to employ one of high intelligence to be a hermit and live in the hermitage for the sole purpose of musing over philosophical matters. The building resembled a tiny cottage, with only one window, a dark wooden door and a flagstone tiled floor. The hermitage served well not only as a place for quiet brooders to contemplate the meaning of life, but for groups of teenagers to push themselves into ruin, which was exactly what we were doing, downing shots of brandy and filling our lungs with delectable smoke in the sparsely furnished room.

I sat next to Jim, as the others were sprawled randomly about the room. I thought about what had just occurred, wondering if it was just a meaningless drunken kiss, if we were we still friends, if it was over now, or if we were more than just friends.

"So what's going on with you two?" Hannah pressed. I was not sure if she had wanted to embarrass me, or was simply asking out of innocent curiosity. Jim looked at me, equally uncertain.

"I don't know…"

"I don't know, either," offered Jim, to which we all fell about laughing, as George topped up our glasses.

The truth of the matter was, we had in fact made it official by force of impulse – the act itself seemed to affirm something – and thankfully, I had lost nothing in the process. We had become something more than friends, and as I knew all along, it was precisely what I had wanted.

It must have been around midnight when my mother found us in the hermitage. Fortunately, there was nothing unorthodox to witness, only an over-intoxicated Polly, and a girl I did not recognise, both sprawled out on a sofa, having lost consciousness. The rest of us had been excitedly discussing how much fun it would have been to have lived in the nineteen twenties.

"I thought I'd find you in here! Oh dear, are Polly and her friend alright?"

Unaware of her presence, we had all suddenly turned round, like rabbits caught in the headlights of a motor car.

"Oh dear, poor Polly – don't worry, nobody's in trouble

– just don't tell her father!" My mother laughed, shaking her head.

That was one of the things I loved about my mother – she knew when to sidestep the rules – and it was further evidence, if needed, that my parents were essentially different sorts. Father, with his austere and authoritarian ways, would have been unable to turn a blind eye, but my mother was liberal in her attitudes; a believer in adventure and squeezing every last drop of enjoyment out of life.

"Is there a reason you were looking for us?" I asked icily, slightly threatened by her unexpected appearance in the room.

"No, but people are beginning to leave, and it's probably about time to call it a night. I'm sorry, but there's not enough space to have all of you lodging here – all of the spare rooms are taken, I'm afraid – but Clarice – do you mind coming and saying goodbye to the Beamishes? They've been asking after you."

Looking bedraggled, makeup now smeared, we stumbled happily out of the hermitage, and into the surprisingly bright, moonlit garden. I could feel a headache beginning as I stood, waving goodbye to our guests – a lingering kiss reserved for Jim – out of sight of my mother, naturally. Although I normally enjoyed it when Hannah and Polly stayed over, tonight, I rather wished it was Jim staying, but there was no use in hoping for that. As we sloped off to bed, giddy with the night's events, I had not a care in the universe.

After that night, Jim and I spent a lot of time together, preferring long walks and good conversation to going dancing, or the theatre. Our talks ranged in topic from the profound, to the inane – but they were always injected with a good dose of humour. Our conversations often turned into heated debates, or even arguments, but good-natured ones. Even in the innocence of our youth, we wanted to make this newfound bond work, so very much.

It was early September; the sun was warm and the breeze cool, and the leaves were still a healthy shade of green. Jim and I were taking a walk in the woods, admiring the old viaduct which loomed above us. We had been discussing, in our own pretentious way, the difference between modern and traditional jazz, when Jim suddenly stopped in his tracks.

"Is it too early to be saying things like 'I love you'?" he said, avoiding eye-contact with me. I felt my heart palpitate faster, but it was wonderful, like falling thousands of metres down from the sky, leaving one's stomach behind. It felt magnificent.

"No." I smiled coyly.

"That's a relief, because I don't think I could stop myself." Now I could not bring myself to look directly at him.

"Really?" I replied. "That's funny, because I was thinking the same thing."

It amazes me how one moment, we can be so clever, accomplished and sophisticated, and then we abandon it all for love, as if we have not noticed by now that it so seldom ends well – the irrationality we are capable of is staggering: Romeo drank poison, Anthony ran a sword through his chest, Queen Victoria mourned for forty years. Is it so hard to accept that our hearts will inevitably shatter into a million pieces, and our tears sting our cheeks as they flow towards the ground?

Hannah, Polly and I were in the café on another rainy Sunday noon, when a couple entered, both dark-skinned and dressed impeccably; I wondered whether they had just come from church. The woman looked around thirty, the husband slightly older. As Jim took their order, they smiled politely at him. She was incredibly demure – too demure, as though she were walking on eggshells. Her husband seemed more relaxed and at one with the world around him; I could see how this dynamic could work well in balancing a relationship – one could see that they were in harmony. However, a group of men, sitting by the window, who had been watching the couple for some time, did not seem at all interested in the subject of harmony.

"I thought I moved here to get away from the nig-nogs," scoffed one of the middle-aged men. "Since when was old Surrey a place for coloureds, anyway?" he continued, this time even louder, almost as if he wished to be overheard. At first, we had all pretended not to notice, as Jim finished serving another customer, and we took another sip of tea, but it was becoming increasingly difficult to ignore the comments.

"Coming to our country, taking *our* houses away from us; just go back to Africa, you wogs!" the same man continued, as the group fell about laughing, obviously finding the bigotry hysterical. By now, Jim had stopped serving. He stood akimbo, glaring at the group.

"Excuse me, gentlemen," he spat out with the utmost contempt, but the group mimicked him as their laughter took on a wild crescendo.

"*Excuse me, gentlemen...* Oh my God, you've gotta be joking! A yank!" cried the ring leader. "Gets better and better by the minute!"

"Get out," Jim hissed through gritted teeth.

"Make me!" came the reply. "And when you've failed at that, you can sod off back to America, you prat!"

"What on earth is going on here?" asked Jim's mother, appearing suddenly in the doorway from the kitchen. But the obnoxious group were far from pacified by her unexpected presence.

"What's to got to do with you, love?"

"Don't worry, I'll take care of this," said Jim tersely, putting down his tray and going to stand between his mother and the group of men. Suddenly, and without warning, the group stood up, chairs scraping as they shoved them away.

"Alright, we're not paying for this crap!" shouted the leader, as they marched out of the café.

"It's okay – your money isn't welcome here, and neither are you!" said Jim's mother curtly, before heading back into the kitchen.

Before anyone could catch their breath, Jim had rushed out of the café. It was only then that I realised what was happening. Without hesitation, the girls and I ran after him, but it was too late; the fighting had already begun. Before I had the chance to intervene, Jim had been punched in the face, with blood now streaming down it – looking a lot worse than it actually was. He rapidly collected himself, and returned the punch with force, laying his attacker out on the floor.

As though a starting gun had been fired, the rest of the group joined in. No matter how strong or resilient Jim was, he was no match against these men, kicking him, punching him in the stomach, spitting in his face. And then I did something completely ridiculous. I took a few steps back, stopped, and then leapt into the calamity at an alarming speed. Before I could regret the decision, I felt my arm being grabbed, and was thrown hard onto the ground, a searing pain shooting through my entire body as I landed on the pavement. As I lay on the ground, the couple who had been the object of the group's taunting came running out of the café to see if I was alright, the woman taking my hand and squeezing it gently in hers.

"You poor thing! Are you okay, dear?" She smelt of peach and bergamot. I nodded my head meekly, looking around to see what had become of Jim and the group of men.

"Have they gone?" I asked. "Where's Jim?"

"They seem to have run away," replied the woman, passing me a crisp, white handkerchief.

I looked around and noticed Jim kneeling, rubbing his eyes. Just at that moment, a monumental crash appeared to tear the skies asunder; the heavens opened, and the rain began pelting down.

"Jim! Are you okay?" I asked, rising to my feet to help him up.

"I'm alright, just a couple of bruises, that's all."

And we had been reduced to this: a sorry display of defeat, a primitive state of disorientation. A woman passed by with her large umbrella and looked down at us pitifully, making a tremendous effort to step around the scene. Ignoring her presence, he sat up.

"I'm sorry, Clare – I didn't mean for that to happen, but I thought I'd left people like that behind, back in Indiana. That kind of behaviour is expected there, but I guess there are idiots wherever you go. They wanted a fight, so I gave them one."

As we sat down inside, Jim's mother dabbed some iodine on a piece of cotton wool, applying it liberally to his cut, and generally fussing over her son.

"So is Indiana really that bad?" I asked.

"Well, let me tell you a story," he continued, taking a sip of tea. "There was a woman who lived in my town; all the men wanted her, and I'm sure she slept with plenty of them, even though she was married. Funny thing was, her husband was completely unaware that she was sleeping around. He treated her like a trophy; he would walk around town with her on his arm, believing she was Lady Luck herself. He took her to nice restaurants, bought her designer clothes – all kinds of materialistic gestures. That was why she married him – he needed a wallet the size of Indiana to fit all his money in. Of course, he believed that she loved him for his sophistication, and that she liked older men, or some-such crap. Really, they were both just white trash.

Anyway, there was a ranch nearby, where the owners had hired two or three black ranch hands. One of them was well-built, and the women agreed that he wasn't exactly bad looking; he had the face, the body, the charm, and so on, but I'm sure he was smart enough to steer clear of the white women, who only spell trouble. But this married woman, she was prepared to break the rules.

One day, they were caught in the act in one of the barns by the ranch owner, who had to admit, if anyone had done any pushing themselves onto the other, it looked like she was the instigator. Anyway, you know what this guy got for his crime? Initially, two years in the slammer – but that wasn't good enough for the husband, who protested at the 'unwarranted mercy' the judge had shown to a 'nigger rapist'. The bastard deserved to swing, he told him. Obviously the state couldn't do that, no matter how well connected the guy claimed to be. The maximum he could get was ten years, and they seemed more than happy to throw the book at him as it already stood.

Still, it wasn't good enough for old Mr Clack – the husband – who tried bribing them with ridiculous amounts of money, but they just wouldn't accept it, thank God. It was just too much of a risk. So he got ten years, and she a beach house in the Hamptons.

The weird thing was, he seemed to be completely oblivious to the fact that his wife was sleeping with most of the guys in town – either that, or he didn't mind – just so long as they were white. But anyway, Clack was still furious that the 'damn nigger' had got off so lightly for 'raping his wife' and he just couldn't let it go. The bastard was free to roam around and breathe in the air of his cosy little cell in the state pen, and it drove him mad.

The word soon got around that he was planning on killing the guy, but then something happened. It could have been that he finally woke up to his wife's infidelity, or maybe he just snapped – I don't know for sure, but one night he gets it in his head that he's going to have to kill them both – not just the ranch hand, but his wife too.

So he starts beating her; then he drags her down to the state prison waving his army issue revolver in the air, shoots the guard, snatches the guy from his cell, and takes both of them down to the nearest churchyard. He'd completely lost his mind by now, so he starts telling them to get down on their knees and beg Christ for forgiveness. He wasn't even a churchgoer, but he'd insist he was a good Christian man if anyone was to ask.

Anyway, finally, he shoots them both in the head and gets some rope from the car; then he hangs them from a tree, side by side, 'where whores and niggers belong'. Now I'm not saying they're all like that in Indiana. Obviously, not everyone's like Clack – but most of them have that mentality

– that whites are superior to blacks. The worst thing is – they're not afraid to show it. It's insane."

I have always seen prejudice as a strange thing; when precisely does one decide that another is inferior based merely on the pigmentation of their skin, or the coarseness of their hair? Is it not ironic to think, for instance, that those soldiers in World War Two, who had belittled the Jamaican Royal Air Force – who helped them to win – were too blind to recognise that they were fighting together against the same evil? An evil based on separation and prejudice.

I now felt that I could better understand how racism worked, and it affected Jim. Due to the encounter with the men in the café, he now knew that the cruel wind of inequality blew on both sides of the Atlantic; its icy gust so cold and bitter, no matter the continent.

★★★

I was called out to the school office one afternoon, during natural science. It was obviously something important, I imagined, for I had never been pulled out of class before.

"I'm really very sorry to have to tell you this, Clarice, but your grandfather has passed away." Mrs Jones paused for a while, allowing the news to sink in, before continuing. "First of all, may I offer my sincerest of condolences," she added. "Naturally, I have spoken to your parents, and we all agree that it's only fair that you should have some time off school."

The news would not register at first. Never having lost anyone close to me before, I had found it hard to be too phased by death; it was something that happened to others, not to me. It wasn't that I believed myself and those around me to be immortal – of course not – but it seemed like something so distant – so removed from my everyday life – that I found it impossible to take it seriously. With the news of Pa's death, however, I was forced to reconsider this naïve view.

I had always admired Pa, my mother's father, who had fought in the First World War, and was something of a poet. His poetry was never published, but without doubt, it deserved to be. Why it wasn't, was perhaps due to the great influx of post-war poetry at the time; people came home horrified – empty – their minds forever recalibrated. And when one is at a loose end, what is better counsel than paper and pen? I suppose many writers' works at the time conveyed the same meanings, repeating and echoing each other, unique only in style; but it was all the same, about the way a mind will never recover from ultimate catastrophe; he questions his sanity, his purpose and his humanity. Pa wrote nothing different, but he wrote well, and I understood.

I caught the four-thirty train into town, where my mother was waiting for me. The brisk February air numbed me as I walked slowly towards her, feeling slightly aloof. I had never had to comfort her before – it had always been the other way around, but suddenly here she was – the woman who had taught me so much, now in need of my support, and although I was not sure what to do, I knew that I owed it to her to be there for her, somehow. We hugged on the platform for what seemed like an age, before making our way out of the station, and back to the car.

The funeral was held a week later at the City of London Cemetery. Pa's wishes were that he should be buried at St. Paul's Cathedral, or Westminster, but despite his heroics during the war, permission was refused. Instead, he lies in the soft green grass of East London, which, although very much a second choice, was still a beautiful spot.

As I stood over the open grave, with the last remaining rays of sunlight playing across the newly dug earth, my heart felt heavy. The scent of freshly cut grass combined with the mordancy of death infiltrated my nostrils, as my eyes glazed over with tears. One of the few people on this earth who had really believed in me – who had guided and supported me – was now gone forever. I should have been able to accept the comfort my mother tried to offer me that day, but I found it impossible. I had always underestimated her as a child, which perhaps prevented me from becoming too attached. The way she would get so overworked over such trivial matters made her seem slightly neurotic at times. With complete disregard for any given situation, she would, without hesitation, shout at my younger brothers over the smallest of violations. Her tellings off were loud, intrusive affairs. It could not have been good for her heart; I was so aware of this, in fact, that I made a point of avoiding contentious issues, so as to not upset her. The whole time that I grew up in her household, it seemed that this was not the life she had wanted. She was living in one world, and thinking in another. Perhaps it upset me a little that neither I, nor my brothers, nor my father, could fill the void that was Robbie's absence. Of course, I still had Jim, and for that, I was very grateful. I had known him for less than a year, but time did not seem to have anything to do with how I felt. When I was with Jim, I did not need faith, guidance or support; we were just a pair of lovers in a world so perfectly obscure, and nothing else mattered. Now that Pa was no longer around, Jim's importance in my world grew enormously.

For a long time after the funeral, I would often wonder where Pa might have gone to. I had entertained the idea that his essence lived on as a ghost; this is probably because at Willow Hill, we had kept a collective library of ghost stories between us. The most memorable was one that Hannah had told us back in our second year. We had stayed up late one October night, frightening each other with tales of being buried alive and haunted houses. As if on cue, the wind was howling outside, as the rain beat against the windowpanes, while we were tucked up in bed with mugs of cocoa, under the dim light of my bedside lamp. One could even hear the rattling of the wind against the bare branches of the late-autumn trees.

"You know," Hannah whispered, trying to keep quiet. "One of the former girls here at the school, back in the nineteenth century, thought that she could see the devil. Everywhere she went, he followed. Apparently, he could take on different forms, too; sometimes, he was a tall, dark figure in a cape with no face, but when he was angry, he changed. His face became worn and wrinkled. Veins showing all over. It terrified her. His nose was bright red, but not in a funny way, like a clown; it looked painful and it was peeling, and his teeth – they were the scariest. There were gaps between each spear, like a great white's jaws. Blood dripped from his mouth and down his chin. The skin on his hands seemed to stretch like fabric pulled across a tight surface, his disgusting yellow nails poking out the ends of his twig-like fingers. As for his eyes, he didn't have any – just empty, black circles that oozed blood; but he could always see her.

He possessed the girl one night, so that she hurt herself. Eventually, the matron realised that something wasn't quite right – there had been too many stories and rumours. She decided she ought to check the situation, and watch the girl carefully. By then, however, it was too late. She walked down the hallway, floorboards creaking as she went, finally arriving outside the girl's dorm – which happens to be the very same one we're sitting in now. As the door creaked open, the matron stopped dead in her tracks; there before her was the girl, crucified; hanging upside-down against the wall, her body covered head to toe in crosses that she had carved into herself.

On stormy nights she's said to wander the corridors, her cries of pain intertwined with the howling of the wind. If you're ever unlucky enough to suddenly feel yourself grow cold, the rumour is that her spirit is passing through you, desperately trying to possess someone – looking for revenge."

We sat in terrified silence, looking at Hannah, who suddenly smiled. "Obviously she can't really, because she's a ghost – she's been trying to possess people for years but she just drifts straight through them!"

We began to giggle, and after a few seconds, we were laughing loudly, albeit nervously. Admittedly, I was impressed with Hannah's storytelling, regardless of whether or not her tale was true, its morbid and gruesome nature had certainly sparked a train of thought, especially so recently after Pa's funeral. It was not that I was becoming perversely fixated on the concept of death in any way, but simply less afraid of it; I was beginning to realise the value of just thinking about it, despite that conclusions could not easily be drawn. Whatever happens when we die, another's death has a great impact on the way we view our own lives, if only for a short period. Some realise its value as a precious and ephemeral entity; others realise its ultimate nothingness, its inherent lack of meaning. I began to see death as a real possibility, a *towards-which*, as Heidegger put it, our actions are continually propelled, and there was something strangely liberating about that.

IV

In the summer of 1957 I turned seventeen. Around this time I was beginning to consider my future options, which in retrospect were remarkably limited. Marriage and motherhood seemed to be the predominant path for many young women at the time, and as my mother had often stressed, there was no reason why I should not have been thinking about it at the ripe young age of seventeen. It all looked rather simple; I would wait a few years, Jim would hopefully propose, I would grin enthusiastically and shriek *Yes! Yes, I do!* and we would have a perfect white wedding in a chapel in the countryside, and all would be well. But the imagination need not restrain itself there; soon after we would be blessed with our first child – our pride, our joy – whose precocious nature would be what all the neighbours were talking about. We would send he or she off to a little village school, by which time we would have had our second child. After perhaps a third, we would marry off our eldest – assuming they did not first attend university – and having raised three children, we would then retire into comfortable lives, and take frequent visits to the south of France. We would die contented beings, with the consolation that perhaps our children might someday contribute to the world a little more than we had.

The only other option, furthering my education, looked a less clear route to success that came with no guarantees, but as long as my grades remained high enough for the following year, I knew I wouldn't have too much trouble getting into university. As much as the idea of staying at home, cooking and drinking tea in the garden with other housewives appealed to me, it all seemed rather limiting. Instead I was considering studying music, so that I could perhaps become a critic, while also composing some of my own material; I revelled in the prospect of writing film scores, and imagined myself one day working on one of Jim's future creations. I wanted to implement melodies, harmonies, textures, rhythms and so forth to move my audience to tears, as other composers have done for me. I am fascinated by the way in which sound affects us, how it can transform an entire atmosphere from dismal to vibrant. I made a habit of putting a scene to every piece of music I listened to; Vivaldi's *Spring* for a farce set in an English rose garden, the clinking of teacups, the twirl of a parasol; Tchaikovsky's *Barcarolle* for a bird's-eye view over a cold expanse of derelict land; Elvis' *Hound Dog* for a group of teenagers running across the beach in the summer, and so on. Dissecting a piece to extract its elements, to find out what it was that had *that* effect, was something I never tired of; and if I could anatomise music and understand its elements, then I could surely put something together too. After all, I had not endured years of music theory for nothing.

By this point in my life I had completed all of the grades on the violin and piano. I adored, like both of my parents, Debussy's piano works, and had learnt to play a few carefully selected favourites. I hoped to one day compose the most effusive pieces of all time, and in doing so, forever change the face of contemporary music, combining the old with the ground-breaking to create something that was both original and yet firmly rooted in its time. I wanted the vivacity of Parker with the innovation of Gershwin; I wanted jazz, I wanted rock and roll, I wanted swing, blues, diatonicism and atonalism; I wanted to gather music from every corner of the earth, from every point in time, to amalgamate and impel a world of creation at my feet. But in spite of all these lofty aspirations, I still had a year of school left, and for the time being, the only plan I had made was to enjoy the summer.

On one particular day that July, an idea in my head had begun to form itself into a tune. It was like the first two notes of *Für Elise* played on strings, yet repeated, and slowed down over a falling motif in the upper register of a scintillating piano. As the components slowly came together, I realised that the tune I was by now humming was *Aquarium* from Saint-Saëns' *Le Carnaval des Animaux*. I hadn't a clue as to why I was humming this precise melody, as I couldn't distinctly remember the last time I had heard it. My father used to play it to me when I was very small, and as melodies tend to do, this one had come back to haunt me. As I heard it play in my mind, I instantly built a film scene around it. If you have ever heard the piece, you will understand how beautiful, enchanting, and wistful it is. I decided to go and look for the record in the attic; after all, it was a hot, lethargic day, and I had little better to do. Humming the eerie tune to myself, I followed the narrow staircase up to the dusty attic, in search of that weathered old cardboard box where I knew it was kept.

Through the small window at the end of the attic, the sun streamed onto the bare floorboards as I moved trance-like across them, towards the stacks of vinyl. After some rummaging, I managed to find the album I was looking for, wedged between Satie and Ravel in the box marked 'Classical'.

I held the record up to the light, and as I did so, the floorboard beneath my feet became loose. In an attempt to put it back in place, I lifted it up, only to find what looked like a large mirror underneath it. Intrigued, I began recklessly pulling up the surrounding boards.

The mirror was oval, full-length and covered in dust and insect carcasses. Consumed by intrigue, I hauled the object out from under the floor, took it to my bedroom, fetched a bucket of water and began to wipe it down. As the debris of years, perhaps decades, was sponged away, the mirror's frame adopted a gold hue, and the previously ambiguous protrusion at its top became an exquisitely sculpted angel. The frame was also elaborately engraved with flowers, birds and leaves, that seemed to grow wildly around the edges of the glass. I wiped off the final traces of dust – the metamorphosis was complete – the mirror was leant up against the wall, facing the bed.

I then had to return to the attic to replace the floorboards, before the gaping hole in the floor was discovered by someone else. Before doing so, however, I noticed another artefact that had evidently been lying beneath the mirror. It was a small, brown leather book, with a name inscribed on the front: Amelia Parriton. Parriton. The name struck a chord within me. It had a familiar ring of grandeur to it. I could almost imagine the type of family it belonged to; there would have been a Lady Parriton – the commander of the house, the typical nineteenth-century literary figure who spoke in epigrammatic wit. She would have been married to Lord Parriton, cultivator of the household's income, and often taken for granted; he would have been employed in politics, or something of the sort. Their children – perhaps Amelia, and maybe an Augusta or a Percival – would most certainly have been taught Latin and advanced mathematics by a private tutor, and would then have gone to Oxford or Cambridge. The household staff would have been copious: a gardener, a cook, maids, and of course, without doubt, a hermit – who lived in the hermitage. As my imagination ran wild, it suddenly struck me: the Parritons had lived here before us, back in the previous century. Indeed, they were the family that had built the hermitage and the conservatory, and all the other Romantic features of the house that I had always so admired.

Picking up the antique book, I opened it onto the first page, the faint scent of weathered paper rising from it like an arcane mist. After all this time, the pages had turned almost brown, and had grown delicate and flimsy, as if on the point of disintegration. At the top of the page Amelia had written the date; the black ink whose intricate loops delicately glided across the paper denoted that it was the seventeenth of February, 1830 – more than a century ago. The entry read as follows:

It is utterly inconceivable! How am I expected to reside in this dreadful attic for the entirety of my life? Why do they not just throw me in the hermitage? At least then I would not have to hear the sound of their voices below. My parents hold the belief that I, an intelligent and grown woman of far sounder judgement than they, am quite mad. Perhaps I am so intelligent that I cannot comprehend my own thoughts, but mad? That is a perverse fallacy! It is not I, but they, who are deranged!

Not two weeks have passed since the terrible accident occurred, and already I feel I have paid a lifetime's penance. I could have saved my brother from drowning, I am sure, if only I had persevered. I did jump in after him, but I could not swim, and the weight of my clothing, and carrying him, impelled me to struggle to the shore in order to save myself. I clambered out of that wretched water, leaving Peter behind, as I ran back to the house, bewildered and terrified. I must have looked a wreck, as Mother studied me accordingly. Stricken with panic, I was still screaming, but the words finally parted from my lips – that poor Peter was drowning. Without hesitation, we sprinted to the lake. However, by the time we had got there, Peter was nowhere to be seen. Mother dived into that cold, murky water, ruining her dress and appearance; I had never seen her act so instinctively in my life.

After what must have been five minutes – although they felt to be fifty – she returned to the bank of the lake – without Peter. By the time Father had initiated a rescue procedure, he could not be revived. Mother and Father directed the blame onto myself, implying that I had pushed him in. Confused and scared, I asked them what they could possibly have meant, but they replied plainly that I was possessed by a daemon which had caused me to do it! The madness! If I have ever been entirely honest in my life, that time is now, and I swear on all that is good, I am by no means possessed. My parents are delusional from grief, and I believe that this is the cause of their accusations; but I will not let myself be blamed for this – not by others, and certainly not by my own conscience.

The events which I have related in this entry have left me upset and wounded, and certainly not accountable.

Closing the book in mild confusion I wondered if this journal entry was genuine, or if it was a joke, perhaps placed there a few years ago for someone like me to find and believe entirely. I wondered if anybody else had stumbled across the mirror and the journal before me. I thought to keep this discovery a secret, so that I could read it without interference. I also wished to protect Amelia's personal thoughts – assuming that she ever existed. After carefully replacing the floorboards, I decided to tell my mother about the mirror; I knew it would interest her, but she had apparently never set eyes on it before.

"It must be worth a decent amount – just look at those beautiful engravings – the amount of work that must have gone into it!" she exclaimed after her initial examination of the object.

"Mother!" I cried in protest. "I don't want to sell it! I was actually hoping I could keep it."

After some minutes bargaining with her, I was allowed to keep the mirror. It fitted in perfectly, matching the general softness and femininity of my bedroom – a design which had been partly dictated by myself, although mostly by my mother. Leaving it slanted against the wall, I adjusted the mirror to be at an angle, causing the afternoon sun to reflect against it, so that the frame glistened with an almost holy light, which would be cast across the room. It was only an oversized looking-glass, but to me it was like a treasure, and as I gazed at my own reflection, I imagined I could sense the spirit of Amelia gazing back at me.

★★★

The evening sky was draped in a thick blanket of purple cloud, shot through with bright pink paths that crossed and overlapped like railway junctions. There were small, empty patches of light blue sky, yet to be polluted by the amethyst smog that sometimes hovered over us, the remnants of London which drifted into our rural lives. Jim and I sat admiring the perfection of this midsummer evening from the warm light of my bedroom. My clothing was minimal; I had undone one too many buttons on my shirt; this was mostly due to the heat, and partly due to the Dutch courage an earlier glass of sherry from my parents' liquor cabinet had afforded me. We had the house to ourselves, without the imposed restrictions of my parents, or the general ruckus of my siblings, which of course meant only one thing. I thought about how things must once have been the same for my parents when they were young lovers, although it was difficult to even imagine such a scenario. It was difficult enough remembering that they had once been young. Parents aside, all that mattered was that for now, I was with Jim.

I could remember my mother once warning me that love – in its truest sense – was very rare. I could recall every word in detail, for it had frightened me back then. What if I was never to find love? But here I sat with Jim, certain that I had found it at the age of just seventeen. Thus far, my life had been a relatively easy one – not pampered, but undeniably easy. I had suffered no tremendous heartbreak; in fact, I had suffered nothing whatsoever that could cause me to either lose or find myself. I knew that one could not continue forever in this way, and I was always tempting fate just thinking about the potential tragedies that lay in wait; but for the time being, at least, they lay only within the realm of contingency, and not in actuality. Here then I was, untouched by pain, unafflicted by sadness, and changed only by the joys of Love. Everything was going accordingly, and we were feeling immortal, as young, mortal lovers do; there was rock and roll playing and a thrill in the air. So engulfed in the moment were we, that it took me completely by surprise to find myself suddenly frozen in fright – and for a reason I could not even comprehend myself. It provoked a terrible stir in the atmosphere, dampening ardour, turning passion to anxiety in an instant.

"What's wrong?" Jim asked, a look of alarm on his face, noticing how I was now staring at the mirror. Feeling slightly foolish, I looked away again.

"It's going to sound ridiculous, but the mirror's unsettling me."

For a moment, there was silence – but then, more out of nervousness than anything else, I began to laugh. My bizarre behaviour, as worrying as it might have appeared, was admittedly rather ridiculous. A smile crept across Jim's face as he joined in with the laughter.

"I had no idea you were that self-conscious," he offered cautiously, not wanting to offend me, and completely misunderstanding. I had no intention of explaining anything then and there; it was not the right time or place; instead, we both just collapsed onto one another, laughing hysterically. Still giggling like a couple of unruly children, we contentedly lay down again, side by side.

Simply being with Jim, just the two of us, but for an awareness in the silence, I found to be far more intimate than any act of lovemaking. The measure of our breath, our lungs absorbing the oxygen in the room, breathing in unison – heavy, full, absolute; our hearts were beating simultaneously. We communicated in silence; he put his arms around me and pulled me closer to him.

I was elated, yet almost sorry, for accepting his love so undeservedly; but even miles deep in adoration for him, even in our closeness, our fingers intertwined with each other's, I still felt somehow distant – both from Jim, and from everything else, as if I wished to sabotage my connections with the world. Inevitably we, as human beings, feel independent from each other, for in reality, that is what we are. We cannot rely on someone else to complete us; it simply does not work that way. Yet how can one long for both solitude and companionship at once? I have a tendency to feel alone, even in the most crowded of places; and yet sometimes, it is a sweet tang of solitude – my tears satisfy my palate for that zestful disposition. But that is only sometimes.

"You know it's been a year since I realised that I loved you," Jim whispered, breaking the silence.

"You won't get bored of me, will you?" I joked.

"That would be impossible," he replied in that reassuring American accent of his. My heart felt so light at that moment, dangerously so.

Later that evening, as we kissed and uttered our goodbyes, I felt I was the luckiest girl alive. I remember him taking hold of my hands as we stood by the gate, and squeezing gently, and as I looked into his eyes, I saw the universe, with everything in it; I saw us, my family, his family, England, America, Earth, stars, moons, suns, galaxies, atoms, Gods, demons and parallel dimensions; each and every secret of the universe was revealed, for no more than a second, within the immeasurable pupils of his eyes.

His gaze had been so potent, so full of love, making me feel like the most beautiful, the most sought-after girl on the planet. With Jim, I knew he loved me for what and who I was – not simply for what I did, or for how I looked. He pulled me close and we kissed. How different it was to that time at the party; now we had confidence, reassurance and absolute trust. My lips tingled as we pulled away; everything did, including my heart, which felt as if it had left my body and poured itself into the world around me, making everything look glorious.

I watched Jim as he drove off into the night, the car's headlights fading as he disappeared down the driveway, the clouds enveloping the moon as he went.

V

The darkness of the country road stretches out ahead, reminding me of back home, of Indiana, but God, I have to stop thinking like that. This is it, this is Home with a capital H now. And yet this emptiness keeps reminding me of that holiday, of being driven across Arizona, on our way to Los Angeles. Night was coming down on us fast, the hilltops basked in a golden glow of sunset; now dark, ominous mounds. The hills – and whatever else was in the distance – may have looked sinister, but there was something comforting about the way the stars shone down on us that night, as if to suggest there really was a God watching over the world, looking out over us. I found it reassuring; I was at one with everything (albeit momentarily).

There is something timeless about being on a seemingly endless stretch of road in the middle of the desert, with nothing but starlight and headlights to guide you. *No matter where in the world you are, if you look up at the night sky, you will see the same stars that everyone else sees*, Father once pointed out. Made me realise just how small and insignificant we really are. That someone else might also be marvelling at those magnificent fiery gems, burning through the vacant night sky, leaves me awestruck...

.Awestruck and in love; it sounds absurdly fictional. Clare – I don't know if she believes me when I tell her that I love her, but it's true, beyond any doubt. What is it in particular that I love about her? Everything… I guess if I had to put it in a nutshell, I would simply say that she's perfect – for me, anyway. What other people may see as imperfections, one of us will find lovable all the same… but she's damn close; wise beyond her years, that girl. Stop overthinking it. Some things are better left unexplained.

Nineteen years into life, I seem always to be reminding myself that I can't possibly know enough of the human condition to believe what I feel is true. Now I'm beginning to realise that I don't actually have to convince anyone of my joy, despair, affection… neither should I try to mask them – the latter being something the English are surprisingly adept at, although I'll never understand why. Men are routinely taught to overlook their emotions; *the emotional world is the domain of the fairer sex*, they say. My peers seem to accept this doctrine without question. I never voiced my opinions in high school, for fear of being ridiculed. I kept mostly to myself and became more interested in writing than in anything else, and thought, *Oh, you'll probably succeed because of it*. But then you get into the real world – same old attitudes; not set in stone, but hard to break.

Then you met Clare. It was a typical rainy Sunday afternoon, the kind of day that makes you thankful to be inside and around so much tea (they drink so much tea in England). Taking their order, I thought that they were just like all the other girls, nudging each other under the table, whispering as soon as I turned my back – typical schoolgirls. Soon I discovered that Hannah was the most vocal of the three. The other two seemed content to sit reserved, chuckling at her banal comments (**oh forgive her, you're not meant to hate your girlfriend's friends**)… *never whisper, and never point; I* thought the British knew manners. Thought I may as well try and get to know them; after all, I was new in town. **You didn't know anyone**. Soon enough, after spending mornings wiping tables down and serving rude customers, to see the girls at the door provided genuine relief; in fact, I would go as far as to say that I was curious to talk to them. Hannah definitely shared my curiosity; whether she was playing the match-maker or the tease, I couldn't tell. A definite ulterior motive was struggling to conceal itself. Whatever her motive, try to forgive and forget. We got talking. I told them about Dad's work, how he wanted me to learn the ropes, to follow in his path and become a successful lawyer. I was surprised; they listened intently, and by the time I had to close up shop I offered them some beers (carefully contrived from the stash downstairs). Somewhere along the way, we got drunk. And then we were chatting, slurring our words, laughing uncontrollably, like the oldest of friends.

The drunken conversation continued. **You found yourself being drawn to Clare; somehow, she stood out from her friends**. Polly was amiable enough, if slightly generic. She laughed, but she didn't make any jokes herself; she agreed with various points raised, but had little to offer herself. She was nice, but that was about all I could see in her. **In other words, she simply was not your type**. Hannah tried too hard, her manner verged on desperate. Clare didn't need to try. She was smart, and she was witty (even if it had taken a couple of beers). There was nothing irritating or egotistical about her; she was cultured, worldly – so impressive. Feel like I've come from a land of ignorance, citizens segregated according to the colour of their skin and what not.

You admired and agreed with the way Clare looked at the world; the way it troubled her that some women were so content within their husbands' shadows. You revered her progressive views, her general lack of

prejudice. It was incredibly refreshing to hear a perspective that wasn't downright questionable. Even her taste in music – not to mention her musical ability – is unparalleled. It is not often that one comes across a fledgling, great composer – even more seldom, a female one. So typical of Clare to break this pattern, where music is chiefly a man's world; aside from a certain number of successful female pop artists, the classical world has long been deprived of a woman's touch. Hasn't deterred her in the slightest; if anything, it seems to make her more determined. Can't help thinking she should seek out Hollywood (where far lesser talents have made their names by composing scores for the motion pictures, the movies). I told her as much too; the potential joys of having people scratch their heads, wondering what the name of that talented composer was; could he possibly be the next Gershwin... the ingenuity of Mozart, and so on... It would soon emerge that Clarice Stratford – a young woman, a young English woman – had rewritten the American national anthem; one day she would exemplify our very era. She's far too modest, of course she is. She'll never take me seriously – although I mean every word of it – and it only makes me love her more. Everything, in all sincerity, seems right about Clare.

But there was that one instance which continues to astonish and baffle me; six months – Jesus, how time flies – *six whole months* ago – all of us – and then Clare, Polly and Hannah. That ridiculous town hall dance thing. In the gloom of January, as well. The most exciting thing round here, I s'pose. We'd all eagerly anticipated the drinking and the dancing. We were already half-drunk before we'd even arrived, bottles of spirits hidden in our coats and bags – I suppose trouble was never going to be too far off. Soon stumbling around, vision blurred, looking for the bathroom as I weaved my way across the dance floor, colliding with other teenagers, all of them dancing like lunatics, couples lurking in the shadows, whispering into each other's ears. Got into the bathroom to escape the noise for a moment or two. Opening the door to leave, that pale, white hand snaked around my neck, pulling me backwards, towards the building's exit, out into a deserted cobblestone square.

Shoved forcefully against a wall. Hannah, shock horror. Her emerald gaze flashing with danger itself. The combination of those particular eyes, her raven-coloured hair and porcelain skin, contrasting her angular features, almost intimidating in their sharp precision. Slowly, she took a few steps towards me, neither aligned nor stable, and definitely drunk. *Jim, how are you?* she slurred, weaving about in front, unsteady on her feet. Dishonourable intentions, of course. I tried to convey as little emotion as possible in my tone, failing. *I'm fine, thank you,* I replied hesitantly. She finally released her grip and leant against the wall beside me. *How are things with Clarice?* A sly hint of sarcasm in her tone; even more uncomfortable, a forced discomfort – I couldn't even find the strength to shuffle further away from her. Like a psychological strength that I lacked manifested in physical weakness? *Yeah... things are fine,* I said, *look, are you all right, Hannah?* Ignoring my response, she continues. *It's okay; you can tell me,* she whispers, edging even closer. I move further away, but she almost has me trapped, her alcoholic breath hanging heavily in the air between us.

I know you better than you think, she goes on, *to begin with, I know you that you are clearly in adoration of me.* "Adoration" of? She has only lived through Austenian heroines. Pretending as if she knows about people and their emotions; unblemished by tears, her complexion is. I just stared back at her, wide-eyed and dumbfounded. *Jim, you've been leading me on since the day we met. Don't think I haven't noticed,* she adds, coquettishly twisting that menacing lock of hair round her finger.

Quickly made for the door – but in vain. All in one swift movement – *one fell swoop* (imagining a bird, falling, swooping through the air, over the fields now dashing past me) – she has me back, spins me round, forces her lips against mine. Both of us seem to freeze at this point, as if cemented to each other for what must be a half-second, before finally, I find the nerve to unclamp her hands from my shirt and storm away.

It leaves me wondering if it hadn't been your fault after all. Could I really have been leading her on? Don't think so. Hannah's the kind of girl that demands to be seen, craving attention at all times. Her mannerisms and expressions tell all; the intensity of her gaze, the prurient lip-biting, the licentious laughter – it does not take a man of great perceptivity to interpret such movements as signs of self-conceit. Certainly, she is no background silhouette; she has colossal confidence, that crushes all else in its path in order to achieve its aim of receiving full attention; and then there are her rare, eye-catching features... but what is a shallow notion of beauty, if it cannot be substantiated by something inner? I doubt her sincerity. I pity her, really; she's delusional – she built all these false impressions that I had taken an interest in her (based on indeterminate situations, and a sad kind of wish to be loved, probably). The very idea that I have been unconsciously leading Hannah on the whole time – simply inconceivable! Was going to tell Clare, but didn't want to distress her – **still don't. You can't do this to her**. A childhood friendship, betrayed so easily, without hesitation and with such risk – she may not ever be able to trust anyone after that. **And it might destroy all faith she has in you**. She might think I really was interested in Hannah, that she had dismissed me... she's probably already told her that lie, and all kinds of other myths.

Everything's fine anyway; Hannah's been colder recently. Probably for the better. Shows she's not attached; but there's this thought gnawing away at the back of my mind, goading me on to tell Clare. What's a bond without trust? **Don't ask mundane questions. When you met her, a better part of**

you emerged that you never knew existed – hold onto it, hold onto her. She's taught you how to love another person unconditionally. She, Clare, oh I love to say her name out loud – "Clare, Clare, Cla*rice*!" – Clarice. She has all those extra qualities, rare gemstones that can only be found by digging incredibly deep into the thick – and what we thought was immovable – earth around us. But even when we are looking for something brilliant, we so rarely find it – our expectations exceed reality. When we do find something amazing, it has usually been stumbled upon; these are the things that we don't expect to have or to find; they find us, and once they do, we should never let them slip away. I am happy now, these are good thoughts. **Turn on the radio.**

VI

I awoke with a start, shuddering with the horrid sensation of cold sweat covering my body, my heart like a bomb about to explode. It was too hot, or was it too cold? I was shaking beneath the sheets: all signs of a fever. There was also a rancid taste in my mouth, and I was dehydrated. The grandfather clock in the hall was clacking loudly, as if it had been plugged into an amplifier and turned up to full volume.

Earlier that night, with Jim, I had felt fine – if anything I had been abuzz with the excitement of being young and in love. I tried to recount what had happened from the time when Jim had left, up until this point, attempting to pinpoint the moment when I had begun to feel so unwell. After saying goodbye, I had practiced a Chopin prelude for about half an hour. At ten-thirty I drew a bath, after which I had made a cup of camomile tea, and then went to sleep with no indication of a brewing fever; but now I felt wretched and light-headed.

"Clarice," a faint and unfamiliar voice whispered. Suddenly wide awake, I sat up abruptly. Reflected in the mirror on the wall, a ghostly-white face gazed back at me. Her delicate frame – fragile, almost translucent – looked as if all life had been sucked from it. Her long, blonde ringlets fell gracefully over her shoulders. Her pale face was sculpted exquisitely, her features like those of a marble bust, with every attribute perfectly proportioned. She was undoubtedly beautiful, but there was something unearthly about her, whilst the long, flowing nightdress she wore gave her a distinctly Victorian appearance.

I sat up in bed, frozen in terror, struggling to make sense of what was happening, grappling with the possible explanations: could it merely be a rather unconventional robbery attempt? How did she know my name? Had I forgotten that I had a friend staying over, or had I just gone insane with the fever? Indeed, it was a surreal situation I had found myself in.

Swiftly, I spun around in an attempt to take the intruder by surprise. I prepared for the worst, clenching both of my fists as I slowly stepped out of the bed – only to find that there was no one there anymore: no reflection in the mirror, no one standing in front of me – nothing. Quickly, I turned around; for all I knew she was creeping up behind – but there was no one there either. I scanned the room frantically, even going so far as to check behind the curtains, but still, there was no one to be found.

I wondered if I was merely imagining things – hallucinating, sleepwalking – despite a lack of history of such a thing in the family. No, I concluded. I needed to go back to sleep, before my tired, fevered brain began to conjure images again; but before I dared lie back down in the comfort of my pillow, I looked once more in the mirror. The young woman had disappeared after all, and all I could do was to dismiss what I had seen, and go back to sleep.

For the next few hours I was in a liminal state, neither awake nor sleeping. The night closed around me, but the summer air hung still, making no passage for a breeze. I rose to get a glass of water, in the hope that it might hydrate me.

Lying back down in the dark, I closed my eyes, trying to think of nothing at all, longing to fall into a deep, fulfilling slumber.

Ding! Ding! Ding! The grandfather clock chimed three times, each chime more piercing than the last. I wondered how such a racket had not woken me before. I decided to take the interruption as a cue to visit the bathroom, having drunk almost a pint of water since going to bed. *Better to go sooner rather than later,* a little voice in my head taunted me. As I turned the bathroom light on, I caught sight of myself in the mirror; dark circles had begun to form under my eyes. I needed sleep. I needed to forget what had just happened, and deal with it in the morning. Eventually, at around four o'clock, I drifted off, or rather, switched off, into a mechanical sleep fuelled no more by the want for escape than the bodily need for rest.

I drifted off for maybe five minutes, before, once again, waking up. My bedclothes were now slightly damp with perspiration, and I was now even more confused and feverish.

"Clarice," came the voice from within the mirror.

"What?" My dry voice cracked as I spoke through parched lips.

"I am Amelia Parriton. I once lived here," it continued, "and I must thank you. You read my journal and salvaged my mirror. I am most grateful to you."

It would have been too easy to attribute what was happening to a fever, certainly. If somebody had related this inexplicable event to me, it would be the conclusion to draw. Nonetheless, this happening seemed as real as being awoken mid-slumber by the piercing shrill of an alarm clock. I stared, speechless, at the unfamiliar woman in the looking-glass. She now subtly swayed, and laughed lightly, sending a cold reverberation around the room.

"I really am so dreadfully sorry." She spoke softly now, her eyes moistened with tears. "This must be hard for you to fathom, but I have been trapped behind the panes of this mirror for many years. When I passed away, the servants took it and stowed it in the attic – although I cannot tell you when that was; I do not even know what year it is now."

"1957," I replied in a monotone, barely realising the words had left my mouth. A look of tired anguish passed across her beautiful, yet pained face. The look in her eyes told me she had endured a thousand perils, whilst in my mind I heard her voice speaking – loudly, urgently – as though she had been waiting a very long time to communicate.

"I do not know how I got here, behind this glass, but I could not bear to sit and ignore you any longer. Do not be frightened; there is nothing to fear. It is not often that one gets to experience a supernatural phenomenon; for the open mind and soul, it is but the greatest attainment of knowledge." She smiled as she spoke, but whether it was meant benevolently or not, I wouldn't dare guess.

"But please, you must believe me," she persisted. "You see, I can perceive what is ahead – in the future. I do not know how, but I know of things that by the laws of physics, I should not know at all." Her words were delivered as though she was cramming in as much as possible, before the window of opportunity slammed shut. I urged myself to wake up, kicking my legs against the bedpost as I did so, feeling my face contorting in frustration. I bit my tongue and blinked my eyelids, as if squeezing all moisture from them, but nothing worked. I was still there, and she was still there, laughing at the lunacy of my rationality.

"I have already told you," the apparition interjected, with such urgency that I had to catch my breath, "this is not a dream, believe me. You must listen – something awful is going to happen."

"What – what do you mean?" I finally returned, "I don't understand."

"There is a girl; a girl with whom you are acquainted."

I nodded, then shook my head. "What are you talking about?"

"She is in danger. You must protect her."

"But what can I do?" I replied, trying to make sense of this terrible conundrum.

"Whatever you can."

"But I don't even know who you're talking about!"

"I know not her name, but she is fair in complexion. Beyond that, I cannot say," she replied despondently, before continuing; "be ready, Clarice, be prepared, for it will be soon – when the sun is out, yet fading. The blue sky wavers, unwilling to depart. A brick building is in sight… it is early autumn, perhaps?"

It was the summer holidays now, and I was going back to my last year at school in September – that much I did know. To be forewarned of a disaster now, in midsummer, I conceived would give me just enough time to digest the bizarre information and prepare for any eventuality – if it were to happen at all, of course. Not wanting her to go before I knew more, I began to hurl questions at her, one after another, challenging her in the most forthright way possible, whilst I had the opportunity.

"Why are you here? Is this what happens when we die – we get trapped?"

She did not seem at all fazed, but just stood there with an alarming coolness about her.

"No, only lost souls like myself stay behind; if you would like, I will attempt to provide an explanation as to how I became trapped behind this glass, but take heed, I know not how long this line of communication may last." I nodded in compliance, for that was all I really wanted – an explanation.

"My mother and father were Catholics, although they would seldom discuss religious matters. I do not know whether it is different now, but England was a place for Protestants back then. I was raised to believe in Purgatory and all of the Catholic customs, but I never truly did; something stopped me from seeing any value in such senseless tradition. To me, religion seemed no more than a set of rules for a stray conscience. My parents were not only devout, but uncompromising in their beliefs – insane, even. Their attempts to manipulate and control me knew no bounds, as they told dreadful tales of what happened to those who did not worship and respect their God. I grew up scared in my own household. Little did they know of the private rebellion in my mind; I first adopted the position that God was all-forgiving, and would not condemn me for my scepticism; but soon after I arrived at the simple conclusion that He was nonexistent. Oh, how the thought made me shudder with delight! I had discovered the way to disobey my mother and father without consequence! Private disbelief was my form of escape."

As I listened, I realised how similar my own views on religion were to hers, despite the century that lay between us, and she smiled as if she could read my very thoughts.

"As you know from reading my diary," she continued with a new sadness in her eyes, "my little brother, Peter, drowned when I was aged just sixteen years. At the time, before the tragedy, I had been wandering from the trammels of a Christian life, and this soon came to my father's attention. According to him, I had done a terrible thing; I had sinned a most dreadful sin. I loved a boy who lived nearby. His mother chanced upon us once, just sitting and talking rather intimately together under an oak tree, but nothing more. She thus mentioned our acquaintance to my father in a passing comment, presumably unaware of the consequences this would bring. Both of my parents condemned me, and I believe were convinced that my relationship with the boy was far more intimate than it truly was. A week later, Peter drowned in a dreadful accident by the lake, and this finally affirmed for them that I was possessed – of that they suddenly had no doubt. The truth was that I tried to save him, Clarice, I tried, but my clothes bore too much weight. I would have drowned myself, and at the time, self-preservation seized my every movement – but now I sorely wish that it had not."

I tried to make sense of the inconceivable idea that the girl in the mirror was no trick of the light, no hallucination; I wanted more than anything to rationalise it in that way, but there was nothing in her appearance that suggested she wasn't there; and it was no dream – of that I was convinced. I could not understand it, and yet there was nothing to misunderstand; I was apparently communicating with the spirit of a girl who had died over a century ago. It was an insane idea; it went against everything I had ever believed. The supernatural does not exist; we are cold, rational, reasonable, and terrified people who can reliably provide a scientific explanation for any paranormal activity. And yet we know so little – how could we come to such ignorant conclusions that nothing exists beyond our very existence? Because scientists have spent years in laboratories discovering physical laws, chemical structures and biological processes, none of which have pointed to the existence of anything so childishly contrived as ghosts. There would be an obvious explanation to the 'apparition' – there always is. Nonetheless, she continued to speak in a consistent manner, her pace having slowed as she became engrossed in her own tale.

"They decided that I had killed Peter simply because I was there and couldn't save him. My mother and father had always shown coldness towards me – I never knew why – but from that point onwards, they did not need to explain it, for they now had a reason. They sent for a priest, and tried all sorts of atrocities to pry the daemon from me, but it remained. Of course there was no daemon there in the first place, but they were truly mad, and their belief unchangeable. They kept me in the attic for four years, telling me that I was not fit for courtship. Every night, I was tormented by guilt, and I had to convince myself that the events which had occurred were not my wrongdoings; yet the knowledge that I could have saved my beloved brother never leaves me for a moment; I must carry that with me forever.

One day, however, I escaped from the attic. Deciding that I would defy my parents, this time outwardly, and realising that I was in more danger in this very house than anywhere else, I planned my exit. There was a set of stairs which ran down from the attic, but the door at the foot was locked from the outside. It was only unlocked when the servants came to deliver my meals, but that was perhaps my best chance of escape; the windows in the attic were simply too high up, and I would either have been caught, or injured, had I attempted to climb down. I waited then for my next meal to arrive. When Mrs Bell brought up the tray, and I claimed to feel nauseous, feigning the typical motions, and pleaded for her to escort me outside for a moment. At first, she thought I was mad, and would refuse to consent. On the discovery that both my mother and father were absent, however, and after a great deal of persuasion, she eventually conceded to escort me down the stairs; but a new sort of terror was spreading across her face, as she disobeyed my father's orders. All the while, I made sure I was walking one step ahead of her, for as we reached the foot of the stairs, I dashed out suddenly, slammed the door shut behind me and ran, quite literally it felt, for my life. I had only another flight of stairs to get down, and then there was the front door, which I was soon out before the rest of the servants could even think to apprehend me. Running down the country lanes with a rejuvenated fear, I made for my destination.

I was running to the only people who I knew would take me in. They were called the Hamiltons, my godparents, who lived just down the lane. Both Mr and Mrs Hamilton were kind people, and I very much enjoyed their company. They had been unable to bear children themselves, and Mrs Hamilton in particular, took great delight in her role as a godmother. They took me in straight away, fed me, provided me with a bath, clothed me with fresh linen, and I found them to be extremely attentive. They listened with great interest to the same story that I have just told you, and seemed to completely understand the situation. Although I had previously believed them to be loyal to my parents, it appeared that I might have been wrong in my assumption, as they began to speak ill of their extreme Catholicism. Perhaps having witnessed how Peter and I had been raised, under the tyranny of our parents' devotion, they recognised our troubles better than I had realised. That was what I believed, but I had barely been under their roof for three days before the belief was horribly challenged by a knock at the door. Standing at the threshold were a number of people, of whom I had no recognition. Before I knew what was happening, I was grabbed and thrown into a horse-drawn cart. Terrified and trembling, I watched the roads and houses with which I was familiar slowly fall away from view.

I was to spend the next and final eight years of my life in a place so abominable, I could scarcely believe it was regulated by human beings. My experiences in the hellish prison were limited to torture, imprisonment and solitary confinement. Many took their own lives in their cells – and who could blame them? But the worst thing was the crying; the continuous sobs of deep lamentation and howls of pain that would last all the night – not physical pain, but emotional torment. There was no way out of this bedlam. We were trapped and isolated, most of us imprisoned for crimes we had not committed. To die was deliverance. Most of the people there were perfectly sane when they had first arrived, detained for the most unjustified of reasons: having children out of wedlock, speech impediments, spinal difficulties – none of which are real signs of insanity, of course. The truth was that this place did not deserve the title of an institution, or even an asylum. It was a swamp, where the debris, scraped from the edges of society, were disposed of to slowly decay. I will never forgive my parents for placing me there.

And so I endured the final years of my life in the so-called asylum, becoming more unhinged as time wore on. Finally, I could take the suffering no longer, and I hanged myself with a bed sheet, tied to a bar across the window. It was the simplest and easiest manner in which to despatch oneself, and the favoured method chosen by so many other patients, also to have carried out the deed. At first, the momentary sensations of regret, guilt and fear were too much for me to bear. Oh, it was dreadful! But then, quite unexpectedly, I experienced greater pleasure than one could ever imagine as I slipped away. If only I could go back and once again absorb that euphoric sense of freedom; those fleeting seconds between life and death – where your heart stops, yet your mind lapses in and out of a fantastical dream… such a blissful, divine glimpse of Heaven it was." She paused for a moment, a look of concern passing across her face. "You look troubled. Are you alright?"

My mind was racing; thoughts were flitting in and out as I tried to take in her words, and at the same time, I was trying desperately to understand why this sad, tormented soul had confided in me. I had so many questions, some ridiculously mundane, like what I was to tell Jim, and how I could even reply to the apparition before me.

"Yes, I'm… bewildered," I contradicted myself, not knowing what to say; and as she implored me to forgive her for unsettling me, I was sure I could detect an element of threat in her tone.

"I need you to understand that I had no other choice but to take my own life; I had to escape the suffering, and I was astonished to find that I had; the darkness that I had felt enveloped by suddenly dispersed. As the last breath departed from my body, a myriad of colours danced around me; spirits ascended, awash with a golden light that consoled me entirely. I heard angelic voices singing melodies Aeolian to the gentle lilt of a harp. I desperately wanted to rise up and join them, but my feet were anchored to the ground, and all I could do was observe the spectacle; but it was all too fleeting. It was not long before my former companions – darkness and isolation – were to revisit; only now, it felt permanent. Time halted, and all I knew was that I was doomed, and the sooner I accepted this fact, the easier it would be to accept my fate, come what may.

I had given up on hope many decades ago, when suddenly, I saw a crack of light where there was none before. As I gazed into the brightness, I felt immediately drawn to it, and as I moved in, closer and closer, I could see a face – blurred at first, but becoming increasingly clear the closer I got, until eventually it was crystal clear. It was you, Clarice. Your darling face had appeared before my eyes, and I knew then that this was the face of my saviour! You pulled me out of that hideous cavern and brought me back to life. For that I shall be forever grateful.

I have watched over you for the past few days and I have grown to adore you, for you have helped to deliver me unto the present moment – the here and now – and I thank you for that."

The thought of her watching my movements unnerved me as I looked around the room, which now seemed to stand still in time. I wondered whether this would be the end of my life as I knew it. I needed time to think, but found myself involuntarily moving towards a decision that I found impossible to refrain from making. And so it was that I let Amelia into my world.

VII

In films, car crashes are often portrayed as spectacular moments of action and possess a kind of heroism. The car does multiple flips in the air like a Catherine wheel, only to land at a complimentary angle, giving the protagonist just enough time to escape, before bursting into dazzling and dancing flames. I was still in my youth when I learnt that such glamour does not apply to the real world. Explosions are unforgiving, trees do not give way, and the roads have no mercy.

I did not see the accident itself, nor did I see the wreckage, but I have run through it a million times in my head. I imagined the sheer panic racing through his veins, with the realisation that he was staring death in the face. I pictured that moment in time – the two cars colliding with crushing force; shards of glass suspended in the air like diamonds, before falling to the ground. Perhaps the worst thing that came to mind was the driver of the other car. One can only imagine how overpowering his sense of guilt must be, to have one's conscience shrouded with persistent self-blame for the loss of another human life. Perhaps one day, I would be able to move on and forget; but this man would never be relieved from his remorse.

"Clarice – are you sitting down, my love?" Jim's mother's voice trembled at the other end of the line. "Something terrible has happened." Her breath sounded heavy and disjointed as she delivered the news that would sink my entire world. I should have guessed as soon as I heard a faint weeping at the other end of the line, even if it was only for a split-second. Jim's mother, Mrs Pray, was a collected lady who wouldn't let slip her emotions for no reason. Immediately, I knew I had become part of a tragedy. The details of what had happened were irrelevant; there was no need for her to say any more. All I could hear, in between sobs, was the static of the line. I could not breathe. My eyes glistened with tears that would not fall, but preferred to sit under the lids, as though the horror was too much even for them.

"I am so dreadfully sorry, Mrs Pray," I eventually spluttered, wishing it didn't sound so feeble; wishing I could have done something, could have been there, despite her assurances that there was nothing anyone could have done.

"He loved you very much, you know," she continued, trying her best to contain herself, but she needn't have bothered. It was perfectly obvious that both her universe, and mine, had fallen apart. I did what I could to stay calm as I tried to console her, but I knew that my words probably had as little an effect on her, as hers had had on me.

I put the receiver down and stared blankly into space. More devastating than the news itself, I found it hard to express any emotion at all to what should have provoked floods of tears. I vaguely knew that it had something to do with my upbringing, that it was not all my own fault, but I still felt appalled at the manner in which I had dismissed Jim's grieving mother. I worried that one day I might pay a terrible price for my constant sense of formality, and a perceived coldness that had developed over the years. I was the product of wealth, boarding school, largely self-interested parents, and the misshapen mindset that would inevitably come with it. It was only after I had put the phone down and had run upstairs to lie on my bed, that I felt a soothing, warm tear trickle down my cheek; I needed to feel its warmth, to taste its salinity as it reached my lips; I needed time alone, to breathe; and as the tears began in earnest to stream down my cheeks, they also washed away any doubts I could have had about how much I cared for Jim.

"Clarice! Who was that on the phone?" I heard my mother call after me. Her shrill tone broke the spell, and as I heard her footsteps approaching the door, I wished to jump out of the window. I could not let her see me cry – not that she would disapprove, but I wouldn't show weakness; I had never wanted her pity. Her face quickly softened as she focused upon the scene; her unbreakable child sitting on the edge of the bed, looking, to all appearances, rather broken. I quickly turned away. I did not want her to see me like this.

"Clarice, is everything alright? Who was that on the phone?" she asked again.

I was shaking, trying to contain myself using every fibre of my being. But I did not speak – not because I didn't want to, but simply because I could not find the strength to articulate words. The grandfather clock amplified itself once again in the hall, resonating through the room. My mother walked around the bed to where I sat, hunched over and biting my lip so that I did not make a noise, staring at the cream-coloured carpet, softly dampening it with tears.

"Whatever is the matter?" Her look of concern had turned into one of grave anxiety, but still I could not reply. She sat down next to me; I could feel the warmth of her hand on my back and a new set of tears forming in my eyes. This unsought pity was insufferable, particularly as I was trying my best to avoid pity of any kind. The sadness I felt was a private affair; I was so consumed by a sudden, sharp emptiness, that I felt I had become it.

"Please tell me what's wrong," she repeated. "Clare? Please, I want to help." Her voice was weak in the midst of my gloom.

"Jim's dead," I finally replied.

Her face dropped as I spoke, as though someone had unplugged it. "What? What on Earth are you talking about? Jim is dead? What do you—"

I broke down in tears right in front of her like a helpless child. In an instant, it did not matter that I was nearly an adult; I certainly did not feel like one as I hugged her back, as though I would never let her go. My mother's comfort was almost too painful to bear, as between sobs I told her what had happened.

I had never needed to make it plain to my mother that I felt strongly towards Jim – it was already obvious. However, I felt that all the explaining in the world would never affirm to her the bond between us; but at that moment, I knew that she had seen beyond any kind of superficiality. From the day he died, whenever she spoke of Jim, it was as though of a deceased martyr. Her over-compensation may have been her way of letting me know that she understood the extent of my loss; either way, I truly appreciated it.

Having lost my grandfather just a few months earlier, I knew what it was to grieve. Often, I would feel light a pang of sadness whenever I thought about Pa, or visited somewhere he had taken me to as a child, or heard a song that he liked; but he had lived a long and fulfilling life. The death of a lover in the prime of his life is an entirely different affair. No matter how strong familial ties, losing Jim left me feeling incomplete; he had everything in front of him. Pa's death, however upsetting, was ultimately the full stop to time on this Earth well spent; the tragedy of Jim's departure from it was something else altogether, and I could only wonder what would happen next. Now that our romantic adventure had died with him, would he, like Pa, also begin to fade and become less real over time, as though nothing had ever happened, as though he had never even existed? Was it possible, that someone who had provided me with so much happiness, could fade away like a pallid moon in the cold morning sky?

VIII

September had arrived and along with it, the start of the new school year. I remember it being around three o'clock in the afternoon when the day's drama unfolded, now stamped in my mind like a pungent scent that refuses to depart. The Queen's boarding house lawn was freshly cut and radiating viridity. The sun, so high in the sky that it looked like a warm, compact ball of golden light, was slowly starting to fade away. I sat amongst the trees, their cool shadows falling this way and that, criss-crossing my slight frame. It was a fine day, with the last remnants of summer keeping autumn at bay, but I was in no mood to appreciate it. During this time of despair, I was finding it hard to see the beauty in anything; in fact, I was finding it hard to even understand the concept of beauty, and I saw an abundance of shadows, rather than rays of light.

Queen's house looked gloomy from where I was sat; the building towered over me, staring down from its large, cheerless windows. The architectural monstrosity had never looked comfortable; in fact, a visitor could be excused for thinking they had mistakenly taken a detour to a hospital.

At this time of day, most of my fellow pupils were outside, playing lacrosse, working in the library, or smoking against one of the numerous outbuildings. The senior girls' boarding house – which I had moved to in the third year – was built during the Long Depression, when trade was low, and misery high. The scarcity of the time was reflected in the building's lack of any ornate detail, either inside or out. The walls were bare and had cracks in them which ran all the way up to the ceiling; the floorboards creaked, and there was an unshakable smell of boiled cabbage, which could well have been hovering since the reign of Queen Victoria. The large, high-ceilinged rooms were always cold, even in the summer. During winter, one would have to pry oneself out of bed in the morning, as if being upturned into an arctic sea. Colds and influenza would spread amongst pupils and staff alike, as rapidly as the ice spread across the pond outside.

As I looked at the imposing sight of Queen's, I remembered happier times with Jim. The lake by my house, where I had written poetry as a child – that was where we had had our most valuable conversations, even if only valuable to ourselves; and within those hermetically sealed moments, we were so content, so grateful for what existed between us, that I had longed for each one to last forever.

"I wonder why older people take our emotions less seriously than their own," Jim had remarked on one such occasion, the sun bathing us in its glorious light as we sat in the old rowing boat, glistening waters and flourishing trees as our backdrop. "It's as if they think everything is so much more superficial at our age, as if our experiences somehow don't really matter." The look on his face suggested to me that this had been on his mind for a while.

"Because they're jealous," I finally replied, after giving it some thought. "They're just bored with their married lives. They yearn for the sense of discovery that we still have. Just because they never found the right person, they assume it's like that for everyone." I looked up at Jim, who was nodding in approval. "People our age are jealous too," I continued. "They would like us to be mistaken in what we feel for each other, just so that we can all be lonely together."

"You could have a point there," Jim said, squeezing my hand and making my heart skip a beat like he always did.

"There's something distressing about lonely people, isn't there?" I speculated. "Like Polly – she's a good person, and she's attractive, but she's so shy – what chance does she have with boys if they don't even notice her?" Jim smiled pitifully, before fixing his eyes on the water, still holding my hand in his. "It kills her, I know it does. She says life's not worth living if you're living it alone. Of course, I told her that wasn't true, but then, how should I know?"

"It's only like that for some people," Jim replied. "Some people are perfectly happy living a life of solitude, and lonely people are only lonely because they have a different perspective to those who aren't. It's not healthy, and it's not how things should be, but it seems like the lonelier you are, the less chance you have of finding anyone at all. It's not the most attractive attribute in the world – it turns people off, you know."

"I wish I could find a suitable partner for everyone that feels unloved," I replied, realising it sounded a little saccharine, but nonetheless with good intentions.

Perhaps I was blessed that I had never felt that sort of longing in my life. I had felt alone, but I had never yearned for true love to come and rescue me. I might have been seventeen, but whilst other teenagers' hormones raged, I never felt overly affected by such things. Yes, I loved Jim, but I could not see my world collapsing without him; I would move on, at least, that was what I had hoped to do, should anything have happened. Young love rarely lasts. It is a generalisation, but one that, in most cases, proves true, but it was not this which gave me reason to question the fortitude of our love; there seemed to me an even greater threat. The truth remained that there was a part of me I could not share with anyone; a kind of distance, even from Jim. I simply valued solitude too much. Somehow, in my naïvety, I saw this as being incompatible with unconditional love. That is not to say that our conversations held any less value than my own analysis; it is only through the exchange of thoughts with another person that our perception can broaden sufficiently, so that the thoughts of each subject feed off each other, linking in a cerebral chain, the end result being the satisfaction of having opened one's mind to a new perspective, and viewing the picture as a whole.

"Well," Jim said, attempting to lighten the mood. He stood up in the boat, making it rock gently. "I don't know about you, but I'm getting in the water," he said, removing his shirt. I dipped my hand into the lake. It was freezing, but before I even had time to say anything, Jim had launched himself into it. Droplets of water sprayed into the air around him, forming a perfect arc, before collapsing back in unison, onto the surface with a triumphant patter.

"How can you do that?" I yelled, "it's so cold!"

Jim laughed, as his head bobbed up out of the water. "Come and test it for yourself!"

"I don't have my swimming stuff... or a towel," I protested.

"You only live a minute away!"

"What if my mother catches us?" Not that she would have thought anything of it, but any conceivable excuse not to plunge into cold water was compelling all kinds of objections.

"Well, if she has a problem, she can tell me," he joked, before disappearing again under the water.

As I began fiddling with the top button of my blouse, all of a sudden, the boat began rocking from side to side. I knew it would not be long before I was in the water, it was just a matter of whether it would be voluntary or not.

"Stop it!" I shrieked, laughing hysterically. The rocking abruptly subsided as Jim smiled earnestly back at me.

"Make me!" he teased. I splashed water at him, but he didn't fight back. Instead he brought his face up to mine as I surrendered, leaning over the boat to kiss him. I already knew what was about to happen. As our lips met, and I felt the warmth of his breath, his fingers on my blouse, I was suddenly tugged into the water after him. I went headfirst into the lake, my feet following behind me, and as I acclimatised to the temperature I felt an immense satisfaction, a totality, as if the lake itself could be my dwelling.

"I hate you!" I screamed playfully, suddenly winded and meaning quite the opposite.

"Race you to the shore!" Jim shouted, as we both splashed and kicked, somehow making it back to dry land, but not before we were both thoroughly drenched.

"God, you're heavy!" Jim exclaimed, grabbing me around the waist, trying to hold me aloft. "I think you're gonna crush me!" he joked, knowing full well I was as light as dust.

"You really know how to win a girl's heart," I replied, pushing him backwards, noticing his unblinking eyes settle upon me.

"You're perfect, did you know that?" he said, after a while. "Perfect!"

"Well, I'm not sure about that, but if you say so, I bow to your greater knowledge; after all, we're taught to respect our elders, aren't we?" I teased.

Good humour aside, in that very moment, that pinnacle in the large expanse of time, intertwined with a million other moments, I could see no reason to disagree with his claim, for I was infinite, we were infinite, and time did not need to exist. All was now, all was perfection – and then the world slowly continued to turn.

I was abruptly awoken from my reminiscence by one of the most distraught sounds I have ever heard. Someone was yelling my name.

"Clare!" the voice screamed again. I looked up to see Doris, her mass of long, blonde hair trailing behind her as she ran towards me. She was drenched, and looking unusually hysterical, frightened, her eyes wide and tearful.

"Come quickly – it's Sheila – she's – she's in the lake!" Doris spluttered breathlessly, taking my arm in an attempt to pull me to my feet. "I think she's dead!"

"What?" I gasped, frantically trying to make sense of her words. "Sheila?"

"Sheila Daniels!"

"Oh my God," I heard myself say, feeling the corners of my mouth turn downwards in horror. I breathed deeply, trying to regain my composure. Sheila Daniels was a girl in our form. Immediately, Amelia's words had forced themselves upon my thoughts; she had warned me of this exact scene less than two months ago; I was sure this was it.

"How? I mean, what?" I yelled. "What happened?"

"I don't know, I just found her there, lying there – face up. I kept calling her name, but there was no response so I panicked and I jumped in and tried to pull her out but-she's-not-*breathing!*"

Without another word, I rose to my feet and began to follow her, both us now running faster than we had ever moved before, into the forest.

By the time we had passed through the trees into a shaded area, it had already grown colder and the sun was out of sight. The wilted purple anemone flowers looked sorrowful in their state, creating a trail of their own as we crushed them underfoot. As we ran through the shadowy trees to the self-contained area that was the lake – a world in itself – everything looked as if it were caving in on us; the trees formed a tunnel around us, and the leaves rattled with the slight touch of the breeze, shaking the whole wood.

Nothing could have prepared me for what I was about to witness. The mere sight of the catastrophe made me so drowsy and numb that morphine could only have enlivened me. There, lying on the muddy bank, was Sheila, her clearly lifeless body prostrate, stiff, dead. It was an unnatural position; her head was tilted too far back, her arms impressible; one flopped to the side, hanging there, attached to her body like a piece of old cloth; the other rested limply beside her. Her damp, white blouse clung to her torso, revealing every contour that lay beneath. Whether it was blood, water, or both that had saturated her, I was unsure, but there was no mistaking the desecration that she had been subjected to; it was obvious that she had been murdered. There must have been around a dozen knife wounds, each randomly rammed into her in the most savage way imaginable, so that she resembled a human pin cushion; this was an alarming detail that Doris, in her panicked state, had failed to mention.

Was it for God's own amusement that I had now experienced three deaths in the space of seven months? Was this a test of my suffering, or was I atoning for some wrongdoing? To have such misfortune thrown upon oneself, at so young an age, did not seem fair. It had to be a joke. It just wasn't plausible. I was half waiting for Wilde's Lady Bracknell to appear and tell me that I had exceeded carelessness, and delved into destruction.

I was overcome with nausea. I thought about all of the times I had ever felt on the brink of vomiting; there were not many, but I remembered the time I discovered an intolerance I had to vodka. I diverted my thoughts to this – it was more bearable. The Russian poison made my stomach writhe just thinking of it. Who could possibly enjoy its preposterous, spearing taste of all things repugnant? How ill it had made me; I had tried it at a dance in the town hall a few months before. One of Jim's friends had brought a bottle with him, from which we were all taking large swigs, and by my third gulp, I had begun to dislike the sharp, saline taste of the water-disguised abomination. I spent the rest of the night wandering around aimlessly, feeling queasy, and leaning on other people; the next morning I had thrown up for about two hours. The nausea I felt from my vodka consumption was so great, that I now cannot think of the substance without reliving the experience. I have tried drinking it since, but anything more than a drop, I simply cannot tolerate. Standing over Sheila's corpse, the same sickening feeling had come over me, but I was not devastated, nor was I fearful, I was simply overwhelmed. Her face was very pretty, that of a film star, a Hollywood treasure. It was the kind of face a mother would envy in her daughter; the kind of face that would sanction for lack of any other talent. She stared back at us, her once sparkling blue eyes now dull and cold, and I could not help but remember what Amelia had said. I asked myself if this was just a coincidence, or if the whole conversation with Amelia was simply a premonitory dream. I began to wonder what I could possibly have done to prevent this tragedy, but now was not the time for pointless speculation.

"Come on, Doris," I said, softly placing my hand upon her shoulder. "There's nothing we can do here – we need to tell someone." At first, she did not respond; only sat on the bank, motionless as the corpse itself.

"I want to stay with her – you go." I felt uncomfortable leaving her, but there was no time to spare. If anyone were to come, I told her, they were to stay there too.

As I ran back towards the school, the tears began to fall, unabated. All I could do was to keep running, despite a desperate urge to collapse and sink into the leafy ground below.

Disconcerted and exasperated, I finally arrived at the

main reception. As I spewed what must have sounded like incoherent gibberish, the school administrator scrutinised me as if I were insane. Whether she understood any of it, I'm not sure, but my panicked state was enough to motivate her to reach for the phone.

Within ten minutes the police and an ambulance had arrived. Doris and I were sent to the school medical centre for the night for observation, the school's staff being unsure how we might have reacted to the event, or how it may have damaged our psyches.

The two of us sat in silence with mugs of cocoa. I had never seen Doris so pensive. I was so naïve, and far too quick to judge. I rarely gave people a second chance, assuming that extroverts who cared too much for their appearance probably cared too little for quiet contemplation, and that this somehow infringed upon their higher faculties, but in some twisted kind of way, with her over-abundant ditziness and frivolity, Doris had done this to herself. I am sure many of our peers would have concurred with my crude assumptions too, but watching her gaze out of the window, so deep in thought, hair falling elegantly over her shoulders like an oil painting, I wondered if my judgements had been a little unfair. Perhaps, instead of critiquing my peers, I should have looked more closely in the mirror, for I could now picture Amelia, standing beside the dead body, her face filled with scorn. I could have prevented a death – I had no clue as to how – but the harrowing jaws of guilt gnawed away at me, eating me alive as the night wore on. I didn't sleep, nor did I eat, I could not concentrate in class, and worst of all, Amelia returned.

It was a few days after Sheila's death. I was alone in the dormitory that I shared with Hannah. It had been yet another warm September day of an Indian summer. I looked out of the window; it was still light outside, at eight-thirty in the evening.

The sky was a soft shade of blue-grey imbued with a tinge of purple. The air was now cool and the troubles, emotions and events of the day were fading. It felt as if I was nearing the end of an era, drained and lethargic, simply from existing. Lying outstretched on my bed, my eyes watered as I yawned. Lazily I rose, and examined my face in the mirror. Tiredness was etched into each and every line; too much frowning, I had thought, and not enough laughter. My lips were thin, and my skin looked pale and slightly blemished. I wondered whether stress had made me appear less attractive; I was not the type of girl who could maintain her prettiness even on a bad day. It looked as if I had been crying; my nose was red and numb around the nostrils, and my eyes were trapped behind a sheen of tears that acted like a flood barrier, waiting only for the right moment to breach its defences. I began to ponder the complexities of the face; I had always thought it slightly unfair that I should have a particularly flat face in comparison to my ancestors. It looked fine from the front, pretty even, but I was never a great admirer of my profile, which always took me by surprise whenever I caught a glimpse of it.

Then it happened. I should have sensed it coming right from when my eyes found the mirror. She appeared, almighty and omniscient. I turned away. It was something I could not be dealing with at that point in time. But before she could exude a single word from her lips, I was out of the door and running down the cold stone stairs, as fast as my legs would carry me, out into the advancing twilight... It is an odd time of day, always occurring at a random hour; one can never pinpoint when exactly twilight ensues; it is a paradox of vagueness, neither here nor there, rather liminal in its temperament. There seems to be a state of mind that comes with it as well – the relishing of solitude perhaps, or not knowing one's place in the grand scheme of everything and anything – even this feeling one cannot pinpoint. Dismayed, I strode swiftly towards the forest. It was the only place where I had a chance of being alone. *Keep walking* was the only thought that then occupied my mind. I wanted the dusk to swallow me up, the trees to engulf me; I wanted to run into that forest and never come out again. Amelia would never find me there – there were no mirrors – but what if I saw her reflection in the lake? I felt insane just contemplating it, yet I knew that if I tried explaining my fears to anyone, it would only confirm what was simply suspicion, in my mind, as truth; if I began to believe I was going mad, then I would surely become mad. But to convince myself that there really was a girl in the mirror with whom I could hold conversations – there was a name for that type of behaviour – *schizophrenia*. Kraepelin had referred to it initially as 'dementia of the young', and the phrase had terrified me. To lose one's grasp of reality in old age was a sign of the end, but to lose it in one's youth was just unthinkable.

Perhaps I could convince myself that Amelia did not exist. I decided I would ignore her; that is what I would do, I had told myself, as I walked down the leafy path. If Amelia did not exist, I would be free from my troubles. Of course, my troubles were not limited to Amelia's appearances, but my other concerns were beginning to pale in comparison to the perplexing nature of this one. Perhaps in six months or so, I would come to terms with the recent deaths that had affected me. I would hopefully come to understand that death was as inevitable as life, and that things could have been so much worse; I could have been born a Jew in Nazi Germany, or in a slum in Bombay, or in poverty in the Soviet Union. But I was born in one of the wealthiest countries in the world; so full of victory, invention, artistic achievement. I was blessed with a wealthy background and all of the commodities that come with it. With a healthier perspective, I would surely realise that it was merely insolence to believe that I was truly suffering. People like me, we never go far in life. We spend too much time thinking and self-pitying. We do not make do with what we have, because we always need something more. We compare ourselves to those who have more, and those who have less are but a distant realm we choose to overlook. When we finally get what we want, it is never good enough, or it is not what we want anymore. With such capricious and fleeting desires, we cannot ever expect to be completely satisfied, and everything that the world has to offer is wasted on people like me. It seems the only way that we can ever be truly happy is to accept that life is suffering, as the Buddhists teach. To take each second as it comes, surely must be the sensible option; we all know it. Those who smile endure so much. The suffering think they do not suffer, fools think they are unbreakable, and to the consistently depressed they are mere parasites. But those who smile are the wisest; they are the only ones who understand life enough to truly enjoy it.

However, on this particular day, happiness had no place. I don't know whether it was the hour, the tall, dark, sinister trees, or that autumn had nearly arrived, but something was rumbling my thoughts, turning them inside out with self-hatred and fear. The trees – they were all bigger than me, and so much stronger. How did they withstand the rain, the scorching summer days and the bitter winter snow, and yet still manage to stand so tall and mighty? The cold would ruthlessly strip them of their comforting foliage that took so long to appear; but the trees would carry on regardless. Year after year, the leaves reappear, then shrivel and fall come autumn, only to start the process all over again the following spring; trees have such resilience. I know that they are only shrubs, but *if a shrub has stronger willpower than me, then what hope is there?* I thought.

As I entered the clearing where the lake lay, like a silk sheet over its aphotic depths, a sense of relief came over me. When I had last visited the lake I had felt enclosed, trapped in its little domain, but now I felt the exact opposite. I dwelled on the perfect roundness of its edges, and the way the bank smoothly slipped down into the shadowy waters. I listened to the crickets chirping in the sedge, and the birds whistling a haunting tune from the trees above. For a few minutes I sat in stillness and let the earth revolve around me at its own pace. I allowed my thoughts to drift away unnoticed, and I finally felt nothing.

I cannot say what it was, possibly being near a lake in solitude, but something reminded me suddenly of the girl I had written a poem about when I was thirteen. I suddenly realised that I envied her. She was so free, so at one with everything and anything that life threw in her path. She simply danced under the summer sky, her golden locks mixing with the perfumed air. I wanted her life for myself. For a moment, I considered the possibility of pursuing such a dream; to free myself from the restrictions of thought. How I longed to be like that, and not constantly absorbed by things that I would rather have ignored, like that day when I had been down at the lake, and my mother had told me to wait until I was sure that I had found 'the one' before committing myself. And I was certain with Jim, but nothing else was. The only certainty I could have in life was that one day death would put an end to all the uncertain contingencies, all the contingent uncertainties, of existence. Now all I could think of was how pathetic I had been to believe that I had found someone I could love eternally at so young an age. For the first time in my life, I saw Jim not as I did when I first met him, on a pedestal somewhere in my dreams. I did not see him as I had when I was in love with him, as the sole being who made me look forward to the next day. I did not see him as I had at the beginning of my grief, an irreplaceable loss. The bleak truth of it was that he was just another person. A great person – one who could have made my life relatively whole – but I knew there were plenty more like him. Of course, they would have slightly different interests, they would talk differently and they would look different, they would be different – but they could make me feel the same way that Jim had. I knew I had to let go of my grief one day. I knew that, essentially, he was just another person that had passed through my life to teach me something new.

Whether my thoughts at this point were positive I cannot tell, but they led me to the final deliberation of the evening; it was a gnawing one that had been eating through the others the whole time, and only came to the forefront once it had been fed. I believe I had been hesitant to think it directly, so it had taken time for the thought to pluck up enough courage to be recognised: what must it be like to drown in that lake? I knew it was not something I wanted to do myself. I knew with all of my heart right then that I had something to live for, just as I knew there was nothing to die for. I do not know why I thought about it. Nonetheless, the image of the water filling my lungs, making it impossible to breathe, began to imprint itself onto my mind. These were not moving pictures – each one was different; the tubes being stuck down my throat in a hospital; having to explain myself to my parents; the look of disappointment and confusion etched into the worried contours of their faces; and then the screen went blank.

I waited a while until I had stopped shaking; only then did I allow myself to retreat back to the house.

It was now completely dark. I was shocked at how long I had been by the lake. During the day, the room had been cool and refreshing, and could easily have served as a hideout from the heat, had it been slightly warmer. Now, as I had forgotten to shut the window, it was uncomfortably chilly. Hannah was not in the room; she was probably out smoking somewhere. I quickly changed into my pyjamas and pulled on my dressing gown, before shutting the window and getting into bed to work my way through *This Side of Paradise*. I had not read more than a sentence when she showed her face.

"Clarice – we must talk, immediately." No. My mind was in denial. This was not happening; it could not be. It was simply impossible; yet when I closed my eyes to block her out, I still felt her overwhelming presence. When I opened them again, hoping she was gone, there she stood, resembling a faded Victorian portrait. And all the while, that clinical yet fictitious sounding word buzzed around the parameters of my thoughts: *schizophrenia*. I did not know enough about psychology to actually diagnose myself, but I was surely experiencing the key symptom, the trademark of the condition – hallucinations. I would not fuel it. I did not respond.

"Oh, please answer me! I mean you no harm, quite the contrary, in fact. Please! I implore you."

I did not reply to her pleading tone. For once, I had the control. If I did not answer, Amelia would eventually tire of her game and disappear from my mind. I knew where I had gone wrong – I had been treating her as a real person as opposed to a figment of my imagination. She carried on, but I was confident that if I was unresponsive, her visits would surely become briefer and less frequent, eventually ceasing altogether.

"You are in danger, believe me. Please, believe in me. Clarice, what can I possibly do to convince you that I am as real as the very ground you walk on?"

I ignored her, and tried to continue reading; but I was too aware of her presence and what she had been trying to tell me – that there were some kind of threat at the school, someone connected to Sheila Daniels, that I should help myself and all those who meant anything to me, by trying to "halt a maniac's progress", as she had said, which had sounded so hyperbolic that it became impossible to believe.

"I am just a messenger, Clarice. But I want to help you," she continued. "Believe in me and we can resolve all of this…" Her words finally trailed off into the night. I drew the curtains, shut off the light and buried my head in the pillow.

I awoke strangely refreshed the next day. Waking up in the English countryside is one of life's priceless luxuries that can give an entire day the reassurance of tranquillity that it needs. On a pleasant day, you do not hear just a few birds singing, but a wondrous orchestra of different chirps; the shrill tweeting of the blackbird, the husky, muffled tones of the wood pigeon and the brassy sounds of the mallards in the pond. The sun does not simply shine, but bathes trees, fields and hilltops in a golden light; there are beautiful places all over the planet, and the grounds of Willow Hill were no exception. I was feeling surprisingly confident that Amelia was just a hallucination, and that I could surely ignore her. Perhaps if she got worse, unbearable, and did not flee, then I would have to look into therapy, but I was determined now not to have the rest of my life destroyed by her and all her prophecies. I wanted nothing more to do with Sheila's death – anyone's death for that matter – and to be done with it.

It was time to move on; no more reminiscing about Jim in the afternoon sun, no more immersion in self-pity. I needed to reinvent myself. It was 1957; rock and roll, as I had known it, was in its last years of glory before its fast-paced lifestyle would come to a sudden halt. We were soon to be done. Our rebellious generation swiftly wanted to grow up. There was nothing more to do with the same old guitar riffs and stop chorus. An age of strange invention was just beyond the horizon, and not only in music. But it was still 1957, and there was no telling of the future. I would have to make do with the slow progression of time and start my own new era right then. I was so fatigued with my old life that I would need to reassess everything; my perception, my attitudes, my experiences – everything. Of course, it had been staring at me in the face this entire time. I knew my problem – I was nothing but an inexperienced schoolgirl. Yes, things had happened to me – my friends, Jim, Sheila, music. Yes, they had all happened *to me*, but I had been so passive. I needed to do something. The girl in the poem, the one whom I had aspired to be like, she did not simply sit around thinking, thinking all day. She travelled the world, and did things that had never even crossed my mind. If I was serious about overcoming the past, I could no longer let it define my future; I needed some sort of basis, a stimulus for growth. We are ever-changing beings, and surely life was to be lived; it is not just a waiting game; waiting to get rich, waiting to fall in love, waiting to die. *What was the point in any of those, when it could all end in a second, at any given moment?* I thought. *When I come to the end of my life, what will I have to say for myself?* The deal had been done. I would start afresh, and see where I ended up.

PART II
1958 – 1968

I

Although now eighteen, I was still naïve in many ways. I will never know whether it was due to or in spite of that naïveté, that I also happened to be enjoying the most carefree time in my life so far. Many an enjoyable afternoon would be spent with fellow students at Bella's, an Italian-run café in Holborn, where we would discuss politics, literature and music, or simply watch the never-ending flow of people floating by in their summer clothes. Bella's was one of the most peaceful places in the city, with its gentle lull of wind chimes, and the hushed voices of intellectuals in the background. Although in the centre of town, it was set back from the high street, at the end of an alleyway, so only the distant sounds of whirring bus engines could be heard from where we sat. In the colder months we would drink our coffee inside, reclining on the maroon leather sofas, keeping warm.

I had a wide circle of acquaintances at the Royal Academy of Music, my closest friends being Mary, Bridget and Tommy. Mary was from Cambridge and had wanted to study composition, Bridget was a girl from Chelsea with a flair for writing choral music, and Tommy came from Birmingham, and played percussion and guitar. I was sharing a room in

95

the halls of Nutford House with Mary, and was pleasantly surprised to find that she wasn't overly eccentric, introverted or bizarre enough that she seemed somewhat unhinged, as is often the way with composers. Thinking in stereotypes like that, however, I was proven to be quite wrong, not to mention hypocritical. After all, I was normal – or at least, I behaved no more strangely than anyone else I had met thus far; no one plunged their heads into buckets of cold water to help them compose; no one, as far as I knew, had any obscure fetishes or phobias, or were fascists. The majority of the students at the Royal Academy were not particularly unusual; they went to lectures and classes, performed at recitals, composed music, fell in love, worked part-time and socialised, just like any other student.

Mary and I quickly took a liking to each other. We would spend time together talking long into the night, and although it transpired that we would not remain close in our second and third years, we had willingly accepted the role of each other's confidantes at the beginning; we knew the other's likes, dislikes, strengths and limits, in a way that only roommates or housemates can perceive.

I had met Tommy in my theory classes. Everybody fought for his approval; he was an instantly likeable character, the type that would never have trouble making friends and could still achieve all the ambitions he had in life, remaining unchanged by the end of it all. He was an enthusiastic student, always energetic and constantly singing the melody or tapping the beat to some jazz song. He had a lively sense of humour as well; there was one young man in our class who was often the target of Tommy's endearing ridicule, but being somewhat slow on the uptake, it was quite possible that he didn't even realise he was being made fun of. He was so ludicrously incompetent, in what seemed like every aspect of life – even music theory – that I often wondered how he could have qualified to get into the Academy. He questioned everything on a Pyrrhonian level, so that it bordered on an irritation. The fact that his questions were of such an asinine calibre never failed to astound me either; he had once asked why chord three cannot be used in Bach chorale. As anyone who has studied music theory in any depth will be aware, chord three cannot be used in Bach chorale, firstly because Bach himself never used it, and secondly because it sounds terrible, creating a dissonance so abhorrent that only Schoënberg might have appreciated it. It was the musical equivalent of asking why we do not bathe in Breakfast tea. Tommy's teasing was the perfect antidote against the ignoramuses of our world, for which we were all very grateful.

Bridget was a revelation. I found myself drawn to her confident demeanour, just as I think she was to my open cordiality. I had met her through Tommy at some social event in the first term, and she had struck me with an attitude about her that proclaimed she did not make apologies for herself. We took an instant liking to one another, as we began to talk about I don't know what – anything you like – and hit it off faster than a batter striking a ball.

My first year at the Royal Academy went almost as quickly as my childhood, leaving only distant memories of simpler times. Looking back now, it just seems a huge blur of chorale and composition. During the ensuing summer, I had seen Hannah and Polly again. Hannah was at Oxford, studying physics and living the kind of sophisticated lifestyle which students from lesser acclaimed universities envy; but despite her academic success, I had always felt that she was the most susceptible to coming 'off the rails', as it were, although the evidence to support such an assertion may have been fairly scant; it was more of a gut instinct. Polly, on the other hand, had taken on both a secretarial job, and a committed relationship, which had not surprised me too much, for although quiet and shy, she had always been the most mature of the three of us; but here we all were, still intact, trying to make a success of life, and most importantly – enjoying it.

I had invited them over to my house, one particularly scorching day in July. I remember being somewhat taken aback by the sight of my childhood friends, and the contrast between them. Hannah looked so much older, whilst Polly had hardly changed, retaining her doll-like, curly blonde hair and soft, childlike features. The only real changes were in her mannerisms, her tone of voice; she now spoke with a newfound confidence with which I was unfamiliar. Her interests too, had changed, were rather more eclectic, but then, it seemed everyone's interests were constantly changing around that time. Growing up seemed to have suited Hannah. She was more attractive than I remembered, and appeared to have traded in her anaemic look for an air of porcelain mystique. I wondered if all the boys were in adoration of her at Oxford. But she no longer teased us the way she used to; her sly smile was wiped from her lips, and replaced with a more solemn mien. I thought I could detect guilt in her eyes – but I didn't know what for. I couldn't have asked, at the risk of sounding presumptuous or suspicious. She had more than just matured, she was hiding something, atoning for it, but I had no idea what.

As we sat having lunch with my parents and brothers, overlooking the immaculate lawn and flowerbeds, a sudden sadness overcame me. The only people who had stayed with me over the years were all sat at that table, and all at once, I was blinking to hold back tears. It was an uncomfortable position to be in, for in fact there was no reason to be sad at all. I wondered if others ever felt this way; surely they did, but was it over nothing in particular? Contemplating my own subjectivity, it did occur to me that perhaps I was wired differently; it seemed inconceivable that anyone else could overthink everything to the extent that I did. And there were thoughts I had which made me suspect a certain unchasteness in my mind – that is, unsolicited carnal thoughts. Since Jim had passed away, I had, as a result of no significant decision, remained sexually inactive, which for some can lead to all manner of problems further down the road. I understood how it felt now – for the nuns, the monks, the young virgins preserving themselves for marriage – to have to fight their urges. Resisting desire, whilst staying loyal to a wish to wait for the right person, had me pitted in direct conflict with myself. Those early days of fooling around with Jim seemed almost unreal in the present. Now, at nearly nineteen, I was beginning to surmise it might be better to simply sleep around, to forget; then I would remind myself that in the comfort of my own thoughts, I could think freely about it, without the ensuing sensations of guilt and regret that would surely come from real-life encounters. After a while, this part of my mind seemed to mould back into a teenager's, as meetings with the male sex became replete with sexual tension; I was able to view everyone through this vulgar kind of sexual filter, through which people could become objectified within a matter of seconds. It was bordering on ridiculous, and it was not as if there was any clear indication that a young woman, thinking about sex on such a regular basis, was acceptable; but if I could be as honest with myself as was possible, then perhaps this would keep further complications at bay.

It was not that my thoughts were driving me to absurd conclusions, or anything like that. After all, it was not as though I acted out of line or did anything particularly bizarre as a result; in fact, I would go as far as to say that I was probably remarkably ordinary, or even boring; over the years, I had become an expert at masking even the slightest eccentricities. I also knew that mood swings, like the one I was experiencing that afternoon, were hardly uncommon – perhaps it was hormones – I would not have been the first to suffer in this way. And the sex controversy – it could easily have been true of everyone. Although I had a tendency to dramatise and overplay, over-analyse my introspection, I could, on a good day, rationalise it back to neutrality.

"You should have brought Will with you, Polly. I'm intrigued to meet him!" Hannah said later that night. The three of us were sat up talking long into the early hours. It was just like old times, during those extensive stretches of summer holiday when we would stay round each other's houses.

"As am I," I rejoined.

"He would have loved to have come, but he's away on business actually," Polly replied, blushing ever so slightly.

"What does he do for a living, again?" Hannah asked, passing round a packet of cigarettes.

"He's a camera assistant. He's actually filming something in Hollywood at the moment – his father worked for Warner Brothers."

"How prodigious!" Hannah exclaimed. "I always wondered what type of man you would end up with. You were so quiet at school, you'd never let on who you liked or disliked!" I sensed a slight discomfort ripple through the room at her words. Perhaps I had misjudged it – maybe Hannah had not changed so much after all. Even now, she could still manage to steer a conversation in the precise direction that it was not willing to go in.

"*I*, on the other hand," she continued, "would never shut up! I was always rambling on about my dream boyfriend, and then there was Clare and Jim…"

Her words fell back on themselves, issuing forth a perplexing silence. It was not that I minded the topic arising. I had overcome all of that; but Hannah and Polly hadn't a clue where they stood in this complex territory. I had never actually discussed it with them, which seems peculiar given that I told them almost everything else, and vice versa; but he had died just before my last year of school, and so as a guilty child avoids the scorn of his parents, we had avoided the topic altogether; it was easier for us to pretend that Jim had never existed. If we could ignore that slight blip in our existences, the line would flatten out, the future would run its course smoothly.

"I always knew you'd end up with the right man, Polly," I said, genuinely happy for her, glad for all of us that anything, and everything, seemed attainable at that point in our lives.

Summer drifted by all too quickly, and I returned to the Academy for my second year. I had decided I needed to fulfil the object I had set myself in school; to embark on a new journey that was rich with experience. My first year, although it had been mostly uneventful, had at least helped me to move on from the trauma that I was still then experiencing. Now that I was starting again, laying out the foundations for the future, I was feeling more optimistic than ever, and with positive thoughts filling my head, I plunged myself straight into an elite pool of scholarly socialites, along with Tommy and Bridget. My friendship with Mary, whom I had got on so well with in the first year, had somewhat dwindled, which I suppose was not all too surprising, seeing as we had been held together more by the fact that we shared a room than anything else. In the second year I was assigned my own room, the privacy of which I infinitely preferred to the claustrophobic intimacy of a shared room.

I began to enjoy myself a little more. The quiet nights of study in my first year at the Academy were over, and now I found myself immersed in a social whirl of bustling party-going. If there was a party to be had, my friends and I would be there, and after the long, quiet summer spent back at home, I was truly quite excited when it was announced that a ball was being thrown in honour of the second and third year students, in Marylebone. It was not that I had *become* a scholarly socialite, conjuring up, as it does, images of pretentious people strolling round extravagant parties in Mayfair and Park Lane, champagne in one hand and a Dunhill International in the other; but that was not to say that I didn't mix with those who did, and their company was anything but dull.

I had been readily anticipating the ball since it was announced; it was as if I had known that the date would be somehow significant; that it would mark the moment at which my life finally accelerated. That weekend I departed the real world, and entered into a soporific, parallel one of endless days and nights that blended intangibly into one another, all to the beat of whichever song was playing. The music never stopped, nor did the flow of alcohol, or the conversation, or the dancing. Each night was a splendid dream which could be shared with whomever one happened to meet, dance with – or even go home with. I was enjoying being young again, really enjoying it. I could not remember a time since childhood when I had ever been so content. Life had become a pageant of simple routines; I would wake up in the morning, shower, dress, have breakfast, attend classes and seminars, perhaps study, then powder my face and slick on some lipstick for whatever the evening had in store. One thing was always guaranteed: no one would be asleep before the clock had struck midnight.

Since my recent transformation into something approaching a social butterfly, I really began to appreciate the art of good conversation, and enjoyed navigating it. Aside from the awkwardness of the usual introductions, and customary opening questions – *What's your name? What do you read? Where are you from?* and so on – the encounter would be surprisingly simple; any stalemate, or lull, would be smoothly handled. If there was a definite chemistry or affinity with another, then evening would roll quickly into night without so much as a blink of an eye.

My life had become like a condensed version of *The Great Gatsby,* except the 1920's glitz and boating trips had been replaced with an academic edge and library expeditions. Conversation had never been so dynamic, largely due to the great variety of people that I was meeting. If one wants to experience extreme opinions and all that lies in-between – go to parties in universities with an ample supply of alcohol, for that is where thoughts are flung about so freely. And why? Because one is surrounded by scholars, and there will inevitably be those who take alarming pleasure in ramming their educated opinions down the throats of all who stand in their path, believing it would be pointless to discuss anything else, when there is opportunity for debate. For those less concerned with voicing their opinions, the night was about other things: dancing until the small hours, finding a potential soulmate, or simply someone who would hold them tight. Whatever your intentions were for the evening, there was one collective purpose for all of us, which was, of course, to have a good time. In the morning, when it was all over, the resulting hangovers, the feeling jaded – none of that mattered, because we were young.

Waking up next to someone you hardly remembered meeting was not uncommon for some either. I had heard all kinds of stories, so many of them from Tommy, who considered himself something of a veteran when it came to losing consciousness mid-encounter. Regularly, he would regale us with tales of his drunken escapades. As he had told me on one occasion, he had woken up next to an extremely attractive girl; so attractive, he could hardly believe his luck. Whilst lying in bed, admiring her comely features the next morning, he had begun to recall snippets of the previous night's conversation, and her talk of marriage, children, and owning a pleasant suburban home. To his horror, he remembered how obsessive she had become with being his future wife. What was worse, he hadn't the faintest idea as to how he had ended up in bed with her, insisting there was no way his actions were voluntary, however much she resembled Marilyn Monroe. As soon as she awoke, she would surely be wanting him to confess his love to her – something that was simply not going to happen. Glad that he had awoken in her bed and not his, he grabbed his clothes and disappeared while she slept. We would find out later, during an awkward encounter with that same girl, that Tommy had been ludicrously drunk, and she had done nothing more than take him home and let him sleep in her bed – as innocent as that. Unlike Tommy, I had difficulty finding myself in situations like that in the first place, and was never faced with the predicament of waking up next to a complete stranger.

Meanwhile, I had developed my own secret passion – London. Whilst others gazed adoringly into the sparkling eyes of those they had just met, I acquainted myself with the city, always searching for the nearest view of the Thames, be it from a balcony, an open window, or a nearby bridge. Whenever unpleasant memories, or the harsh words of others came to their attack, I now had an escape; the cool city breeze on my skin, the comforting rumble of passing traffic, the romance of twinkling lights. Whenever the oppressive thoughts returned, though, I found this as a time to cry. It had never really been commonplace for me to shed tears, but lately, it had become more frequent. Perhaps it made sense; I was now socialising with an ever-increasing number of people, and spending whatever time I had with myself agonising over stupid things I had said, and smart things I had not said. Those breezy nights by the Thames produced a bittersweet sadness in me, often reducing me to a wreck, and yet, oddly enough, I could not have asked for any other place to be.

One evening as I stood looking out across the Chelsea Embankment, someone emerged from the party that I had been at minutes before. He must have been in his mid-thirties, perhaps older, with dark hair that was slightly unkempt, as if someone had ruffled it and he had forgotten to smoothen it out.

"Good evening," the stranger said.

"Hello," I replied, recognising his face from earlier on.

"Beautiful, isn't it?" he continued, gesturing at the river and the plain of indigo which formed its backdrop.

"It is. I love just watching the city go by at night," I said abstractedly, letting the Thames dance before my eyes in mesmeric show.

"Sometimes it's good to look up at the sky and remember that whatever it is that you're chasing, running from or forgetting is always eclipsed by what's going on up there; it will be all that is constant, when we come to the end. It's a strange thought, isn't it? Because we act like it isn't obvious."

"Yes," I replied, "it really is." It was as if my present musings were being pieced together, put into words and spoken aloud for me by this stranger-philosopher. I had wanted the conversation to continue, but before I had a chance to think of anything witty to respond with, he had bid me goodnight and disappeared indoors. I never saw him again.

On the first of May, 1960, a U-2 spy plane was shot down over the Soviet Union, and Eisenhower tried to convince the world that it was a weather research plane. It also happened to be the day that Bridget, Tommy and I decided to travel to the United States in the following summer. Given the circumstances, I can understand why our friends and relatives had shivered at the plan, but although relations between North America and the Soviet Union were growing increasingly turbulent, it seemed obvious to me that there was no real danger in our midst.

Whilst we were still young and air travel had become

slightly more affordable, not even the threat of conflict had deterred us. As far as we were concerned, the United States was the promised land; it was bigger, the landscapes were more diverse, people smiled more – at least, that's how it appeared in the movies. The plan was to go the following summer, having attained our degrees, and to do a grand tour of the west coast. We would, with our meagre part-time work and the money we would have saved, be able to produce enough to travel to the land of the free. The aim was quite simple: this was my chance to do something by my own instigation; it was something that I wanted, not something I felt obligated to do as yet another rung on a ladder. No one had told me to travel to America, but there I was, with the rigour of my father in the boardroom, practically initiating the idea. So it was decided: we were going to the United States.

Stepping off the aeroplane in Los Angeles, I became suddenly aware of the reality of the situation. Visitors, travellers, tourists – whatever category we fitted into, we were merely foreign observers, briefly looking into the lives of those around us; a man in military attire, possibly returning from some ungodly battle with communism; a group of men from a different world entirely, in lavishly tailored suits, holding shiny new briefcases; women with designer handbags, headscarves and scarlet lipstick; and then us, our heavy bags loaded with vigour, our voices brimming with excitement, our eyes sparkling with innocence.

Having saved extensively for the past year whilst working part-time jobs, and being the privileged young people that we were – with a fair amount of help from our parents – we had managed to find enough money between us to finance our journey completely. The most expensive purchase – a necessity rather than a luxury – would be a vehicle. We were looking for an old, high mileage camper van; something that was mechanically sound, rather than a work of art – which was why we had asked the taxi driver to drop us off, with our luggage, at the nearest motor dealer, twenty minutes from LAX.

The site was adorned with countless rusty old vehicles; Fords, Chevys, Cadillacs – all good old American brand names. Most of them seemed good enough to drive, yet they were hardly in their prime. That they had once graced billboards, with images of them cruising along the scenic highways of this prosperous country was of little relevance, now that they were all parked rather unceremoniously on this turf.

"We're looking for a lot of mileage – the cheaper the better," Tommy said, approaching the dealer – 'Ted', according to his name tag – a kindly looking old man with a round, owl-like, bespectacled face.

"Lots of mileage for a low price," Ted registered, taking off his cap and lazily scratching his head.

"You see, we're going to be touring the west over the next couple of weeks," Bridget began.

"Ah, to be young again," Ted rejoined, gazing for a moment into the distance.

"It's such a fabulous idea, thanks to Clare here. She really planted the seed in all of our heads…" I coughed, trying to get her attention. Her somewhat vexatious habit of going off on a detailed tangent, for no good reason, was only going to delay us. She glanced at me, but continued, unabashed. "Anyway… we're going to need a vehicle that's comfortable, and we don't mind if it's rather tarnished – we're going to be camping most of the time, and…" Her words trailed off as she noticed Tommy kicking the tyres of an old Chevrolet conversion.

"How much is that one going for over there? It looks perfect!" she exclaimed, as we joined Tommy in looking at the old Chevy. In reality, it was just a run-down heap, but in our eyes, it was a stylish jewel of the road. The dealer – who had been outmanoeuvred, credit to Bridget's domineering tone, quickly examined the van, adverting to various points of interest as he went; the wooden trim, the V8 engine, the idiosyncratic sunroof, and so on.

"Ah, yeah – the land yacht. Okay, how does three-forty sound? She's ready to go – ready to drive away," he said, grinning broadly, aware that a sale looked assured.

"Well, that seals the deal, as far as I'm concerned!" a relieved looking Tommy chimed, amazed at its price – we had anticipated having to spend a great deal more. Beaming, we all shook hands with Ted. Bridget, in particular, looked jubilant, just like she always seemed to, whenever things went her way – not that I minded – the Chevrolet really did seem quite the bargain. It did not bother us that it looked a little shabby around the tail, or that it was a conversion rather than a custom job – it only added to our sense of adventure; and the fact that we would probably be refunded when we eventually sold it on, made it an accomplishment all round – presuming it made it in one piece. Whilst our plans for getting around might not quite have been of the same calibre as Homer's *Odyssey*, we were doing just fine, on our exiguous budget.

Bridget batted her long, lacquered eyelashes at Ted for the final time, before linking arms with me, and ambling jovially to the front of the camper. Tommy paid the dealer in cash, who disappeared inside for a moment, returning later with a receipt, and a map.

"You might find this useful – it's a lot more detailed than the travel guides," he said, handing it to me. "If you just follow this route – you see, I've marked it – that should get you all around Arizona, Nevada, North California, and back here again."

Happily reassured that Americans were the most accommodating of all mankind, we thanked him profusely, and drove off into the afternoon sun. Ideally, we had wanted to travel the entire country, and explore New York, New England, and Chicago, but the expense was simply too much. Instead, we stayed between the West Coast and Wyoming. As for our standard of living for those two weeks, it was just as well we weren't expecting to be travelling in luxury. In some ways, it resembled the unwashed, uninhibited lifestyle of the Beats. Depending on our spirits, for most nights we slept in the camper shell, occasionally assembling the tents if we were staying in one location for more than a night. To treat ourselves, we had once or twice booked into a motel to catch up on lost sleep. Sometimes, we just slept under the stars, and those nights were always the most memorable. There really is nothing quite like lying beneath a sky scattered with stars on a moonlit night, cocooned in the warmth of a sleeping bag, beside the embers of a dying campfire.

We arrived at a campsite late one afternoon, the receding sunlight causing the hills to glow and radiate the purest of golds. As dusk fell, we lit a fire and cooked baked beans and sausages, and although we could have been eating exactly the same food back at home, everything tasted different, just as the air tasted different, felt different, smelled different. Everything was unavoidably foreign, which added to the thrill of our adventure.

"Well, I think a toast is in order," Tommy proposed, raising his bottle of Budweiser.

"Yes!" Bridget cried with enthusiasm, also raising her bottle. "To us! To the United States of America!"

The next morning after breakfast we resumed our travels, continuing eastward through Palm Springs, and into Phoenix, Arizona. Already, I had begun to notice the racial battle that was occurring in the country, aware that many liked to dislike, segregate and stereotype. To know that what Jim had described from his birthplace in Indiana was worse than what I was witnessing in western America, was a blow to my conscience in itself. It is one thing hearing of someone else's reality, with an inevitable inability to truly empathise, and quite another to live this reality. Suddenly, it springs into action, and one feels foolish for choosing to ignore it before, as if it did not actually exist until then. In England, I would sometimes glimpse a sign that read: *No blacks, no dogs, no Irish*, just as in the States, there would be signs reading: *No dogs, negroes, Mexicans*; but in America, that was the least of it; I knew that in some states, this was just a standard public requirement. Buses were segregated, abuse was uttered under the breath of a few, and yet I knew that this still held nothing over the notorious brutality of the Deep South.

In Arizona, as we lay on our backs studying the darkened sky, the night air cool, fresh and musty in our nostrils, we witnessed a meteor shower – a truly incredible sight. Shooting stars criss-crossed the blue-black sky, as though putting on a display just for our own eyes. I had never seen such an abundance of shooting stars, that darted like fireworks, spluttering on and off every few seconds. The static ones were equally impressive, twinkling, burning, like fiery jewels, adorning their vast backdrop; where one star faded, another immediately appeared. The chirping of crickets, and the occasional sweep of a breeze that rustled patches of long grass around us, were the only indication that we were not lying at the core of silence. Suddenly, I became aware of my own breathing, ever-resonant in my chest; the deep inhalation and exhalation of life. I had never felt more at peace, despite an underlying sadness that seemed to live within my bones; if it had been my function to distil and bottle melancholia, this would have been the source. It was like looking at one's own life from some external viewpoint; and I came to realise – or rather, to remember, for possibly the millionth time – that we are all but specks of dust, scattered chaotically across the earth's surface. And yet – and yet – even as seemingly minor specks, everything we do, or fail to do, produces a consequence of universal effect. And as I lay there, I suppose it was unavoidable that certain thoughts would return to trouble me, whether or not I anticipated it, or wanted it; those overwhelming thoughts that would slowly destruct my being, but that I also seemed to thrive on.

After Phoenix, we visited the Grand Canyon and Las Vegas before heading up to Utah. Driving through, we had seen its famous red rocks, and wide desert landscapes. Central Utah held more colourful sights in store, with its many trees that skirt the boundaries of canyons; and to the north, the landscape changes yet again to evergreen forests and snow-capped mountains. It was in Fishlake National Forest, one of Utah's most remote locations, that I truly witnessed the enormity and diversity of nature. While there, I had closely watched the behaviour of many animals in their natural habitats. Having only ever done this within the confines of my garden at home, a variety of unfamiliar and wild animals was a novelty which fascinated me. I had once visited London Zoo when I was four or five. I do not remember much of the experience, but I do retain one or two very vivid images from it; I sometimes recall the excitement of being so close to a real life lion cub, a small child myself. I remember the freshness in those little cubs' enormous new eyes, yet to witness the cruel truths of living and dying. Few of them had grown teeth, not yet having developed the need to kill, and their roar was inchoate, resembling more a pitiful groan; without a reason to roar, with no one to impress and no one to threaten, they were the embodiment of innocence, even to my own infant eyes. Some of them had begun to grow darker patches of fur on their heads, soon to be filled with knowledge of survival – and not long after that, they would live only for routine, knowing they would at least be provided for. Escaping was out of the question, if they were only to be killed or dragged back to their cages as a result; they may as well just have carried on where they were. To this day I have never seen more helplessness than in the faces of those lion cubs. I also remember the cheetahs;

so full of wisdom, but with a look of resignation in their eyes. The adult cheetahs would lazily slump themselves across a tree branch and simply stare into the eyes of onlookers. They did not make noise or run around merrily as the lion cubs had, but simply lay there, as if in the knowledge that they were not truly free. Now, as I observed the elk peacefully grazing, and the mountain lion cubs frolicking under the trees, their elders basking in the sunlight, I saw that there was very little to be said for captivity.

Despite the beauty of the national parks, the spectacle that is Las Vegas, and not to mention the varying Californian territory, veering as it does between plain suburbia, beautiful beaches, and the incredible forests of its northern parts – it was in San Francisco I wanted to stay forever. I loved the sloping streets that verged on dangerous, its diverse music scene that was a novelty to me, and simply looking over the dazzling ocean from the Golden Gate Bridge. We had enjoyed an afternoon taking photographs on one of the beaches there; my favourite was one of Bridget twirling in the sea, her skirt spread out like a parachute, hair lifted by the wind, as Tommy and I sat on the shore, laughing at her haphazard ways. Fortunately, we managed – all three of us – to keep our relationships on a purely platonic level, which was just as well. Coming from an all-girls' school, I fought for many years against a conviction that men and women could never just be friends, but as the years passed, this conviction was continually undermined. I can only imagine the ensuing disaster if Bridget or myself had somehow fallen for Tommy; but there were no surreptitious romantic walks, whispered words, or secrets, and as a result, not a single feud developed over the course of our trip.

Los Angeles greeted us for the second time with cloudless skies and summer heat. Buildings glistened in the sun, radiating a grand sense of importance. Baseball was the topic of the day, occupying most of the conversation in every bar, for earlier in the year, the Los Angeles Angels had come into existence, and now they were doing well. However, I was never remotely interested in matters of sport, unlike Tommy, who found great delight in discussing the latest scores with anyone who displayed a modicum of interest. Bridget and I decided that our time was better spent exploring Hollywood, where an entire street was lined with men and women all holding leads, on the end of which were black cats. I had heard the stories, of course, of Hollywood's people and their bizarre behaviour, and how they preferred carrying their dogs to walking them – but I had not expected to be witnessing black cats on leashes. After a few seconds of confusion, it soon became apparent that the cats and their owners were actually queuing for an audition. The sea of people – and cats – seemed utterly absurd; these proud owners, fussing over their cosseted pets, all in the belief that it was their animal, and theirs alone, which possessed that certain *je ne sais quoi* which would land them the role. Their belief was so robust that they were willing to stand in a queue for hours on end, and for such a small financial reward. For some, things were not going splendidly; one poor man was having to prise his cat out of a plant box, where it had been looking to do its business, whilst an overweight woman in a fur coat struggled with her wriggling feline, as it slipped from her grasp, making a grand escape, laddering her tights and tearing her dress in the process. Bridget and I couldn't help but giggle to ourselves at this farce of a scene.

We proceeded to stroll down the boulevard, the pageantry of it exceeding anything we might have previously called glamorous. There was not a celebrity in sight, and yet the place was bursting with fame; there were lights everywhere, which at night would illuminate the streets with loud, flashing colours. The handprints and footprints of movie stars that we all once idolised were impressed permanently into the pavement, and people drove slick cars; and yet, indeed I failed to find any substance to this world, for it had lacked a sense of reality in a way that no other place did. Hollywood really is a saddening rendezvous for those who have packed up entire lives, and moved thousands of miles away to achieve what most often remains a dream – either for lack of talent, looks, or connections; or perhaps it was just a case of Marilyn Monroe being spotted first. They spend whatever money they can on looking the part, scour newspapers day after day in search of a small acting or modelling job, or gig – just in case that famous record producer shows up and signs them right away. What one hears is true: many will spend the rest of their lives doing menial jobs on the slush piles of Hollywood. But hearing is one thing, seeing quite another.

We wondered what it would be like to travel across the rest of the country; it would be quite an experience, driving through the ranching communities of Texas, across Alabama's rustic landscapes, to the very tip of Key West, and back. We would see the forests of West Virginia, which I have heard are truly spectacular, and would contrast wildly with our final stop in the city that never sleeps. Perhaps one day, I mused, I would be able to make that journey.

We spent our final two days in Los Angeles. The night before flying home, we had decided to visit a bar called Margarita's, which claimed to produce 'THE BEST COCKTAILS IN TOWN!' As Tommy sat at the bar, watching a crucial game of baseball, Bridget and I settled at a table in the corner. Before embarking on our travels, we had not been particularly close; it was not that we hadn't spent time together before, discussing current events, music and general gossip, but we never discussed anything much other than that. As a result, I had never really known that much about her, for she was trapped behind an exterior which did her little justice. She was similar to Polly in a way, but in the reverse; whereas Polly had been crippled by shyness, Bridget was stricken with a false confidence, emanating, as she did, a dull superstratum of vogue and hauteur, which did nothing more than mask the reality that she possessed neither of these features. The character she chose to portray was created from an upbringing in an aristocratic family, and was thus easy for her to execute. It was only since travelling together, that I slowly began to realise who she really was. Now, though, as we conversed over martinis, it finally occurred to me that the young woman I was now talking to was entirely different to the one I had met back in the days of Bach chorale. I had learnt that she was scared to love, the reason for which I could only suspect was rooted in insecurity; how the insecurity came about, I do not know.

"I'm just not good enough!" she had cried, her words cushioned by the cheers of baseball fans. I knew that responding to a statement such as this bordered on impossible; to reply with 'don't be so ridiculous' would only lead to a list of reasons why the remark should not be perceived as ridiculous, and to agree is but the greatest *faux pas* one could imagine. I chose the former.

"No, Clare, honestly – it's true. I don't even know why it's important to me, but it's torture; I'm just not what men want. I'm never anyone's first choice."

"Why would you even think that?" I responded. "From the moment I met you, I've never known you to say something like that. You just breathe confidence – why are you suddenly doubting yourself? Besides, I would have thought that being as good-looking as you are would make you a lot of people's first choice!" This last remark had been a vapid attempt to lighten the mood, in the midst of having no idea what to say.

"I don't know whether you're just saying that to make me feel better, or if you do mean it, but being good-looking isn't enough; any man worth having will choose not only the best-looking, but the interesting and intelligent girl, and that's just not me. That's why he left; she was beautiful, inside and out, and I only have myself to blame for not even coming close to that."

She was making this troublesome for both of us. I too had worried about my individual worth, but I had never let these anxieties feast upon my mind, as Bridget had. Admittedly, now and then I would have my woes, but I would not allow myself to make something that was in fact so absurd interfere with my life in this way. But some troubles are deep-seated, and they affect us beyond what anyone else could ever understand.

"God, you must think I'm so shallow. Sorry, forget I mentioned it. I won't burden you with this any longer. Let's just enjoy tonight."

"It's not shallow at all," I said. "It's not that you're not good enough – it's them, they're not. Do you really want to waste your time on someone who isn't worth it?" I may as well have said, *You just haven't met the right person yet*, for all the use I knew these dismal reassurances to be.

"No, I suppose not," she replied. "I suppose I just haven't met the right person yet." She refused to discuss the matter any further. I gave her some final words of encouragement, as she sighed, and the band played on, and we continued to drink until our heads spun and all we could hear was the sound of our own blood rushing about up there.

By the time we had returned to England's green and pleasant land, I was changed. I thought of nothing but going back to live in California. Everywhere in England seemed grey, flat and dull in comparison to the vibrancy of San Francisco. I was entirely unmotivated, unwed, and now unemployed, having finished my final year of education. Now that I was alone in the world with not an inkling of what I should do, I was more vulnerable than ever; and all along I had known that it is only a matter of time before one's demons return to haunt them.

It had been a quiet afternoon in San Francisco, an unexceptional day of work. I had been writing a review of Frank Sinatra's new album, *All Alone*, which as can be interpreted from the title, is woebegone in its theme. Despite Sinatra's unassailable talent, this was not one of his most acclaimed creations. I was now taking a break, lounging on the sofa with a glass of iced tea and a book. The radio was on, over the subdued sound of the city outside, which seemed a calm haven for my bustling mind. Abruptly, the programme I had been listening to was interrupted by an announcement:

"Good evening, my fellow citizens," President Kennedy began, his flat tone trickling through the transmission.

After the announcement, I was left thoughtful for a moment, contemplating the words *Cuba*, *Soviet* and *worldwide nuclear war*. The situation that had just been described was designed to terrify, and I dabbled in my mind with the idea of another sweeping world war. As I often felt with any life-threatening situation, if I were to die, it would not necessarily be a bad thing, for I was somewhat agnostic when it came to life after death, being quite content to wait and see; if there is anything I have learnt in life, it is that having faith in one's expectations is indeed futile. In this case, if I were killed, it would be for the better, as nothing could be worse than survival in a post-nuclear world. The planet would deteriorate, until it was devoured entirely by our ocean's blackened waves; the end of the world would no longer be nigh – it would have arrived. If America had been obliterated first, it would not have come as a great surprise to me; since the end of the Second World War, perhaps buoyed by its supreme power, the United States seemed to have been going round in circles, achieving nothing but an assortment of enemies; being a spectator to this was tiring.

The following day, a nebulous tension circulated the city. The question that inhabited the minds of many concerned whether it would all be blowing over or blowing up, but the majority of people continued with their routines, as one can only ever do. I had heard that there was more unease on the eastern side of the country, but people generally knew not to panic. Of course, there were exceptions to this, for example, the man next door who hoarded food and purchased a gas mask, before locking himself in his house for a week. I remember how the crisis dominated the news for a while, before it eventually subsided, and the tension that had so tightly grasped the planet, relaxed.

At the time of the Cuban missile crisis, I had already been living in San Francisco for two months. On returning from my trip to America, my mind had been occupied day and night with a craving to go back, to live in a country so large that I could simply disappear at any moment. Everyone's business was their own and there was no domineering culture to judge anyone by; people just guilelessly went about whatever they were doing. One has to have lived on a small island or in a small town to understand the value of anonymity, or even what it truly entails. In English villages, the line between what is commonplace and gossip-worthy is abundantly clear; if a woman so much as wears an outdated hat in a shop, it will most likely arise in conversation at dinner. This was less so in the big cities of the States.

Not only did I see the appeal of anonymity, but I craved the balmy air and sun-washed sand of the West Coast. I longed for each day to be different, and each night to feel the soft breeze upon my skin. I dreamed of bustling streets, full of every kind of person. I wanted to see the Golden Gate Bridge from a window, and sometimes, to see only the summit of its towers, emerging from the fog. I was dying in this forlorn country, which was nothing but a constant reminder of death and incomprehensible events. I had to escape.

Since I had returned from my trip with Tommy and Bridget, I had remained unemployed for a short while – although it felt like years. Despite now having a degree, it made finding a career that I wanted to pursue, let alone actually pursuing it, no simpler. When I began my studies at the Royal Academy, I had wanted to write scores for films, but by the end of my three years, my engrossment had shifted to music criticism; I now wanted to write about music that inspired me. While at the Academy, I had rather inconveniently discovered that composition was not my strongest feat. At first, I believed my musical ability, and knowledge of music theory, could sustain me – and it did; but I lacked the originality and novelty of my fellow students, let alone the great composers. When I was younger, I believed that I had an aptitude for composition, but now I recognised that this belief was based upon the astonishment of my elders – the astonishment that I could compose and perform an intelligible melody in my childhood, not that I was particularly expert at it. My belief was finally called into question when I started composing seriously at the Academy. I would listen to the creations of other students, feeling the acute envy of being unable to parallel their natural talent.

Having heard fantastical melodies and beauteous harmonies, I would then retire to the *Bösendorfer* to formulate my own, but my mindless stabbing at the keys never produced so much as a relatively decent piece of work. The only truly commendable music that I produced was not my own; if I played anything which sounded at all inspiring, it was because it had automatically wavered into a fragment of Mozart. To my good fortune, I received a considerable amount of help from my tutors when it came to composing a final piece – so much so, that the music I produced was hardly composed by myself at all.

Having endured three years of this, I resolved that I would most probably never compose anything again in my life. If my path had been in literature, I would have been the reader, and not the writer. Because my path was musical, I was not fearful of becoming the writer, just so long as it was not harmonies, melodies or lyrics that I was producing. Once it was established that I might be better suited to reviewing music, I decided to follow this path, and see where it led me. After several weeks of rejections from the various British publications I had submitted work to, I thought to broaden my search, and look overseas. All along, I had been determined to start my career exactly where I had wanted to be: in San Francisco. As a freelance journalist, working for whomever I could, I felt confident that I might be able to start making a small living out of it. The only issue was getting there. It had been easy travelling in the summer, for I had saved up a large sum of money; but now, I was on my own, and there was not a chance that I would dare ask for anything from my parents. However, out of desperation to fulfil my plans, I eventually – and rather inevitably – accepted their kind offer to pay for my flight – provided that I stay in England for at least a few more months. It was an offer I couldn't refuse.

"Your father and I want nothing more than for you to

be happy, and we think it's great that you've already decided what you want to do – we're very happy about that – we owe you this," my mother appealed as we sipped tea in the conservatory. "No one can blame you for wanting to relocate; we all need to get out into the world and discover ourselves at some point."

"No, no, you don't owe me anything," I replied. "This is something I want to do and I'm going to have to work for it, like everyone else. Trust me, I'll do whatever it takes for a change of scenery."

"Don't be ridiculous, Clarice!" my father remarked. "We're paying for your flight, and that's final. You can do whatever you want once you're there, but we're not going to sit back and watch you struggle. The least we can do is pay your travel costs. Let us do this, and don't even think about it." As if to emphasise his point, he gestured towards the expensive adornments that graced the walls, and the gilt-edged miniatures on the side table. He was right, of course, and if that was what they truly wanted to do, I was not going to stop them.

I continued working a secretarial job until the end of the summer, and tried in the meantime not to get involved with anything or anyone who might have kept me there; I was in a kind of oblivion. As late August arrived, like a butterfly being unpinned, the glass case was dismantled, and I at last held limitless freedom in both hands. It did not occur to me, however, that a butterfly's freedom is intensely ephemeral.

Although my first visit to San Francisco had been an exciting novelty, this time I truly immersed myself in the environment; I let the city breeze wash over my face, and the sound of the traffic alert all of my senses. I savoured the smell of exotic foods as I passed various restaurants. I wanted to let this place become my home. Having rented an apartment in the Haight-Ashbury district, at a good price, I started to feel settled. I was pleased with the surprisingly spacious – if a little rundown – wooden structured apartment, secretly praying that I could afford to continue living there.

As it transpired, finances eventually became the least of my troubles. As a freelance journalist, I started to make a name for myself, which helped enormously when it came to being paid. It had not taken me long to grasp what the music of this city was all about. It always has been, and always will be, unrivalled in its thirst for new and ground-breaking music. San Francisco may not have produced Elvis or The Beatles, but it had its fair share of talent. The best music is not measured by how popular it can become; it is no dedicated follower of fashion, and does not insist upon being controversial. The best music, as with all art, is created through observation; the artist must be able to both deconstruct and reconstruct the world around them, in order to understand it – or rather, not to understand anything at all; from what is observed, the artist must gather a combination of emotions, which in turn gives life to great art.

I came to the city just a few years before it became known as the pivot of countercultural music, but melodious composition had been running through its streets for decades. At the time that I arrived, the American folk revival was at its climax, led by The Kingston Trio, and of course, there was the city's ever-great jazz scene, with Brubeck's almost minimalist refrains and Guaraldi's distinctive sound. His nineteen fifty-seven album, *A Flower is a Lovesome Thing*, emanates the sounds of Miles Davis, Debussy and Webern all at once.

I had a vivid and enthusiastic outlook on the music that surrounds us; I suppose that is how I became successful in what I did – and in gaining a name for myself, I became increasingly sociable. Soon enough, I was attending every party in town, draining cocktail glasses and feasting on fondue, while I drunkenly related musical points to strangers; after all, I had little image to maintain, being widely unknown, and my celebrity matching none of those around me. When I first arrived in the States, I feared that I would be incredibly lonely, not knowing much about America's people. Despite that Jim had been American, and I had visited the country before, I still suspected a transatlantic language barrier to exist. We would inevitably have our differences, the American people and I – after all, we came from different sides of the world. I am not referring to major disparities, such as linguistic and moral ones, just the smaller, idiosyncratic customs; but my fears were soon abolished when I came to realise that I was quickly making acquaintances, perhaps faster than I had ever done in England.

During my first two weeks in the city, I relied perhaps too heavily on relations at home to sustain me, and I began to miss Tommy and Bridget. At the time I left, Tommy was living in a cramped flat near Soho, writing music and poetry, and intoxicating his body. Bridget had become something of a recluse, having fallen into a pit of despair after an idea had planted itself in her head that no man would ever love her; and why she had thought this, I will never know. Since returning from our trip, we had become incredibly close, sharing our deepest thoughts and spending time in each others' company. As the fingers of the women we knew became, one by one, girdled in expensive rings, until ours were the only ones left, Bridget became increasingly despondent. I tried numerous times to comfort her, quick to mention that I was equally alone; but sometimes, her qualms would be so dominating that even I became afraid of eternal loneliness. However, I was still in no hurry to be paired; unlike Bridget, I didn't experience the gnawing agony of lying awake until four in the morning, terrified of dying alone. But I have heard about this feeling one too many times to claim utter immunity to it. As Bridget eventually began to drag my spirits down with hers, further into this bottomless crevasse, I had to let her go. By that time, I knew I was moving away, so it was a matter of holding on by my fingertips until my leave came. She barely slept, and lost many things: her appetite, her healthy glow, her curves, strands of hair, the character that she had spent her life perfecting. By May, we barely spoke. She did not want to see anyone; her own self-loathing had inevitably led to her withdrawal. She stayed inside most days and nights, and we no longer set dates to meet. Having little understanding of her situation, and only so much sympathy, I gave up. If only I could reverse time and pick my dearest friend up from her gaunt knees, sit her on the softest chair of the finest fabric, wipe her tears, hold her tight and tell her repeatedly that her life was not over, oh, I would.

By the time I crossed the Atlantic, I had lost all contact with Bridget forever, whether I realised it or not. I will never know if any person is granted a happy ending; had I not lost touch with her, my mind might be at peace. Tommy had lost contact with her too and, like myself, later regretted not leaving space for her in his life. On the other hand, I had managed to sustain communication with Polly and Hannah, who were now both married, Polly even having a little girl.

It was a full moon on the night that I met Jillian. I remember this detail because of the emotions that stirred within me when I first looked upon that luminous sphere. It was significantly bigger than usual, and I remember that the sky had been especially beautiful that night; every kind of blue, perhaps even Hume's missing shade, had painted it; midnight blended into sapphire, which fused itself with steel, and the moon was ringed with a turquoise aura, partially covered by thin, smoky layers of cloud. A multitude of vivid stars dotted the celestial sphere, creating a magnitude of awe within me. I had been in America for a week now, and had ventured out to a local bar. It was a small, but packed, place where some unknown folk singer was playing; whatever happened to him, I don't know, but I can hazard a guess that his music never made it into a record shop. Aware that I was doing something that would normally have been out of my comfort zone, I had nonetheless developed a kind of carelessness, which I gradually learnt to carry with me into just about every uncomfortable situation; but at the same time, I had admittedly felt rather lonesome that night, being the foreigner that I was, and not quite fitting in. I knew that I had to stop thinking of myself as a foreigner, for I was in fact part of the city now; but before I had time to dwell on the matter, I was approached by a girl who was equally alone – a comforting sight in a crowded room.

"Excuse me, do you mind if I sit here? This place is packed!" the young woman exclaimed.

"No, of course," I responded.

She looked to be around my age, perhaps younger, but her expression and demeanour more resembled somebody who has acquiesced years of experience.

"Do you come here often?" she asked with a smile, a perfectly aligned set of teeth contrasting marvellously against her bold red lips.

"No, this is my first time here. I've just moved, actually."

"Oh, really? From *England*…?" she presumed, my accent apparently telling all.

"Just last week, actually." Her cobalt eyes lit up as I had said it. She then smiled again.

"Well, I hope you're enjoying life here, so far. I'm Jillian, by the way," she held out a delicate, manicured hand for me to shake.

In our conversation, we had learnt that we were neighbours, living just down the street from each other. And like I had once been, she was a student of music.

"Not the best performance I've seen here, I must say," she said, looking over at the dreary folk singer, who was limply strumming his acoustic. "Normally they have better acts upstairs. I go there alone some nights, just to watch and absorb the music." There was something so wistful in her eyes, I suspected that her studies were not the only reason she came to the bar alone in the evenings. Over the course of time, Jillian and I would regularly meet up there, and she gradually disclosed her story to me. I met many others in San Francisco: neighbours, colleagues, friends made at events and after-parties. *How irrational*, I had thought, to think that I would be isolating myself by moving to the city.

In the year that I moved, my lifestyle progressively began to change. I cannot quantify the exact moment that I myself changed, but at some point, I slipped out of the prim ways which had always governed me, the notions of propriety that I was raised on. As each day passed, I became more insouciant; I even slept with someone I barely knew, which I had never done before. It had also been the first time since I was with Jim. Admittedly, I doubt I would have done it if I had been sober. A new friend had thrown a party in the Haight, in the spring of nineteen sixty-three. The Beatles – *this new band from England* – were on the record player, the drink was flowing, and cigarette smoke swirled around in the air. I remember sitting on a sofa, talking to this friend about music, when he suggested that we go and get high together. Of course, I readily agreed to follow him to a charmingly dilapidated room, best suited to the kind of person I was fast becoming.

The white walls were almost bare, but for a few black and white photographs, stuck to it with tape. There was double bed with a knitted blanket covering the duvet; on one side of the bed stood a wooden chair, with a rosary draped over it – undoubtedly for aesthetic, rather than religious purposes – and on the other side, a lamp rested on the bare floorboards. Propped up against the wall was some framed typography, which read: *Qu'est-ce que tu fais dans la vie?* The moonlight shone a shade of phthalo through the window, bathing the room in an unearthly glow. He sat down on the floor, leaning against the bed, and began to roll ·a joint. I sat beside him as he asked me if I too was a regular smoker, lighting up, and leaning in very close to me. He was somewhat amused at the fact that for the entire time that I had been living in San Francisco, I had only smoked one joint – although in retrospect, it was quite the achievement. As a result, he was convinced that I was chaste in the world of herbs, although my days at the Academy would evince otherwise; but to him, I was his uncorrupted temptation, and I was not unwilling to go along with that. Nonchalant as I was, the idea delighted me, that I was perceived as different. I knew well that my mixing of alcohol with grass was a guaranteed high, so I quickly lost track of time. At first, we were talking animatedly; after that, we were laughing. The Beatles suddenly got louder – the harmonies were amazing – and then we were laughing hysterically. The music became a distant background noise, wavering in and out of focus, Lennon's resonant vocals reverberating off every wall; I realised just how much I had drunk beforehand, and just how strong this joint really was. It felt like I was in my teens again, and it was wonderful. We edged closer.

We didn't even finish the damned thing. In a surreal wash-over of time we were suddenly on the bed, removing each other's clothes, and kissing like we really loved each other. It had felt so good; I had forgotten what it was to be craved. He pinned me down, grabbed my leg, I gripped the duvet, and time became obsolete. It was probably over in a second, but a second and a millennium were one and the same. And for a moment afterwards, this brief, post-orgasmic moment that felt to be eternity, I fell into a crazy dream where I was dazzled by stars and magnificent colours. At that moment, despite what the philosophers claim, I experienced infinity.

Admittedly, I felt I should have regretted it in the morning, what I knew to be a reckless act of pure passion, but at the same time, I could not quite muster the shame that I was 'supposed' to feel. As it happened, we barely spoke to each other again after that night.

I mark the day that John F. Kennedy died as when things really started to change. What madness this country had seen – war, missiles, an assassination – I certainly had not expected life here to be so disrupted by its politics. Even so, I would have predicted a nuclear war before I did the events of my own life.

IV

The acute strings sounded at an alarming rate – *back-forth-back* – and again with the lower octave – *back-forth-back* – like the stabbing of a knife – *back-forth-back*. Over and over again until she was an ensanguined corpse, sliding down the bathroom wall to a sinister tremolo. It was the scene that defined modern horror. When I eventually saw *Psycho*, five years after its debut, it affected me in a way that is hard to describe, drawing from my mind a most bizarre response. Norman Bates had been portrayed as a well-disposed yet awkward character; rather amiable, but perhaps slightly overplaying the role of the congenial host. After having gained some degree of trust from his victim, he would then, of course, brutally murder them. Norman Bates, however, could not help himself, for he had no recollection of his crimes. A split personality; it troubled me that this disorder was as real as any other psychological condition. I tried to keep at arm's length an uneasy feeling that I had something in common with Bates. It was ridiculous, surely, but nonetheless, I struggled to suppress it with all my might. Having invaded my consciousness, though, it refused to budge. If it really was possible to simply forget who you were – and more worryingly, what you had been up to – then surely no one was truly safe. That the dividing line between sanity and madness was so thin, frightened me, and for some reason compelled me to resurrect an event long since buried – the murder of Sheila Daniels, all those years ago; the girl whose death was merely coincidental and had nothing to do with myself; except – except for the fact that I had seen her drowned body, her shirt transparent from being submerged, revealing the wounds beneath, her movie star face now lifeless and cold, and yet still horrifically beautiful, even in death. An unbearable shudder shot through my spine, rattling every bone as it went. My eyes were now fixated upon the floor, and I could not will them to move. It was simply too uncanny, I thought, that I had been warned of the tragedy – warned, that is, by a phantom, imagined or not – but when does a hallucination become a premonition? Perhaps when events proceed to happen, exactly as foretold. I could still recall her every word, and how she had described the girl as 'fair'; Sheila Daniels was the fairest girl I had known, with her light blonde hair and pale skin – 'fair' was certainly no exaggeration. I vaguely remembered that she had had ambitions to appear on the silver screen; she certainly had the face for it, but it was also a face that had long awaited a tragic end. For the first time, I had actually sat and pondered her death, and more specifically, how it was that she met her end that day.

As much as it fascinated me, it also pained me to have to cast my mind back to that dreadful moment: the soaked clothes, the debilitated limbs, perhaps from struggling against her murderer and the multitudinous wounds, her dead eyes. I remember running manically back to the school, across the playing fields, the courtyard, barely able to see where I was going, as tears cascaded down my cheeks, little rivulets snaking their way into my eyes and making them sting. In my blind panic, I could hardly relate what I had seen to the secretary. I recalled being shut up in the medical centre with

Doris before the police had even arrived; it had been the longest night of my life, giving my overworked mind *carte blanche* to re-examine again, the dead girl's Pre-Raphaelite features. Detailed images of both Sheila and Amelia spun through my head, over and over again, superimposing themselves, one on top of the other, until eventually they all lost meaning.

Despite the grief it was causing me, I simply had to remember what had happened. Drawing on faded memories from the year 1957, which in turn helped release further, previously dormant snippets of information, I began to piece the events together.

The day after the tragedy, it was all over the newspapers, and Sheila's face began to appear on the front pages of every publication. It remained a featured story for weeks after that, gradually occupying less print space as the months rolled on. Her killer was never found. They searched the entire lake and all around it for evidence, but not a trace was ever uncovered; no weapons, implements, lost garments or possessions. There was no horrid succession of murders in which others were killed, it was just Sheila, and it made no sense to any of us at school. We had racked our brains; we had asked ourselves the obvious questions: Had she been mixing with dubious sorts from outside the school? Had she been having difficulties at home, and turned to the wrong person for advice? Some of our questions were so outlandish – a theory arose that she was the offering of a sacrifice, another that she was part of a gang of criminals – but we asked them anyway. Suffice to say, all we had wanted to do was make sense of the brutality of the crime.

The police wanted to interview a number of students, as is normal in an investigation such as this. Doris and I were interviewed together by a detective. At first, he was rather optimistic that we had been in such close proximity, but eventually he looked dismayed by the fact that neither of us possessed any helpful information whatsoever. From that point, the lake was out of bounds to all but the police – not that it prevented me from continuing my usual contemplation there. Eight years later, and I still had so many questions: why hadn't Sheila's murderer hidden the body? How could it have possibly matched Amelia's prolepsis so accurately? And the biggest question of all – why would anyone want to hurt her? Whatever questions I had, had always remained unanswered. Then seemingly for no reason at all – ironically during Hitchcock's shower scene – strange ideas began to occur to me, as though being implanted in my head, the main one being: what if, like Norman Bates, I had unconsciously wiped a terrible crime from memory? I wanted to stop thinking, but my imagination had run wild: *what if I had murdered someone, taken another's life because of my own madness, and all of this, prompted by a psychotic personality? What if she had manipulated me into killing an innocent girl? No* – I had to tell myself, I was overthinking it. Jumping to the conclusion that I had committed the murder was more irrational than the act itself.

I lit a cigarette and made myself a gin and tonic, sinking back into the armchair with a sigh. It was funny, I thought, how a trip to the cinema had caused me such torment. It probably meant that it would be wise to retire for the night soon. My mother had always said that sleep was the finest cure for when one is upset, and she would often inflict this philosophy on my brothers when they were having one of their temper tantrums. To lay my head down at last on a yielding, white pillow and shut my eyes for a few moments was indeed blissful. Now, all I needed to occupy myself with was rest, for my self-accusations had exacted a great deal of mental energy. Yet as soon as I began to think of sleep, I felt the weight of an incubus at the foot of the bed, my brain roused by a thousand distractions.

It was never quite dark enough in my bedroom. My eyes

were irritatingly adept at adjusting to curtains drawn, making everything a midnight shade of blue. Objects partially obscured in various corners of the room cast foreboding shadows on the wall, as if something – or someone – was waiting to emerge at any second, with gleaming eyes and teeth to match. It both amuses and baffles me that no amount of rational thought can remove these flickers of childhood that are retained within us. We know that there is no such thing as the monster under the bed, and we will walk freely around in the dark when necessary – but the image still lingers, left over from the days when ghouls and vampires were as real as our mothers' touch; it only takes a creak in the floorboard to realise it.

This is what I thought of as I lay in bed, more as a distraction than anything else. A trivial diversion from myself, and what was really troubling me. Memories were flooding through the sluice gates; but they were no longer concerning Sheila or Amelia. It was worse than that; they were capable of making my current life seem hollow and unfulfilling, despite having achieved the freedom that I had so long sought after. I had found myself overcome with a painful yearning for moments that could never be transcended, and would always be nothing more than glorified fragments of an already broken whole; for really, it had been inevitable that it was all bound to collapse. My life had been so ordinary until the tragedy of death had struck, and it hit a lot harder than I had ever wanted to admit; I had been surprisingly successful in protecting my adolescent self from the difficult, uncomfortable thoughts that followed Jim's fate. I had blocked and filtered out thoughts on an almost minute-by-minute basis, and it had stayed that way well into adulthood. Now, though, I was thinking freely about Jim for the first time since his death. I could recall scenes that I previously would have avoided; that terrible phone call from his mother, her voice ringing like death bells in panic, shock, and disbelief. But I had no interest in reminiscing about tragedy; there was no use in that. I was simply observing the bittersweet longing that only love lost can inspire, filling the void with the memory of my first kiss. That it was with the boy I should have married was heartbreaking, though, and that was where the wound lay.

The love that we crave burns like the furnaces of the gods. Its flames will overthrow Zeus, incinerate Poseidon's trident to dust, drive Hades from the underworld. We want passion erupting from the heart's Vesuvius, and anticipation that suffuses the mind's core, like lava. We want to hang on the precipice of existence, the threshold of combustion – and when we are there, we feel immortal. We know that we can be thoughtless and antagonistic at times, but we also know that our imperfections are outweighed by whatever foolish reason our lovers have for loving us. We might lose each other one day; but that day is not today. In the past I had fantasised about my future with Jim, I could not help it. We would live in a capacious apartment with white walls and large windows, through which the sunlight would always shine. We would live in one of the great cities – London, Paris, New York – anywhere, just so long as it was not another small town filled with even smaller minds. The concept of Love, at least the way I have seen it, has never been about finding the person who will make life an adventure, but about having someone to share the adventure with; and yet, it was only when I was alone that the adventure gained any momentum – until the next time that a song played on the radio, sending a shiver down my spine; until the next time that I glimpsed a face in shop window, forcing me to look twice; and until the next time that someone mentioned Indiana, or a car accident, I could move on, and forget. At last, I closed my eyes and fell asleep.

V

Soon after relocating to San Francisco, I developed a taste for coffee. This was due in part to my boyfriend, Clint, and his penchant for the world of stimulants – legal or otherwise. The pleasant inevitability of that warm, rich liquid, with its exquisite aroma, always lifted my spirits, and it was not long before Clint's recreational habits began to draw me in too. The prospective risks of taking such substances were fast overcome by their more powerful and harmonious effects. Whether the substance was solid, liquid, gas, green, white, mellow yellow, psychedelic or hallucinogenic, it ceased to matter. If someone had proclaimed it to broaden the mind or induce a good time, then I was there. More importantly, we told ourselves that taking drugs was an act of protest; we, naturally – much like everyone else in the Haight – abhorred the country's involvement in Vietnam.

"Well I'm thrilled someone's sorting out those communists," Clint remarked sardonically. He was sat on the sofa lighting a joint, with the news blaring from the radio. I always had to be aware of his tumultuous temperament; with passionate beliefs, steered by whatever chemical had been absorbed, his behaviour was not always predictable. A mild, indifferent being he was not – but then no one was really themselves, we were all too busy being high.

Being so far removed from the war in Vietnam, I had found it hard to envisage, but it soon began to plague our screens, manifest itself in conversation, and fill the streets with placards and clamour. I was strongly opposed to the war, unsure where the necessity of it lay. Never before had I realised its horrors, but after seeing the news clips and the graphic photographs being wired daily from war correspondents, it soon became like a recurring nightmare from which there was no escape. Often I would switch on the television, only to see footage of yet another young soldier being napalmed or blown to pieces before my eyes. This was ultra-violence, something I had only seen in the movies and read about in history books; but now it was real – nonetheless surreal – and unavoidably occurring as I sat there breathing.

I noticed the rumblings of something brewing a few years after moving to the States. A low-level disruption seemed to be building momentum; a sudden insurgence of musicians, who sang words of peace and love, the constant nearby redolence of marijuana, the talk of burning draft cards. Then came the peace protesters, most of them on the line between adolescence and adulthood, between curiosity and compliance, wanderlust and wisdom. Hair was grown long and unclasped at last, blowing in the wind. Collared shirts and knee-length skirts were replaced with looser garments and homemade jewellery. It was as if I had gone to sleep in one world and awoken in another, and what had previously been an act of protest from a minute fraction of society quickly became an ubiquitous fashion trend.

As communes began to appear in and around the city, many of their colourfully attired inhabitants began organising events known as 'acid tests'. I had the privilege of being able to cover a few of these; one of the most popular was The Trips Festival, which Clint and I went to in 1966. Clint naturally intended on getting as stoned as was humanly possible. I however, wished to remain relatively sober; I needed to be cautious of what I ingested, if I was to be writing about the festival. It seemed ridiculous, the notion of attending an acid test and avoiding acid at all costs, but there was such little reported evidence of what actually happened at these events; I wanted to see this one for what it truly was, stripped of psychoactive influence.

Slightly overwhelmed by the light show, and the extraordinarily loud music, I thought to at least comply and pretend to be high on something. Everyone was so dazed, it was unlikely they would notice. I quickly swallowed some punch and wondered if these people had experienced much difficulty in their metamorphosis – that is, into these drug-taking, peace-making flower children. It all seemed rather unnatural to me; not the concept itself, but the transformation. It was classic trend-setting on a grander scale. Everyone at the Trips seemed so uniform, all dancing spaced-out with their eyes closed. I had not expected to feel so excluded. After about half an hour of sober disenchantment, I noticed that mushrooms now grew from the cup Clint was drinking from. I looked away, blinked, then looked again – the mushrooms were still there. He continued sipping at his punch, seemingly unaware of the fungal growth that was starting to cause me some alarm. Sensing my staring at him, he shot me a confounded glance.

"You okay, Clare?" he asked.

I didn't respond, instead turning my head and choosing to focus on the music, which was strange – getting louder and louder until I could do nothing but focus on it alone. I knew exactly what was happening. By this time in my life, I been on a couple of trips already, and had not intended to make a frequent event of it, thoroughly disliking the hallucinations. For me, they were neither enjoyable nor enlightening, but a harrowing reminder of my youth, which I had strived hard to forget; and now this illusion I had made for myself – that I had never seen anything beyond the limits of everyday experience – was totally shattered by an experiment in a laboratory.

Clint was grinning ear to ear as he gazed into my eyes. "Clare… can you hear me? Good trip?"

Again, I heard the question, but could not reply. I was seeing in double vision and mushrooms were sprouting out of everything; the light show – if indeed it was the light show – bathed revellers in a throng of colours, increasing my loss of perspective, making everything pulsate as the crowd heaved in front of me: magenta noses, indigo hair, sulphur mouths. Their eyes – colossal, glinting, endless, black eyes, like cavernous pits that had been drilled into their skulls, were all staring at me, extracting my soul from my body, draining the life from me. *No, I will not let this be a bad trip*, I told myself – which happened to be one of the last things I remembered from that night. I had been one of some six-thousand with their drink spiked, and consequently I had to abandon the possibly career-defining article that I had been planning on writing. Clint was also affected, and began to hallucinate shortly after me; I vaguely recall trying to confront him, imploring him to give me back my soul – God knows what he thought I was trying to say. Sometimes, I wonder whether the events that did unfurl that night might have made a more interesting read than my proposed article.

Rather inevitably, it did not take me very long to pick up something resembling a drug habit, although my carefree indulgences were nothing compared to the monopolising dependencies of those around me. To Jillian, for example, the appeal of losing herself in a hazy mirage was simply too irresistible. I had watched her disintegrate during the time I had known her.

As I suspected from our first meeting, Jillian had suffered

a loss in her life, which seemed to follow her like a second shadow. I don't know why, but I have always been drawn to the most troubled people, always fascinated by tales of affliction. The reason for my innate interest in such things is quite possibly the result of some unconscious mission to continually prove that an untroubled being cannot exist – and Jillian was no exception. When she was in her last year of high school, she had fallen in love with her best friend. She had known him since middle school, and they had shared years of hot summer afternoons, passing notes across the classroom, whispering behind the teacher's back, laughing until their stomachs ached. They talked about things which only the most intimate friends do – the extent of their desire to just leave their small town and travel, their wildest and most abstract dreams, what it might feel like to die, and so on. But by the time she had realised that she truly loved him, he was already holding hands and exchanging kisses with another girl. They went their separate ways. I remember her saying to me how much she regretted not telling him, how it was too late and they would never be. She had believed in soul mates, and that he might have been hers, but I thought to see it that way was to limit oneself to a single chance at love – an inevitable disaster. Comparing her case to my own, I could not decide which was worse: awakening to find that the person you love has drifted indeterminately from your world, or to find that they have been removed from it forever. When all is said and done, it amounted to much the same thing.

In the world of white rabbits and magic dragons, of filter tips and acid trips, Jillian found that her troubles – romantic tragedies and all others – could be easily abandoned. Rather than drowning her sorrows in a bar on Saturday nights, she could now leave them behind completely, or have them so distorted that she would no longer recognise them, and in the solitude of her own apartment, there was no humdrum folk music, no heinous older men, no overpowering ambience of desperation. Within a couple of years she seemed a different person. How rapidly she had changed from that sombre, fair-haired student to a spaced-out, sylphlike songwriter. It was not just Jillian either – many of the people I had known in San Francisco became ghosts of their former selves. Of course, the self can never disappear completely, but minds were becoming occupied with something else – something not necessarily bad, but different. It was very easy to see the appeal in trading in one's monotonous work for the opportunity to live in an optimist's utopia. Nonetheless, while we were gathering up mushrooms and giving up materialism, people were still dying in the undergrowth of Vietnam.

Clint was beginning to detest everything that the 'hippies' had become, but back in the summer of nineteen sixty-five, he was enjoying something of a honeymoon with this new way of life. I had met him at a party hosted by none other than the celebrated 'cook', Owsley Stanley, a true psychedelic kingpin of San Francisco.

One of the first things that struck me as I walked into that party were people's eyes. As I was coming down from a recent trip at the time, these windows to the soul had captured my attention – and on this particular evening, all souls were dancing in a diamond sky. It was not so much the augmented pupil sizes that fascinated me, but how enhanced they appeared in their drug-induced states; a pair of large hazels became a swirling vortex of earthy brown, surrounded by a mix of greens; eyes of the most oceanic blue sent waves of energy across to everyone in their line of vision; a pair of luminous green eyes were chaotically speckled, yellow and black. I tried not to stare too closely into these retinal gazes, but I was mesmerised and strangely drawn in.

"O'Sullivan!" my friend Donald called across the room, to a man with shoulder-skimming hair who was drawing deeply on a cigarette. Letting the smoke drift gradually from his lips, he turned to face us. I could not help but of course notice his eyes, so dark they verged on black, so penetrating I momentarily forgot my surroundings. But what I also noticed was the warmth and generosity of his smile. It was the type of smile that does not go unnoticed; a smile completely stripped of pretence.

"Nichols!" the man cried, embracing his companion. There was something about this young man's tranquil kind of charisma that I found compelling. From the way the other partygoers appeared to be always half-watching him, I suspected I wasn't alone in my admiration; and that everyone who knew the man seemed to revere him, gave him a pre-eminence over the rest of the room. In other words, I was intrigued.

"Good God, I don't even know how I recognised you, you've grown your hair!" Donald exclaimed.

"Speak for yourself!" came the reply, as the two of them launched into a conversation, reeling off the names of people I had never heard of before.

Clint O'Sullivan had not only struck me as being well-mannered and charismatic, but he was also very handsome – and in a less pretentious, more rugged kind of way, than so many of the other long-haired nonconformists. There was nothing distinctly quirky or mysterious about him – there didn't need to be; the unavoidable gravitas his of presence was more than enough to elicit a second glance. The dark-eyed Mediterranean complexion hinted at a Hispanic bloodline, and I guessed him to be around thirty. From what I could catch of the conversation, he was very much the accomplished traveller – or at least he spoke with the perspective of a well-travelled man.

I watched as the people in our group began to slip away one by one, joining a different conversational current. Ever since my days at the Academy, I had enjoyed observing the natural order of conversation. I found that estuaries of people often divided themselves into little streams, and those streams, into tributaries, ending up either in a two-way dialogue, or solitary as the ocean itself. As I spoke to O'Sullivan, however, I had no intention of taking the solitary route. Instead, I arrested the opportunity to continue the conversation alone. As he recounted a recent trip to Rome, I became so captivated by him, that everyone else could have left the room, and I would have remained completely oblivious.

"I would recommend travelling to anyone who can afford it," he said, leaning back into the sofa we had retired to. "Until you've been outside your home country, a part of your mind will always remain closed; it's quite depressing, really."

"But true," I added.

"Yeah… true indeed. No matter how many other life experiences you might have, if you never get to explore the world beyond your familiarity, you deny yourself an important rite of passage."

Delighted that he was taking an interest in me, I answered his questions about my own travels, feeling pleased with myself that I indeed had such stories to relate. I could feel myself falling for him, despite having known him for just half an hour, and I could only hope that he was falling too. I told him about my road trip across the western states, convinced that this would aid my image as a seasoned traveller. I had been on the road, had opened my mind to the wonders of… what I then remembered was a very small slice of the nation that he himself lived in, and probably detested at that. He must have sensed my unease as I realised this, for he suddenly interrupted me.

"You know, it's so interesting to hear your perspective on this country; it helps to look at things from a distance sometimes," he said, his mellow tone sounding oddly irresistible under the influence of a psychedelic. I was relishing the attention he was giving me. It didn't matter that I was probably just another face to him, that he most likely spoke to everyone in a similar manner, or that he may have had an ulterior motive. Whatever reason there was for not becoming drawn in, it did not interest me in the slightest.

It occurred to me in hindsight just how badly losing Jim had affected me. In my late teens, whilst other girls had been daydreaming endlessly of boys, whose minds they probably didn't even cross in a day, I had lost all interest in romance. I had not allowed myself the luxury of it, limiting my desires solely to those of the flesh; I did this to such an extent that for a long time I convinced myself that I would never need to experience love again. This moment, however, was triggering a re-mapping of my understanding, placing me back on the path to normality, whatever that may be. But it felt all wrong. It was not that I found it strange that I should desire a man, but was it supposed to feel this profound? Had we never seen each other again, I dread to think of the hours in thought I might have dedicated to him.

As our conversation grew and diversified, we entered into a self-contained bubble; I had even forgotten about the tab of acid he had earlier placed on my tongue. It was only when I noticed the glow that had enveloped Clint like a shroud, with its lustrous spectrum of rainbow colours, that I sensed I might be viewing things with a heightened sense of awareness. The aura moved in soft waves, gently encompassing each guest in turn, as though greeting them. Sounds became affected too; individual voices stood out at different points, while everything in the background subsided, as though each one was in a wide open space. I had never taken much of an interest in the machinations of cerebral function before, but this experience compelled me, if only for its duration, to consider what exactly was happening. I knew that LSD distorted one's perception of information, causing the hallucinations; but it was not so much the biochemical changes which perplexed me, as much as where the content of the hallucinations, came from. A scientist would have us believe that these phantasmagoria were past sensory information, disarranged and interpolated into reality. I would have hastily accepted this theory, if I had a reasonable idea of the real and the imaginary, but due to strange visions in the night, long ago, I knew I could never be certain. My problem with this explanation was that it failed to explain why so many users reported a sudden influx of creativity, spiritual enlightenment, or even, in some cases, telepathy. I had to know whether it was merely the tendency of the mind to delve into these exact corners of the imagination when given the opportunity, and if so, why? The answers did not come to me that night. My first trip inspired no symphonies, oil-paintings or poetic ballads; neither did I see Gods, angels, or demons. Perhaps it was not meant to be; but through my own mediocrity, I had already come to the conclusion that my experience was more important than anything I could ever achieve.

While swimming in an aberration of consciousness, time became unquantifiable and our conversation so complex, that it could only have been understood by ourselves. All night we discussed the wildest ideas, and I am not certain whether we communicated through words or thought. I knew then, miles from my habitual order of thinking, that there was an inexplicable connection between this man and I. For the first time since I was sixteen, I was feeling something that had been long forgotten in my mind: hope. It had never occurred to me that I would be emotionally able to connect with anyone who wasn't Jim – yet here I was – it felt so real – how could I have been mistaken? Nonetheless, a part of me would always wander alone, even in the most intimate situations; but I had grown to learn that this is an integral part of the human condition, not the anomaly that I once thought it was.

But speaking to someone I was so deeply interested in, more interested than I had been in years, I once again felt very alive.

Clint was a man of such enormous merit, that any girl unable to see that, or not to have fallen for him right away, would have been, in my opinion, rather dim. He was so unlike the others, conforming to no group, including the nonconformists. He had travelled to so many places, studied at Yale, had established himself as a beacon in the field of political philosophy. Every student knew his name and read his essays, and yet he was only thirty years old. His ideas were remarkable, his ideologies even more so. Like every individual who has ever drawn my volatile attention, he was his own person.

I didn't understand what he saw in me at first. After a lot of thought, I concluded that the attraction was based on the fact that we were similar enough to hold a stimulating conversation, but different enough to impel a fascinating one. Both of us had felt the necessity to transcend our self-limiting boundaries, for we both knew it was too simple to fall supine on a couch of privileged security. Both of us felt that our default positions in life allowed us to achieve whatever we wanted to, and felt the ever-lingering presence of failure to do so. We were both well educated, and we both knew that good manners got you to good places. These points aside, however, our minds were otherwise foreign cities to be explored. We mystified each other; and while I was absorbed in his intellect, his mode of thought, his mere presence, he seemed equally enthralled by my musical obsessions, my view of the past, and my interest in all things esoteric. How fortunate I was, I thought to myself, to have loved and been loved in return, not once, but twice.

The ensuing year flew by in a whirl of consciousness-expanding reverie. The people we were associating with were mostly various groups of young, experimental 'bohemians', as people called us. We were the kings of Californian sunshine, and incredibly good fun. It was a year of debauchery and divine philosophy, hedonism and hallucinogens. No one had wanted it to end, and my heart and mind had never been so open. We smoked, we talked, we danced, we mused, wrote, read, loved, laughed and enlightened ourselves. Clint and I sometimes disagreed, but we would agree to disagree – it was always a civil affair; our arguments were mere trivialities, like minor potholes in a road, made worthwhile by everything else that occurred on the journey. Our social circle was thriving; not a twenty-four hour period went by without seeing at least some friends. It was like being a student again, as if my youth had been dug up from its barren tomb and brought back to me in pristine condition.

The small things – these are the things that make the days count: waking up next to the person you love, smoking a joint in bed and bursting into raucous laughter at nothing much, because life is essentially hilarious; staying up until the early hours, discussing things never to be broached in daylight – a delightful, often illuminating pursuit, for conundrums that only made sense in the dark. All of these things I took pleasure in, and more – the beauty in trees, flowers, and even the streets upon which I walked. Contentment had let itself into my world, and I had to admit to myself, I was happy. I was even enjoying a little taste of fame, or at least, being talked about – both for my writing, and because of Clint. Everyone seemed to be discussing us; how we were so well-suited to one another, how good we looked together, that we were made for each other, and so on. To think that it was an acid trip that had been the source of our relationship was both absurd, and completely fitting.

It did not matter that one day we would grow old, that the substances would rot our beautiful minds, that my ambitions were wasting away. We lived only in the present, which is but a series of waves: some are light and gentle, others harsh and abrasive, as they lap up against us, immersing us completely in the flow of life's current. The past are waves already broken, the future is an unconquerable horizon. One may as well frolic in the glistening pool of today; dive, plunge, float – which is exactly what I was doing. And I was reminded of a line from *Othello* – so perfect and pure in its simplicity – *If it were now to die, 'twere now to be most happy.*

VI

It was all moving so fast – the drugs, the music, time itself – that I had barely registered what was happening. Like an animal in its hibernaculum, I had buried myself in indulgences whilst the world continued to turn. All the while, I had noticed Clint falling further and further away from his respected position in the world of academia. Whether or not anyone else had realised this was beyond my knowledge. Initially, he would inhale, ingest and – perhaps once or twice – inject substances to become *metaphysically enlightened*, as he proclaimed, but as time progressed, he began to change. Mushrooms and acid were no longer a luxury, but a necessity; he seemed to survive off acid and cigarettes alone, and I don't know how he did it. Of course, it was all in the mind, but it is amazing how shrewdly the mind can turn a blind eye to itself. This had a severe effect upon me. I was made into a minuscule excerpt of his life, becoming a listener to his exhaustive complaints about the war, the hippies and the government. Sometimes, I had wanted to grab him by his hair and bash his head against the wall, in the hope that it would fix him. More often, I wanted to scream so loud that I could not hear myself think, until

149

my lungs had been emptied of breath enough to scream, and I could collapse onto the floor.

By degrees, Clint began to abandon parts of his life, adopting the habits of an addict. I did not dare count the times that I found him lying paralysed on the bed of the apartment, arms splayed out, the duvet littered with drug paraphernalia. It was like living alone, with only his physical presence and the residue of an addiction to confirm that I was not; and I was so tired of it, but there was nothing in leaving him. I would feel equally empty, perhaps even more so, for then I really would be alone. I knew there was more danger in solitude than there was in this.

My escape was the ocean; it has always fascinated me how changeable it is, at the same time constant and ancient, yet it never fails to inspire the senses. When the waters are light blue, and the soft whitecaps of the waves curl gently inwards, one can so easily slip into a serene forgetfulness. Everything becomes possible, the imagination leads the way. If one listens to nothing but the sound of the oscillating tide, mermaid voices might be heard on the wind. At the shore, it did not matter that I was falling apart under the weight of my discontent. It bothered me that I could feel myself dying sometimes; my head ached to the extent that I felt brain cells imploding, I was never rested enough to do anything with the vigour that I used to, and the deep circles beneath my eyes were becoming more prominent, more permanent. No amount of makeup or caffeine could conceal those awful engravings; they appeared to be carved deep into the skin.

In spite of all of this, I maintained an impregnable loyalty towards Clint. Although I could almost hate him, I suspected that somewhere beneath the layers of narcissism was the Clint I knew and liked; yet I find myself saying 'loved' with difficulty. For all the intimacy and experiences we shared, there was something not right, and almost unreal, about us.

Clare and Clint; we sounded too fictional, too perfect, when in reality there was nothing perfect about us at all, and it was all fabricated; we were only interested in the person we had met in '65 and how we might salvage them.

One night there was a storm. Enormous black clouds rolled up above, consuming any light in the sky, before parting to allow the rain to descend. It swept across the city like a mighty wave, soaking every building in its path, leaving split drops splattered across the windowpane. It was two in the morning. I lay awake while Clint slept next to me. A half-thought would have crossed my mind about how enchanting he looked while he slept, had I been next to someone else; but when I looked at him sleeping, his breathing heavy, his chest rising and falling with each inhalation and exhalation, his eyes closed, unaware, his heart elsewhere, I wanted to run into the storm.

I began to fantasise about us perhaps one day having filled the void. Perhaps one day, he would come home from giving a lecture, and as he walked through the door he would advance towards me instead of his hashish. He would look into my eyes and see *me* and his lips would slowly part to say: *I missed you*. This was just a foolish reverie, a ridiculous ideal that would never come to fruition; but I could not see that far ahead, and he could not see beyond the purple haze that clouded and obscured everything.

The uninterrupted pattering of the rain was somewhat comforting. It reminded me of when I was growing up, when the sound meant that crying was permitted because the world too was crying; yet I was grown now, and did not shed even a quarter of the tears I did then. I was at that moment unoccupied with any particular emotion whatsoever, only a sense of duty to amend this piteous relationship. Suddenly, the sky let forth a great boom of thunder, unsettling the entire room. I love the thunder. It excites every bone in my body, for it is far greater, far more sublime than that imperceptible 'I'.

Again, it rolled under the floorboards and resounded through the walls, subsided, and left me with nothing but the beating of my own heart, and the distant breathing of Clint.

I was alone; I always had been and I always would be alone. The reason I had felt a distance between myself and others was because that distance physically existed. We are born alone, we die alone and everything that happens in between – we are alone. Others may share experiences with us, but it is ultimately in isolation that we are left to feel, reflect, speculate, anticipate, that is why we can depend on no one but ourselves. But what happens when the self becomes unreliable? Can it ever really become unreliable? For it is just about the only thing that we can see from each obscure angle; but even then, are there angles we manage to overlook?

The room was illuminated by a scintillation of lightning, like the blinding flash of a camera; and then, darkness. Clint stirred in his sleep. The thunder roared again, causing the wind to howl through the walls of the apartment. He abruptly sat up in bed as though someone had shouted in his ear. For about ten seconds, he simply stared ahead, seemingly amnesic of time and place, oblivious to my presence. He then turned his head to face me, and smiled. It was the first time this had happened in weeks, and I almost could not believe that I had seen it; after all, my judgement was slightly clouded by my imagining just minutes before of the day when I would see it. I took this as an opportunity to connect with him once again.

"Clint."

"God, I just had the worst nightmare," he said, sinking back down into his pillow again, now staring at the ceiling. "I was swimming around in this muddy water, looking for the light, the surface, but I couldn't see a thing; I thought I was gonna drown."

I went to put my arms around him, and he passively accepted my embrace, but I received nothing in return; I could have been lying with an empty pillow. As a lover, I had never wanted to invade his space, and I never had, so this was not enough to irritate anyone. At times like this, he was almost unresponsive to anything I did, as if taking my existence for granted. Perhaps it is selfish to expect anything more, but I could not help feeling that I was no longer wanted; and even then, I was determined to rectify anything we had. I did not know why; if a real affinity between us existed, then surely I wouldn't be missing him when he was lying right next to me. But then it was two in the morning, and the strangest occurrences happen in the early hours.

Another flash of lightning lit up the bedroom. The words surged from within, leading to the devastating question:

"Do you still love me?"

It was silent for too long. I did not quite know whether I had said anything at all. And then he answered almost mechanically, as if reading from a script:

"Of course I do, Clare." There was not the slightest variance in his expression as he said it. I couldn't help believing that he truly did not care. In case he hadn't heard what I meant by the question, I asked again.

"Do you really?" This time he turned to face me, his eyes focusing upon mine.

"You think I don't?"

I knew I had to be careful. Saying the right words to him was like walking through a minefield. He had never done anything to hurt me, he never even shouted, but his powerful expression and the passion with which he spoke terrified me. But I told the truth anyway.

"Yes. It feels like you're pushing me away. It's as if you don't even care." Now it was his turn to pull me close, and he did. I could not bring myself to fall for it.

"Clare, what do I have to do to convince you?"

I sat up in a strange kind of dismay.

"You've changed, Clint," I found myself revealing sombrely. "I want you to be the man I met two years ago – the one who actually gave a damn."

"Oh, you mean when we were both tripping out of our skulls? I can't believe what you're saying."

The wind beat against the windowpane and stirred through the streets outside. It was then that I realised how foolish I had been. What blindness had possessed me to suppose that drugs would not drastically mutate everything I experienced and everything I was?

"So what now?" I said, suddenly feeling bored, so dreadfully bored of life. I was met with silence for a few moments, and the suffocating darkness of a room which seemed to be closing in upon us.

"I don't know," came the eventual reply. Neither of us said anything after that; Clint lay absolutely still, up until the moment when he suddenly turned over, facing away from me. I watched him, waiting – for what, I did not know – but when nothing happened, when he did nothing more, I lay down and faced the other way. Our backs to each other, I cried silent tears; they were in perfect synchronism with the rain outside.

I was awoken by the effulgent sunlight, soaking through the curtains. Even in my sleep I had been thinking about Clint, knowing that something had to be done. I looked at the clock, unpleasantly surprised to find that I was awake at six o'clock on a Saturday morning. Rapidly recalling our conversation from the previous night, I felt something descend within me; attempting to confront him clearly had not worked. I would need to find a different way of reigniting something that was quite possibly burnt out from the start. I pulled on a dressing gown and went to make some coffee. As I sat by the kitchen window with my coffee and a cigarette, I thought about how life might have turned out had I chosen cats; after all, cats are far more adorable than men; but, of course, one cannot love a cat the same way one loves a man. Perhaps, I thought, when I am old and resentful, I shall get a cat. There must have been a reason, I thought, why old spinsters surround themselves with those mewing balls of fur.

The truth is that solitude will eventually become unbearable, and while another human being may not satiate the hunger for contentment, they are a fruitful diversion from the recesses of the ego; selflessness, cherishing, honour, respect and intimacy all result from the narcissistic drive for escape. No matter how much we try to convince ourselves otherwise, it still remains that everything we do is an attempt to rid ourselves of this pain. But now I was back to where I had started, trapped once again with no one but myself – and I saw this as an important battle to fight, one I was determined not to lose.

I spent the day at the typewriter, reviewing a new album by The Temptations. It was an uplifting piece of work; the drums were rousing, the brass was vibrant and the vocals bright, having all the musical ingredients of a party. It immediately reminded me of the music of my youth, and how limited we really were back then. There were only really three main genres that we were exposed to in the fifties, which were jazz, blues, and rock and roll. There was pop music, but even that was just an umbrella term for the trinity. Ten years later and the definition of 'genre' had exploded; there now existed psychedelic rock, a massive folk revival, and every variation of pop; bubblegum pop, sunshine pop, baroque pop – and of course all of the music that had come before it. The world seemed a much broader place than it had ever been.

Clint had spent the day smoking pot somewhere in a park with George Harrison, enlightening others about the wrongs of capitalism. At seven o'clock that evening, a solution finally occurred to me: I would surprise him. People need spontaneity.

I would cook his favourite dish and we would eat by candlelight next to the big windows at the front of the apartment; this felt ridiculous, my devising a plan as if we were a middle-aged couple attempting to resuscitate our marriage. What was worse, I could not even remember what his favourite dish was. I scrapped the idea promptly, feeling foolish, knowing that he felt nothing at all whilst I was falling apart. The agitation was boiling over inside me; I could feel my face getting physically hotter with the frustration of losing a battle which would keep us both from falling over the edge, I thought. Sinking back into my chair, tearing the piece of music I was composing in two, I relinquished every morsel of good sense I had.

Twenty minutes, five shots of whisky and a strong joint later, I felt better already. I had not been drunk in a while, and I had forgotten what it was like to believe that *bibero ergo sum* was epistemologically true, that I could achieve anything, that I was invincible. I meandered into the living room. Clint was sat reading *Why We Can't Wait*, and Detroit was burning on the television. As he saw me, an unexpected smile began to form across his face. Perhaps he had truly considered what I had said the previous night, even though all I had done was make myself look foolish. Mindlessly and thoroughly intoxicated, I found myself slipping out of my sundress and into his arms. All I wanted at that current moment were his lips on mine, enticed by the close proximity of our faces. He kissed me slowly, about to unhook the clasp of my bra, when he suddenly refrained.

"Have you been drinking?" he asked, somewhat taken aback. I laughed imperiously at the suggestion.

"No," I grinned, leaning in to kiss him again – except this time he disengaged himself from me with a slight air of indignation.

"You know what, I'm not in the mood," he said, as if deeply demoralised. Infuriated by his refusal and struggling to stand still, I lapsed into a state of insolence.

"Really? Are you on your fucking period or something?"

"Clare, you're drunk."

"But it's okay to be stoned all the time?" I found his hypocrisy unpalatable, and it stemmed from an alleged belief that whilst certain substances were mind-expanding, others were precisely the opposite, and sacrilegious because of it. Drink fell into the latter category, and due to its unique combination of properties and wide availability, was considered the most dishonourable tool in The Man's great agenda to stupefy a nation. Perhaps so, but sometimes I wanted to be stupefied; Clint regarded this as the ultimate weakness, regardless of his own constant trance – regardless also, of all the times he would take up the bottle whenever the mood struck him, or of all the times drinking together was part of the fun.

The ultimate quandary here was his way of life being no longer compatible with my own. He was in fact no different from anyone else in the Haight, on a constant trip, going nowhere. Perhaps what exasperated me the most was that we were slightly too old now for the lifestyle we had chosen. How was it that a man of such marked philosophical acuity could resent a stereotype which he fulfilled in himself? Yet perhaps he was just as confused as everyone else, lost between hedonism, an existential crisis and the New Left. I, on the other hand, was becoming increasingly desperate to escape this life before its lack of direction killed me. And it was as if we didn't love each other anymore. I found myself with no alternative choice but to confront him at that moment.

"Why do you distance yourself from me? Why does our life together only work when it suits you?"

He said he didn't have the slightest idea what I was talking about, although I could not bring myself to believe him. "Are you honestly not concerned about the fact that our lives are going nowhere, because you can't bear to encounter reality? The only reason we can even afford this place is because I pay for it with the wages I've earned while you sit around all day getting high; I can only wonder what it is about the real world that you can't face."

I knew then that I had crossed a boundary I had never crossed before. As if thinking intently about something, Clint fell onto the sofa, then raised his eyes to me.

"Tell me, Clare, what is reality?" His tone was so immensely patronising, I knew that whatever I responded with would be inadequate.

"Look, we both know what I mean by reality – it's when you're not stoned, when you're not hallucinating, and when you're not dreaming."

"That may be your definition, but it's not mine. Reality isn't just the world around you, it's also how you perceive it; now if I want to perceive my reality in technicolor, I will. I thought you of all people would understand that."

Had I been sober, my reaction most certainly would have been different; but in my inebriation, I felt that I had been struck with an arrow of intellect, dropping to my knees and burying my face in my hands, sighing what seemed like an accumulation of every sorrow I had ever felt. This was the first indication I had received that my thoughts were worth anything to Clint, and it was painful to know it. Ashamed, I stood up, put my dress back on and made for the door.

"I'm going for a walk," I said resolutely.

"No you're not – you're not even walking in a straight line," he objected, coming to prevent me from leaving; yet I focused my eyes on him and spoke sincerely for possibly the first time that day:

"I just need to regain my senses. I'll be fine – I'm coming back," I responded, shutting the door firmly behind me as I went.

There is nothing more comforting than the warmth of the city's air on your face, as you step into the evening. I had been overcome with a sudden urge to drive to the beach, regardless of my drunken state. The sun would be setting soon, and I wished to see it from the shore, so I started up the car, driving to the seafront with not a care for life or death.

By the time I had reached the white sands of Ocean Beach, my head was slightly clearer. The sun was just beginning to set, shining a pathway over the water, the colour of a tiger's eyes. It was a Saturday evening, and to avoid the bustle of men, women and teenagers in love, I had to walk further down the beach than usual. There is something in a Saturday night which makes it different from any other. Even with no preoccupations, there is always an inexplicable inkling of hope in it, the universal night of enjoyment; yet now, feeling a ridiculous sentimentality in my stupor, I could not hope for anything more than what was before me; that is, the illimitable orange sky, and the smooth sand in which my feet made imprints, before disappearing under the incessant tide, and the countless waves that spanned for miles across the horizon. I sat on the shore of Ocean Beach long enough for the sun to set, the sky to turn from orange to leaden, and the clouds to enshroud the disc of fire that was slowly sinking behind the sea. I too, was sinking on this voyage. I was a hypocrite, constantly mulling over Clint's addictions, which were no more than those of the great artists, whilst I myself was addicted to sadness; and sadness has destroyed far more souls than drugs ever could. And I had my poison too, just when it suited me. I was not interested in living forever, or staying high until I died, so I sinned as I pleased and moved on; but I still resented my hypocrisy, and it was not my place to judge the choices of anyone but myself. In bitter truth, I was grappling with a situation with the worst possible attitude, and was yet to have explained to Clint what exactly troubled me; did I really expect him to change, when honestly, neither of us had the faintest intimation of what needed altering? Even if we did, there would still be no reason for him to change the person he was and the life he had chosen.

If I wished so greatly not to be a part of Clint's life, then walking out of it would be the logical thing to do; but it was only with this in mind that I realised how unwilling I was to walk out. The richness of my own existence would be hugely diminished in his absence, and perhaps his would be in mine; imagining how real a possibility this was becoming, the thought of him leaving made me stumble on the spot. Even if I left with my life still wholly intact, I would be alone; but it was not loneliness that I feared, only insanity; for I knew, and had always known, that I would never be free from my past.

VII

When living in a dream, one does not age at the same rate as the rest of the world. Many of our acquaintances spent the Christmas of 1967 with their new families, leading a life which was now alien to my own. Meanwhile, Clint and I neither wanted nor needed such drastic change. We were perfectly satisfied in the company of those who had not withdrawn from withdrawal. Since the summer, I had made decided efforts to enter onto Clint's level again, and found that once I had, I felt significantly happier. I might have regretted not getting married, having children, investing in my future retirement, even leaving California every once in a while, if I had not been so enamoured with everything that surrounded me.

Throughout my time in San Francisco, I had been communicating with friends and relatives in England, but neither they nor I had yet crossed the Atlantic. My parents were quick to send me off – they always had been – but not so eager to receive me back. My friends vowed one day to come and visit me, and I to visit them, but being so rapt in our own circumstances, these were empty promises. However, what I had managed to do was stay in touch with everyone I cared about – apart from Bridget. Since I had left the country, my mother and father had barely changed at all; in fact, the house seemed to have changed more than they had; Mother had finally installed the tennis court that she had wished for since she was a child. In one of her letters, she expressed her sheer delight in the fact that she would no longer have to use the courts at the club. A swimming pool had also been created, to be used on the rare occasion of a British heatwave. My bedroom was now a guest room, as if they needed another one. *At least make it into something functional*, I thought; a library, an artist's studio, a billiards room, a nursery – anything but another guest room.

My younger brother now lived in London, playing a real-life game of *Monopoly*. Like my father, he was ruthless in business, which must have been very profitable, and, I suspect, lonely. Much to my parents' displeasure, my youngest brother had dropped out of Leeds, moved back to the south, and having inherited the musical gene, was writing and performing songs, indulging in a lifestyle not entirely different from my own; but from what I gather, his was wilder, ungrounded, and lethal, involving a great deal more drugs and partying. Freddie had always been the ungovernable one; from the moment he entered the world, he screamed like a kettle that needs to be taken off the hob. As a toddler, he could not be left alone for more than two seconds, for he would unquestionably cause some form of destruction. He was the reckless teenager, the embodiment of rebellion, and nothing could impose itself between his will and his actions. He lives up to my every expectation, doing everything that I was afraid to.

Tommy now lived in Paris with his girlfriend, and often requested that I go and visit him sometime, although it never seemed to be the right time. Polly was the same as she had ever been, happily married a long time ago, now with a son as well as a daughter. I had met her daughter back when she was a baby that could melt even a heart brocaded with the thickest cynicism. She had inherited her father's features, and she was beautiful, for both of her parents were too. They would spoil her and bring her up on love and kindness – and whatever her experiences would be, she would only know how to deal with them in the most gentle manner. I am a godmother to both of Polly's children; they were the closest I could get to having a child of my own, without actually having one. She sent me a picture of her son when he was a week old; he looked more like her, with cartoon eyes that seemed to twinkle, even in the picture. Hannah, too, had a family – a daughter of two years and a husband who owned a large estate in the country, due to his father's success in the celluloid industry. All this change, I thought, in the space of a decade; more had changed in one decade than I imagined possible in a lifetime.

Christmas and the New Year were spent with a constant stream of friends from across the country. How I spent my Decembers in America were considerably different from my childhood and adolescence. A part of me did miss seeing my entire family over a two-week period of eating, drinking and merriment; I wholeheartedly missed being next to a glowing fire, as the cold wind outside rapped against the windows and doors, and eddied around chimney tops. In San Francisco, one does not hope for a white Christmas, and yet, wherever I was in the world, it would always be a time of immoderation.

I began once again to take pride in people mentioning that Clint and I were 'so good together', and questions of marriage from friends even began to arise. I had not considered the prospect of marriage until then, and wondered whether Clint had either. It was certainly possible that in the future we would be married. Not that I cared much for the title, but a wedding did sound like good fun. We had been to one that July in Novato; the reception was held at the ranch of the bride and groom. She wore a crown of white flowers, and he a white and gold kaftan, with strings of beads, loosely inspired by parts of Asia. The guests danced all night under the moonlit sky, high as the stars themselves. There was something charming about this occasion, which almost made me want to get married, but I knew that Clint would be opposed to the idea altogether, and I myself was not too concerned with it, the concept of a contract seeming a highly unromantic gesture.

I ended 1967 with Clint, Jillian, and her boyfriend, Frank. We said our farewells to The Summer of Love, Sgt. Pepper and *Surrealistic Pillow* by taking a road trip to New York. On New Year's Eve, standing on a rooftop terrace and looking out towards the Empire State Building, Jillian and I watched the firework display together, numbed by the brisk air.

"You and Clint seem so peaceful together. It makes me so happy to think that it's all worked out for us, you know? We found people who can make us feel... incredible," she mused, her smile lighting up the mood, like the fireworks illuminating the night sky.

"We really did. So you think Frank might be 'the one'?" I asked, not so much because I believed in such a thing as 'the one', but because I suspected that she did.

"Definitely – I can just feel it in every bone, every artery, vein, cell – I know that he's the one for me... a soulmate, if you believe in such a thing."

"That's amazing – how do you know?" I exaggerated, feeling my stomach drop at her use of the word *soulmate*.

"I don't know – you just find yourself loving that person more than you could ever love yourself. I would die for him – that's how much he's changed my life. And if I were to lose him, I feel like I would die. I can't go back to where I was before; he means more to me than anything."

"Apart from me, of course!" I joked.

"Of course!"

At that moment, I felt a perplexing sensation, for I was

not certain that I felt this way about Clint. I had never given the matter much consideration, and I thought then to leap from the roof of the apartment simply to prove to myself that I would die for him; of course I knew that this was all wrong, that no woman's life depended upon any man, but still I could not shake the feeling that perhaps there were such things as soulmates, and Clint was not mine. Unsure and scared, I walked cautiously into the New Year with one eye open.

It was early January, and we had recently returned from our trip across the country. The apartment was almost silent; December's parties were over, the wine drained, the holly brittle, the fire burnt out, and everyone had resigned to the comfort of their sparsely populated homes. It was not particularly cold, yet I felt a chill biting at my feet as I sat by the window, watching Clint leave the building.

Most of the time I felt as distant from reality as Lucifer must have felt from heaven. I believed that I could separate myself from it for a short while, and swiftly return as I pleased; yet once I began to enter a different world more frequently, the one I knew and disliked began itself to morph out of ordered chaos and into the colours of a dream. I gained an odd pleasure in being able to see the world as it was and as it was not, knowing that neither perspective had authority over the other. Perhaps if I had had to maintain a lifestyle that required accepting solidity, I could grow to hate the earth as we are taught to see it; but I was part of whatever existence I wanted to be part of, and I believed I could never grow to resent that. Clint had been right all along; a substantial part of our reality depends upon how we perceive it. He once told me that Kant had concluded that the world around us exists independently of ourselves, and that our knowledge comes to rest in experience of it – and this is all we can know. I thus deduce that what we impose upon the world, and how we understand it, whether it is a place of beauty or of evil, only we can decide. I have always found this sphere of matter to be one of extraordinary beauty. It is one of extraordinary evil too, and of continual pain, and overwhelming pleasure; but here we stand, with a remarkable acceptance of its workings, making sense out of the senseless.

By observing my state of living, it would not have been difficult for one to presume that I was somewhat dismantled from this world. Had I willingly flung myself into a stable life and that alone, I might have ordered my surroundings as I did when I was younger; I would have a colour scheme, matching linen, an aversion to clutter; yet the bed on which I now sat was unmade, the blinds were slightly askew, and I was not entirely fond of the moss green paint on the walls. However, I certainly did not care enough to change these features, for I was only ever half-there. Due to this, very little was particularly important to me; there was Clint, and there were drugs, and a few close friends, but that was all. To be without ambition was refreshing – I was sombre, for I knew that there were things I was not doing or achieving – but I was simultaneously content. The silence of the room was startled by a female voice.

"I had always known that you would end up here. I can read you like a book."

Despite the years that had passed, I recognised the voice immediately, its detached, ethereal lilt all too familiar. I turned around and was confronted with an appearance that I thought I might never see again.

There she stood in the full-length mirror, her hair like an aura, glowing in the natural light. I couldn't breathe. I could not will my lips to move or my eyes to blink; everything was numb but for my heart, which hammered at my ribcage, filling the mind with its noise. It only occurred to me in retrospect that Amelia had not changed at all in the decade which separated this meeting from the last. Nothing in her appearance betrayed any evidence of ageing, and she still wore that long nightdress, and her ringlets still framed an extraordinarily beautiful face.

"There is no need to be afraid. I will not hurt you."

I closed my eyes for a few moments, but she was still there when I opened them, gently swaying in her nightdress. It made no sense – I knew this to be no drug-induced vision. However, I also knew that I was not 'sane', in any conventional sense. I have heard that acknowledging one's own insanity frees them from it; but I had acknowledged mine years ago – precisely to free myself from Amelia – yet here she was.

"Leave me alone," I pleaded, horrified.

"Why? You awoke me from a prolonged slumber; now I am awakening you from yours."

I cannot say how, but I knew then with certainty that she was a figment of my imagination. Perhaps I knew that no matter how blurry the lines are between the real and the imaginary, they nonetheless exist; there are simply things which everyone else sees, and things which they do not – and I knew that no one else would ever see Amelia. I knew what this realisation entailed: I would have to acquiesce that this young woman was a hallucination, fabricated by myself. And why had I fabricated her? Undoubtedly in order to cope with some unconscious trauma that I could neither face nor remember. I knew had to ignore her, no matter how vehemently she persisted. It occurred to me that Amelia had only ever made an appearance when I was alone. Perhaps if she came when there was someone else in the room – and they remained oblivious to her presence – then I could once and for all privately diagnose myself as schizophrenic, lock the evidence away, and resume my life as usual. Whatever happened, I knew that for now I had to assume that Amelia was a disease of the brain, re-conjured by my recent exploration of chemistry; but when about ten seconds later she disappeared, there was also that faint hope I wouldn't have to assume anything at all.

I resolved to stop taking hallucinogens; it was simply too dangerous for someone with my history, and not to mention mindless. I cut down on smoking pot, only doing so occasionally. I was prepared to do anything to avoid this symptom of madness called 'Amelia'; but I soon began to crave it all back – the metallic rainbows, the feeling of being underwater, where the only sound that can be heard is an unworldly echo of the universe. I gave myself no pity for it; it was entirely my own doing, my own idiocy. If I was going to ruin myself in this way, then I was a fool. So as I craved a great escape, a release from the confines of actuality, I condemned myself for it, as a nun hopelessly condemns her sexual desires. I, however, was abstaining for something far more sacred than God – it was my sanity in question.

A week passed; it passed painfully slowly, and felt more like a month. It was a long blur of coffee, cigarettes and writing, and it did not take long for the tedium of it to embed itself in my skull, numbing the imagination against its own power. Music became my only escape; and only music could transport me elsewhere, for perhaps three, or five, or twenty-five unsurpassed minutes. As a comparison, many have praised the magnificence of the novel – of words which can, in one instance, pervade the very being of the reader with the sense of its own irony, and in the next, reduce them to a state of utter disorientation at their own absence of knowledge. It is an art form which has had monumental effects on both the self and the world, and yet could never affect me so greatly as music; not even drugs had that kind of power over me. My attachment to it at this time was somewhat therapeutic. I was listening to just about everything and anything: Aretha Franklin's fervent voice, its brim running over with soul; the pure, fiery energy of the Doors, infused with poetic electricity;

the iconic harmonies of *California Dreamin'* that will haunt the ears of its listeners forever; these sounds were like heroin to me, sustaining my soul through inanition.

It was the end of the week, and I lay awake contemplating Amelia. Aware that I was not going to sleep anytime soon, I went to the bathroom. As I glanced in the mirror in the pale moonlight, I felt and saw all colour drain from my face. For a brief moment, I wondered how it was possible that she had appeared – I had abstained from hallucinogens completely, and yet I was still hallucinating. I quickly reminded myself that this was a problem that spanned far further back than recent years; I started to wish it had only been a matter of a bad trip.

The world seemed to spin ever quicker, as I became increasingly nauseous. I thought. *If my mind can manipulate me, then surely I can in turn manipulate my mind*. It was not necessarily by choice that I could think of nothing but where I wanted to be right then: on the road with Clint, as far away as possible from any place that I knew. It was now sickeningly ironic that San Francisco, the place of my nightmares, really had once been the subject of my dreams. My tale told nothing new, only a story of human folly. I burst open the windows, letting the wind ripple through my hair and night shirt, feeling the freshness of the dark against me, lifting my arms to let the breeze brush over my fingertips, as if cleansing me head-to-toe. The world still seemed to spin somewhat, or perhaps I was dizzy; I felt myself fall to the ground, until I was lying there on the cold tiles, clasping my knees.

You can't ignore me forever, Clarice. Her wild phantom voice slid across the tiles, seeping into my head like an unsolicited thought.

"You're right, I can't," I replied. The floor seemed to move beneath me. I heard the motion of bedsheets in the other room, and then quiet. I was then struck by a moment of *eureka*. "I presume you have something to tell me," I heard myself say.

I do. I think my words shall please you, Clarice, for I think it is quite possible that you shall be freed from your suffering, soon; it will all be in good time.

I was shocked by this statement. I had not expected to hear anything like it, but I was nonetheless terrified at these words that were filled with ambiguity. Her previous prediction had not been false, whether she was a figment of thought or not; but I would not let her dubious forecasts affect me. I spoke with a morbid sarcasm, that came from my unstable nerves.

"Really? How so?" I said with a chuckle.

That I cannot tell. Only time can tell.

"What? Can you speak louder please?" I jested with her. Again, I heard movement in the bedroom.

I cannot see.

A foot descended upon the floor; I asked pointless, trivial questions. The footsteps got closer; Amelia answered, this time louder. Closer again. My pulse quickened; a rush of adrenaline. The footsteps faded away towards the bedroom door; he must have been going to get a glass of water. How funny it must have been for him, to wake up in the middle of the night, to overhear his insane girlfriend talking to herself; if we were not both so accustomed to acid trips, he might have seen this as a point of concern.

"How can I escape you?" I sighed.

You can't. She laughed coldly.

"But there must be a way,"

It's not that simple, Clarice. I'm in your head.

I had never heard anything like it; I quite literally could not believe it. The closest condition to this I could think of was schizophrenia, and yet I had always pictured schizophrenics as irrational, deluded, lost souls, their heads were too crowded with confusion to make sense of anything at all; but as far as I was concerned, no one had ever suspected me of being delusional, and I didn't feel overcrowded with information – only invaded at times by a singular hallucination. I had no idea whether a condition such as mine could even exist.

I had also been suspicious as to why there had been a decade's hiatus between one bout of hallucinations and the next. None of it could be explained, but Amelia had to be right. She could not have been anywhere other than in my mind. I couldn't restrain myself, and began to sob helplessly like a child. I heard footsteps coming into the bedroom, towards the bed, and then back towards me; a knock on the door. Amelia was gone.

"Clare, are you okay?"

I attempted to wipe my tears away, but my voice cracked as I spoke:

"I'm fine." He opened the door.

"Hey, what's wrong?" he said, and I suddenly remembered being seventeen years old, hunched over on my bed and crying over Jim. Clint came over and sat down on the floor beside me.

"I can't begin to explain to you what is happening right now."

He put his arms around me, which seemed to act as a shield against the external horrors that seemed to congregate around me. He kissed the top of my head, and it filled me with a warmth that permeated through my entire being.

"Whatever it is, you will be fine. You're stronger than you think," he reassured me. "But tell me what is happening." I couldn't find an adequate lie to tell, but I was equally incapable of telling the truth. Oh, I trusted him, but I wanted him to trust me – and yet the truth is only a rational thing; I didn't know if rational was something I could really be.

"There's something wrong with me," I said, and there was no regressing. I had jumped, and was now falling through the sky, through layers and layers of cold white cloud, rapidly falling to his overwhelming response:

"Something wrong? Is it serious?"

"Not like that. It's not a disease."

"Well then, what is it?"

"I'm crazy." He looked at me uneasily.

"What? Aren't we all?" he said, half-smiling in what I can only assume was sheer relief, and deep confusion. "What makes you say that?" I was still suspended in the air, inches above the ground, which I would hit the moment I spoke.

"No – I really am crazy – I see things."

Clint's expression dropped from a look of intrigued concern to absolute consternation. I saw he wished he hadn't heard; I wished I hadn't said it. I had undeniably hit the ground.

I had to tell him about everything – Amelia, Sheila, my suspicions – tell him everything and watch him listen. Like a deserted beach in the early hours of the morning, we sat in cold silence, waiting; I know not whether for sunrise or storm.

★★★

"Clarice, why won't you kiss me?" he had said the next morning. He had attempted a tender kiss on his way out of the apartment, to which I was unresponsive. "Well, I suppose I'll go then," he added awkwardly, and once again met by silence, slipped quietly out the front door. His warmth was making me grow colder; preparing myself for the all possible outcomes of my revelation, I had failed to consider that Clint would respond with compassion. It had thrown me off, and now I was left in silence to ruminate over what I had done. While attending to all the thoughts flying about in my

172

head, I ran a bath. Despite Clint's show of understanding, I couldn't help but think that he was behaving with a certain inauthenticity; and I could not help but wish that I was capable of returning it. It was no fun being so dispassionate, so remote and unmoved; and while I felt pity for him, it was a kind of condescension, as if ultimately it was his fault for trying to kiss me. Hot water gushed from the tap, filling the room with steam.

★★★

I sat in the lukewarm bath, nose and mouth pressed against my knee. I had fallen off the edge of the cliff I had been precariously walking for the past decade, and to simply climb back over it was out of the question; I had slipped too far from the brink to even make an attempt. I felt paranoid. Did everyone else have that feeling; that feeling I got when I was alone, curled up and vulnerable? One could so easily begin to rock, but no, everyone knows that only the unhinged rock back and forth, muttering to an imaginary higher power which they do not even believe in, bitter pleas to be released from their suffering – *oh please, Jesus Christ oh please.* Perhaps it was only a matter of weeks before I would become that figure.

★★★

I lay on the bed in my towel with a cigarette, inhaling the thick, white smoke that would hopefully kill me someday. It twisted in the air, meandering within itself, teasing me as I lay paralysed, body enslaved to the mind. It was as if I was no longer living; I wondered what the point of having a life was, if one did not care to live it. But there was no force forbidding me from living in this sense, only the prison in which I moved. Agitated, I got dressed. Nothing was stopping me from catching the next flight to South America, Europe or Asia and beginning a new life; it was something I wished to do, but lacked the motivation.

Often these days I find myself wondering *what if...* what if I had boarded the next flight to India, leaving everything and everyone I knew behind me? Perhaps I would have been able to begin afresh there, amongst the spices, the sunsets, the ancient psyche of that arcane land. And what if I had dropped some acid right then and there? I had an acute sensation that I would never have returned from that trip. And what if I had never seen Amelia in the first place? I can only dream of how different everything might have been. Perhaps I would not have been in San Francisco, living with Clint, filling my days with trips and dreams and acoustic guitars, painted cars, coloured stars. Perhaps I would be married in England; wealthier, healthier, learning from my children's tears, and feeling abstract fears that I could never quite pinpoint. Perhaps I would still be in close contact with people from my younger years. Perhaps, perhaps – it was all rather dubious.

In actual fact, there was nothing preventing me from changing my circumstances, only, I felt that a dreaded recapitulation was inevitable. I would always be an empty vessel through which my tireless analyses erupted within themselves, imploding over and over, until I was empty again and the process could recur continually; it was my way of preventing myself from becoming too content. I wanted to be content; I wanted to feel a lightness in my step as I ascended the stair, a brightness in my eyes as I glimpsed myself in a passing mirror, but an unknown part of me, unlocated, unmarked and utterly minuscule, felt a staggering danger in being content, as if synonymous with emptiness itself. I suppose this is what it feels like to be neurotic. But I did not want to be neurotic, and so immature, and I had forgotten what it was like to have a moral compass, a sense of security and purpose.

I needed to step out of myself. If I expected not to go insane, then a distraction would surely be the solution, and this meant participating in life a little more willingly. Perhaps I would regain my pace, perhaps I would fall farther behind, perhaps I would find a secret clearing; perhaps, perhaps.

VIII

The summer arrived quickly; the madness of spring had been and gone, and finally the mild air rested pleasantly on my skin. The Golden Gate Bridge was characteristically ensconced in a white fog, and the city was bustling with tourists. Between then and the previous summer – the Summer of Love – San Francisco had gained a reputation like never before; it was the place to be for the young, the wild, the lovers, the artists, the freethinkers. So the city heaved with summer festivities and daily activities, while I stood in the dark apartment, the five o'clock sun concealed by a passing cloud.

I was in front of the mirror holding up dresses against my figure. That night I was attending a party thrown by January Green, a close friend who had just sealed a record deal. For the musicians, these deals are few and far, but for outsiders like myself – the journalists, the critics, the promoters – they have an inevitable regularity to them, like the day preceding the night; artists were always celebrating their new contracts.

I was well-suited to music journalism, for I have always been the listener. I need something to hear, deconstruct, analyse, understand and feel; it is an area in which I find myself diving, exploring its tremendous depths, and not merely floating; yet I cannot muster in myself what it is to be an extraordinary creator of art. What many seem to agree on is that geniuses are born, not made. In this vein, whether they accept it or not, a genius can never escape the pressure of their resplendent mind, which is what links them so intrinsically to insanity. Creativity and madness coalesce like paint on a canvas, and yet they are equally capable of standing alone. It was obvious to me that I would never encounter a creative spark in my body, so I clung to being a listener, for my relation to music and my understanding of it was something of which I could be certain.

Suddenly, I felt a hand on my waist, and was snapped out of this contemplation.

"Hey baby," came Clint's voice, and I could feel the heat hanging between his lips and my ear. He began to kiss my neck when I felt an abrupt repulsion, moving away as a vague look of confusion passed across his face. "I'm sorry, I didn't realise—"

"It's always sex," I muttered, unable to look at him.

"What?"

"Sex. We use it to avoid every obstacle we don't feel like overcoming. Why does it only happen when one of us is unhappy?"

He did not reply for a few seconds; we both knew it was the truth. Since I had told him about my past, he had only sunk further into himself, and I had done likewise; and the simplicity of our physical intimacy helped to create the illusion that we didn't have to talk about anything.

"Well perhaps if you weren't so impossible to talk to—" Clint objected.

"Me? I'm not the one who's constantly shutting myself up in a niche of self-pity – I'm not the one making basic communication some kind of exerted effort!"

"But that's the thing – you *are*. You just sit here all day in this goddamn apartment, wondering about what you could do to make things better for yourself while not actually doing anything at all, and I have to live with it and not say a word because it's not what you want to hear."

"I have to get ready for this party," I said dryly, resenting the denseness our sour relationship had thrust upon him.

Clint's words stuck in my head for the remainder of the day. The wine at the party took on undertones of fire which set my blood pressure rising, as I struggled to forget what he had said. The sad thing was it was true, and to think that I had criticised him for sitting around doing nothing was utterly hypocritical; and now, he had not a care in the world, it seemed, idly exchanging witticisms with an older man, as I strained to keep eye-contact and hold a conversation with anyone.

"Well, he's only very recently started to adjust, which is a shame really, because we'll be shipping him back in a few years time for Harrow – and then Julia will probably be sent back as well, which just leaves Ben – we can't get rid of him quite yet, *ha ha!* They're being cared for by a nanny at the moment – I couldn't possibly drag them all the way here from L.A.," the young mother said, flipping her hair back from her face.

"Oh!" I responded, a great exertion on my part to muster enthusiasm. "So how do you know January?"

"Well, you see it's a funny story. Back in '54, we were placed in a dorm together with a couple of other girls at Cobham – and oh, how she *cried!* All day and all night, and of course her parents lived in Florida. God knows why they sent her to school in England – I think they thought it would discipline her, *ha ha!* Of course, as you can see, it didn't exactly amend her. Anyway, they were utterly fuming when they found out their money had gone to waste, and the school discovered her smoking pot on the roof. Anyway, to cut a long story short, somehow we've both ended up on the West Coast."

"How funny!" I said, somewhat mirroring the rehearsed artificiality of her demeanour. She had been relentlessly talking only of herself and her children for a full ten minutes, I daresay she hadn't noticed. Now I was exhausted from listening, and as if summoned by the power of thought, a pale hand lightly took my forearm. The scent of orange blossom – or was it moonflower – gently wafted around my senses. I turned to face January, who was looking radiant in the light of her record deal.

"Clare, when did you get here?" she said.

"Oh, only about a quarter of an hour ago – congratulations, how are you?" and all the other precursive remarks.

"Thank you! Ah, I'm feeling... wonderful! And yourself? I must say, you look well, but then you are loved so well! Such a beautiful evening, isn't it?" She hugged me, so that I was embraced by the scent of the delicate flower of her perfume. I now noticed that her accent was rich with the flavour of English literature, or perhaps I was just imagining it, after the revelation that she had been educated in England. There was something about January which made you trust her; she always focused her full attention on whomever she was talking to, as if they were the only person in the room.

"Champagne?"

Two hours later, having avoided Clint to the best of my ability, I was approached once again by January. By the evidence of her graceless walking and raucous laughter which could be heard from across the garden, she was most certainly drunk, and not so refined as she had been at eight o'clock. She fumbled for a moment in her clutch bag and presented me with a rolled joint – which was something I had not touched for months. I had been around all too much pot in that time, and had without fail resisted the urge to smoke it. I had developed a surprising level-headedness over recent months, somewhat ensuing from all the chaos before it; but the balmy June evening and fizzing champagne triggered something within me that couldn't refuse; after all, I too was most certainly drunk.

As the night reached its inexorability, we began to pour our hearts out to one another, as drunk people do, and I was invaded by a fascination at the world; the kind that comes with being high.

"Wow – look at the stars!"

"It's as if they're kissing the sky, the way they glint like that."

It was truly romantic: the stars, the hibiscus, the jasmine twisting around the bird fountain where the water lay, soaking up the night. Whereas I had been stilted before in resentment and coldness, I now luxuriously fell across the quiet bench, away from the clamour of the party. Everything beyond this little corner in which we sat, surrounded by flowers and shrubs, raised a little from the main patio, was seemingly nonexistent; only this vignette, of which we were the subjects, needed to exist.

But then she asked after Clint.

"How is he? I haven't spoken to him all night."

"Oh," I said wistfully, "well, he's alright, I suppose." A sadness had overcome me with the heaviness of the drink and the joint. It was a dreamlike, pensive sadness, one that requires a degree of calm and repletion to accompany it. I liken it to the sadness of Lamia in her marriage to Lycius; under the layers of mellifluous pleasure, she knew that a cold diminuendo awaited her. Yes, like a drug, I was utterly addicted to it.

"Clare, what's wrong?" A look of concern overspread her sun-freckled face.

"You don't want to hear about our stupid fights…" My voice trailed off into the warm breeze that suddenly brushed across the garden. I lost my train of thought entirely, as all of a sudden I found the entire situation hilarious. I let forth a peculiar chuckle, beaming like a fool. January burst out laughing maniacally too.

"Why are we laughing?" she said.

"I don't know, why are we laughing?" I said.

When we had partially regained our senses, we resumed our conversation.

"It's ridiculous, isn't it? Clint and I are falling out of love with each other and neither of us are willing to admit it!"

"You just did." It only then fully occurred to me, with nothing to obscure this fact, that we were ill-fated.

"I had no idea that there was anything like that going on between you two," January continued. I sighed and sank further into the bench.

"It's all show – but even then, we continue it when there's no one else around. We're trying to convince ourselves that everything is okay, when it's obviously not – and then when I try to confront him about it – not even confront him, just *talk* to him, he either accuses me of being difficult or tries to seduce me!" I laughed as I said it, because it was so trivial. Surely there were greater complexities to be concerned with.

"Oh *God*, don't even go there – Kenny does that all the time." There were certainly greater complexities to be concerned with... but *what were they again*?

A plane passed overhead. A champagne flute clinked with another. A hand felt the curve of her buttocks and squeezed, and she kept a straight face. A man in Resurrection City shot by a police officer. A Vietnamese village destroyed. All of this in a single second, and in a moment of disorientation, I could not quite bring to mind what I was meant to be doing in amongst all of this, for I was raised to believe that I could achieve anything and nothing all at once.

"Sorry, this isn't about me," January apologised. "So is this the end?"

I nodded silently, but I could not tell her the whole truth, which was all too easy in the time and place. I knew what her reaction would be, needless to say it; the weight of the revelation would cause a real plummeting sensation within her, instantly disrupting the evening. She would then, endeavouring to regain her high, liberate that last ounce of a chuckle left in her, before responding. *Are you sure you weren't just tripping?* And then, realising my solemnity, her whole impression of who I was would be entirely subverted. I could not trust her, or anyone for that matter, to keep such an astonishing piece of information to themselves; the word would soon spread, and hence, I had more to lose than I had ever understood before. With this in mind, I gave her a vague response about how we discovered that the person we loved was not who we thought they were – which I suppose was just as true.

"Well if you're so unhappy with each other, then why not just end it now?"

"You're probably right... is that *Rock Around the Clock*?" I abruptly exclaimed, newly animated. The last time this song had been played at a party, I had been no more than eighteen. Hearing it here and now, in this large venue with drinks, and drugs, and lights, cameras, action, it sounded remarkably dated, as if from a different era – like the Charleston or the waltz. Yet we were in a new era – the world had been turned inside out in just ten years, and that was terrifying; but this song transported me back to the night of my sixteenth birthday party, as I had carelessly flung myself into the arms of what I believed to be paradise. And for a brief moment, I once again felt young and insouciant, as if there was no need to be otherwise.

***

It was the sound of voices in the street that awoke me. Last night's events had left me exhausted; I must be growing too old for parties, I thought. Sometimes, it astounded me to think that I was twenty-eight already. There was once a time when I was younger than the musicians I worshipped, so full of hope for what I might have achieved by the time I was their age. Now I was the age that Elvis had once been, that Hendrix had not even yet reached. With these concerns crowding my thoughts, I was reluctant to drive south today with Clint. We were going to visit an old friend of his, a professor and writer whom he had met in Paris, and his wife. This man was apparently one of the most respected figures in modern philosophy, and had inspired Clint in writing his own dissertation.

Like many students fresh out of academia, Clint had once concluded that American society was much too materialist for an individual to truly flourish in. As a result, he moved to Paris for a short while. To him, Paris seemed the logical destination; it had a rich cultural history, he spoke a reasonable amount of French, the majority of the philosophers he admired were French, and in those days he wore a beret. He still owned it and kept it hidden away safely, like a relic from battle. Not to anyone's surprise, he fit into Paris like a jigsaw piece that had been missing for the past twenty years. He found its most bohemian *rues* as a spy detects his target. There, he associated himself with the renowned intellectuals and had a romance with a beautiful French woman. When I saw his old photographs of her, with her long, chestnut hair, and a face like a Michelangelo carving, I couldn't help feeling an inferiority in myself. Together, they spent time in little bookshops and cafés in Montmartre, and sat in the Jardin du Luxembourg on sunny afternoons, before the long, drunken evenings ensued. Clint's tales of Paris filled me with envy.

One night, in a bar in Saint-Germain-des-Prés, he met Humphrey Bolton, a plump, middle-aged American. Clint had been speaking in English with another man, discussing Bertrand Russell's *In Praise of Idleness*. The conversation, naturally, had intrigued Humphrey, a self-acclaimed philosopher. Being a tourist with not a single qualm at his age, Humphrey joined them, and from that point had always remained in Clint's life. Had I been on satisfactory terms with Clint, I would have been overjoyed with leaving the city for a day or two. However, my unwillingness to spend the most part of the day with him, in the confinement of an automobile, had made the idea somewhat unappealing.

Humphrey and his wife, Marla, lived in Ojai, east of Santa Barbara. On the sun-baked streets were flower stalls, quaint art galleries and youthful girls with tanned skin and lambent smiles. Their house blended in effortlessly with its surroundings, promoting that tranquil lifestyle and upscale simplicity of suburban Californians. The whitewashed walls were wholly bare, and one or two monochrome photographs rested on the mantelpiece, beside some Middle Eastern candle-holders. Everything else appeared to be beige: the window-frames and shutters, the thin gauze curtains at the threshold, the blanket draped over the sofa. This home had the appearance of belonging to someone who wished for order, serenity.

We were greeted by Marla, a beige-looking woman whose appearance matched her home's interior design in every sense. She was far from what I had expected. A man who spent late nights in Parisian bars and, I had heard, smoked cigars with the likes of Sartre and Marcuse, I imagined would be married to a more colourful, striking specimen, but when Marla answered the door, she had scrutinised our faces for a moment, before half-smiling and greeting us rather phlegmatically. We had then stood in the white and beige living room, before Humphrey entered and received us with considerably more enthusiasm. He embraced Clint heartily, and expressed his delight at our arrival, having all the aspects of a cheerful man who could cajole his way through life, and avoid taking any of it too seriously.

Over iced tea, we sat on the back porch and spoke about what we had done, what we were doing, and what we would do for the rest of our lives. I soon learned why Marla had a need for order in her surroundings: for the last thirty years she had worked on a psychiatric ward. As she spoke of her career, little could she have known of the uneasiness that it stirred within me. The people she described, they sounded all too familiar; an awful part of me had wanted her to describe them as deranged lunatics, simply so my mind could be at rest, but I knew that any intangible wire which separated me from one who hears voices or sees people did not exist. For many years, Amelia had been a dormant chimera of my past, resting in unconscious silence. It was not her reappearance, but my own mistakes, which had brought her into being; I had told Clint about her, had said those irretrievable words – *I'm crazy* – and now she was a secret to be kept, and one that I so desperately wished to expose. More troubling was the trust I had placed in him not to expose it. How could one store up such tantalising knowledge in their mind, allowing it to percolate into every crevice and as it does, say nothing? I did not expect Clint to reveal anything – far from it. I was not concerned that he would ever tell a living soul, but I knew that at any moment, he could, and that was enough; I waited.

"The line between what can and can't be diagnosed as a mental health problem is incredibly thin," Marla said.

During dinner, the conversation shifted towards the many achievements of Humphrey Bolton.

"I had grown up wanting to explore the planet, like any young boy at the time. I dreamed of one day exploring the Amazon rainforest and the ancient Egyptian temples. It was the earth's mysteries I wished to uncover, and naturally, I believed that exploring it would allow me to do just that; but at some point in my adolescence, I wanted to do more; I had always wondered about matters that were not limited to the confines of the world as it is, but the world as it could be – a world that cannot be seen just with the human eye. In my younger years, I had dabbled with the possibility of a utopian society, or another dimension in itself. The possibility of a world beyond that which is, was real in my mind. I had ideas for the future, and I never stopped questioning how everything came to be," he explained animatedly. "I suppose that's how I got so interested in philosophy," he added nonchalantly, as Marla listened intently to the story she had certainly heard a hundred times before.

"But it was a good thirty years after obtaining my PhD, before my most successful work, *A Critique of Modern Western Capitalism*, was published, and I must say, it received far more praise than I had ever anticipated. Let me tell you – when you're fifty years old and haven't made so much as an imprint on the surface of history, you don't hope for much more than a comfortable retirement, so this came as a great surprise. Anyway, to cut a long story short, after the success of my book Marla and I took a holiday in Mexico. Of course, back home few people recognised me – as you would know, philosophers tend only to be known within select circles – so imagine my shock when I was approached by someone who had read my book and recognised me – in Mexico!" Humphrey began to laugh at this before we had even had a chance to process it, which you could tell he instantly regretted.

"So there we were, sitting out the front of a café in Mexico City, being approached by a man who had simply been walking down the street with his wife, until now. He was quite robust, walking almost certainly towards our table, and Marla and I could only sit in astonishment at this odd, but also frightening, situation. Is this how these Mexicans rob people, I thought, in *broad daylight?*"

Again, we meekly chuckled at this joke before we really knew what it was.

"But then he said, in impressive English," Humphrey proceeded to carry out a poor imitation of a South American accent, "'Excuse me, I hope you don't mind my intrusion, but I believe you are Dr Bolton?' Well, startled as I was, I could only confirm his belief, gathering that he must have been a student of mine at some point. Anyway, he said, 'You are a great inspiration to me – *A Critique of Modern Western Capitalism* has influenced a lot of my own writing.' Of course, I was now completely dumbfounded!" He paused, as if considering the credulity of his words to himself.

"I went on to ask him how he had come by my work; he was obviously very well-read. When I asked him what kind of writing he did, he closed up a little, answering vaguely, and referring to Marxism and poetry in the same sentence. You could tell he was beginning to regret coming to talk to us. I decided not to scrutinise him any further, and so I bid him good day and good luck with his writing, before he walked off again with his wife. Of course, the reason he had let me believe that he was a Marxist poet, whatever the hell that is, was because he was secretly planning to overthrow Batista in Cuba!" Being sure to give the right response, I quickly gasped and said a surprised "really?" but Clint and Marla had obviously heard it before, and my exaggerated reaction caught their attention – for Humphrey had not yet finished the tale. Nonetheless, he raised his tone, reaching the climax of his story:

"You don't forget the face of Che Guevara! Soon enough, he was world-famous – and he had come over simply to tell me how influential my book had been. Now that's what I would aspire to – humility – forget the politics. Of course, this left me with the biggest question of all: to what extent did my book contribute towards that revolution?"

Whether or not the story was entirely true, Humphrey's question was still a very interesting one; had Marx known what his manifesto would do to Russia, would he have written it at all? Can a book be held accountable for anything?

Humphrey went on to exult about his connections with Marcuse, displaying a curious preoccupation with his luminaries, and when he spoke of his own life, it was as if he was performing a dramatic monologue. Had all of this been six months earlier, I would have glanced for a brief moment at Clint, exchanging a private joke and a subtle smile; but now the fabric of our intimacy was torn, without the means to be sewn back up again. I no longer had a desire to make amends – to myself, or to him – and that left me with a hideous emptiness. I could only wonder whether his feelings, or lack of them, matched mine.

Later that night we lay silently in bed, both mimicking sleep; something gnawed at his mind too, but I knew not what. The masses of greenery that filled the guest room seemed to trap us within it; the leaves that looked dark blue in the night lurched over the sides of surfaces. Behind closed eyes, I longed to be at home; not in San Francisco, but England. I missed the verdurous hills, and the musty woodland scent that travels through an open window on a summer's morning. I missed the Medieval castles, the Tudor cottages, and the Gothic mansions that grotesquely imitated their European counterparts. Yet more than its luscious hills and historical architecture, I missed its people most dearly; I had not seen my parents in six years, and despite our frequent communication, I knew that six could turn to twelve all too easily, and they would not be around forever. Then there were my old friends, all now grown up, so different from the young and vivacious students I had once known. Despite the urge to return and visit them, there was not much that frightened me more than the prospect of doing so. After all, it had been six years, and I had forgotten so much of what it had been like at home; but worse than that, it would be humiliating. I had left the country in the hope of finding myself, being inspired, perhaps even inspiring others – yet I had achieved none of it. If anything, I was more lost than I was before, and somehow, I felt I knew less about everything. To go back would simply be to admit defeat.

I drifted into an uneasy sleep and dreamt of travelling home, over ink-blue seas and onto grassy moorland. Eventually I came to an old hill that I knew belonged to the distant past – to centuries ago. Reaching the tangled hilltop, I was presented with a vast view of the grey sea, blending into the sky above it. Continuously I ran into the tide and let it carry me out to the ancient stone boulders that stood between the shore and the horizon, and back again to the brown sand; it had felt so significant, yet I could connect it with nothing.

We barely spoke a word to each other the next morning. Our arguments had been harsh, belligerent and loud, but this time we had reached the point of exhaustion. I thanked some anonymous higher power that we were leaving Humphrey's today, for I did not have the energy to be socialising with people I barely knew. This, however, was at the expense of another day in the car with Clint, and despite Humphrey's egotism and Marla's glacial quality, I momentarily found myself wishing to linger at breakfast.

Humphrey had started to talk again about his time in Paris, describing the beauty of the Eiffel Tower at dusk, glowing a rosy gold against the darkening sky, the Seine rippling quietly below. He spoke of the art galleries with such pretence that it left me with no choice but to conclude that he had spent no more than two weeks in Paris.

"Oh, and the French eat with such sophistication," Marla added. "Their lives revolve around food, but it's all in moderation – that's why the women are so trim; and they don't start the day off with a bunch of fried food like we do over here. When we were in Paris we would have one or two slices of French bread, with honey or cheese, and some fruit – and it was amazing how good you'd feel afterwards, as opposed to having a fried egg and bacon." We all hesitated for a moment over the cooked breakfast before us.

We ate and said our farewells to the couple that had somehow slipped from my expectations; Clint had spoken of Humphrey was as if he were an idol, someone to aspire to, although I struggled to see him in this light; but they had a history which spanned back almost a decade, and there were undoubtedly great things about Humphrey that I would never know.

"So did you like Humphrey and Marla?" Clint asked me on our drive back over the brightening highway.

"Yeah, very nice people. Humphrey was a character." A sportive smirk flashed across his face for a split-second.

"And what about Marla?" he asked.

"She was nice." After a moment of hesitation, as I searched for something more to say, he laughed.

"I think she's a little odd, too."

"I don't know," I replied, "but I imagine working in an psychiatric ward for that long would make anyone a little odd."

"Yeah, I guess you're right," he concurred. The conversation ended there, for like a scorched desert, it's cracked earth deprived of rain, the essence of discourse was as dry as dust. Suddenly the air became excessively heavy as all of this began to feel horribly inevitable. For a large part of my life, I'd had only a faint idea of the workings of love, and before meeting Clint, I had lacked any understanding of it in the long term. I had loved Jim, but that was before hardship had hit us, before we had grown tired of one another's ways, before we had fallen out of love. When I was with him, I had believed myself to be more knowledgable than others in matters of the heart, but by the late sixties, I was more disillusioned than ever.

The feelings I had once held towards Clint were somehow vanished and unobtainable.

On we drove, through the sweltering day and into the late afternoon, over the dusty roads of Salinas, which I had once read about in *Of Mice and Men* as a schoolgirl in her dormitory, the April showers pouring down on the pink roses outside, dreaming of one day leaving the rain; yet here I was in the stifling heat, the parched air beating against my face, and all I could think about was rainfall; light, dewy drops sprinkling from the sun, gloriously replenishing the scorched arena through which we drove.

Arriving in San Francisco, I felt alienated still; alienated from those around me, the city, the entire country. It now felt as if I had only moved here possessed by some whimsical state of mind that had romanticised the entire affair. I had had ideas of freedom, healthy ambitions, dreams that would come true, which now all looked utterly ridiculous. Often we miss the essentiality, the entire meaning of something that, when realised, we wonder, *How could I have missed that?* Common sense is called into question, for it was always so undeniable before. I myself had missed the manifest truth that I could have travelled to the South Pole and I would still be no further away from my past; for I now understood that the past recurs in the mind, the clutches of which one cannot escape by mere migration. As soon as we entered the apartment, Clint slammed the door behind us.

"Clare, what's going on?" he interrogated me, as if unable to contain his agitation. I was astonished, unsure of how to respond. "'Cause if it's gonna be like this then I don't know if I can stick around."

"You really do have no idea what's happening, Clint! You never even ask me if I'm okay – you never take any kind of interest in me at all!"

"Bullshit!" he responded, infuriated. "Don't make me the

191

self-interested one here, okay? Because that's you – you know, perhaps if you just spent a little more time asking me what *I'm* going through, then maybe I would do likewise, but to be honest, you're impossible to communicate with anymore!" His eyes were inflamed, almost tearful with anger. "What happened to you?" The veins in his neck jutted out as if he were exploding, which only upset me further.

"You know exactly what happened," I snapped, as if breaking into smithereens; suddenly, everything I knew was scattered around me, and I couldn't think of anything to say. Through the silence, which held us for a second, he spoke, and he knew this was the end.

"Yeah, I do – you went fucking crazy."

I was overcome with the most horrifying sensation; I felt like a child on a windy boat deck, slipping over the railing, falling further and further into the darkness, the endless abyss of the ocean, as the ship sailed onwards and I was left there in the company of no one but sharks. It was then, and only then, that I madly wished to reconcile our trust. I wanted to collapse onto the floor with him and kiss him slowly, as if it would fix the fighting and the despair, but I knew that was now an impossibility; there was no life-rope to which I could cling – I was simply drowning, and I surrendered helplessly to the void in which I was trapped.

I could barely muster the courage to speak my next words.

"I'm leaving. Please, never speak to me again."

I did not even think to gather my belongings. At an alarming pace I was driving to the beach, propelled by inexplicable impulses.

My thoughts were more ordered by the time I had reached the shore, but I kept having to remind myself that what I was doing was for the better, and now my circumstances could only improve. I was lonely, yes, more than I had ever been before, but that could change as swiftly as the tide. I saw two lovers on the shore, they could not have been more than eighteen or nineteen, but there they stood, embracing as if their lives depended solely on the strength of the other's arms. Her head was buried in his shoulder, and I could only wonder what it was that compelled them to cling so tightly together. The wind now carried a chill on it, which brushed against my face and found its way to my heart, as I contemplated the lovers, feeling only the bitterness of a woman who has been wounded by Cupid's arrows one too many times. And it scared me, no, terrified me, that I had some dreadful instinct in the pit of my stomach, that there were more years behind me than there were ahead. Perhaps I wouldn't die in the literal sense until I was greyed and hunched, but as I looked out over the cooling horizon, I saw no desire floating above the waves, no ambition – nothing but the echoes of a life that seemed to belong to someone else, but they were my memories – and yet even those from five minutes ago seemed to have been reclaimed by someone else.

I walked to a more deserted part of the beach. Sitting on a rock, I lit a cigarette and remembered the day that Kennedy was shot. I had marked that day as my life's turning point, and I allowed it to be as symbolic as it really was. I thought about what it more precisely symbolised – although I already knew the answer, and I was entirely done with seeking answers; doing so had long kept me in the past, and as I had promised myself many years ago, I would always move forward. I would walk fearlessly into the morrow, however fruitless it may appear; for my thought was that after miles of aridity and dried hope, sooner or later the landscape must surely change.

So the night arrived, and the city lit up and danced on, as I inhaled the world, exhaled and singed it with cigarette smoke; and for the first time in what felt like years, whatever it was that had so cunningly seized me, loosened its grip.

PART III
1969

I

There was something so tranquillising about the way the rain pattered onto the gravel, permeating petrichor, and invigorating the senses. It was April, when the bright-eyed and bushy-tailed awaken to blooming roses and vivid greenery, which, in their sprightly innocence, mock the muted skies above. The birdsong is always at its purest in the springtime, shrill and clear; the birds do not know misery, for it can so easily cease to exist in their world, once winter has passed. The wildlife has an extraordinary knack for starting over again, I have noticed – a skill which our own species noticeably lacks. Perhaps if it were not for our astonishing tendency to render what is so simple unintelligible, perhaps if we just – stopped – and reminded ourselves that life is only a matter of breathing, we might be more captivated by it.

I had become more at ease in recent weeks. It felt as if I had finally been given the space to come to terms with everything. I was bizarrely content in my circumstances, in a place overflowing with desolation and hysteria, instability so deeply rooted into its grounds – and yet never before had I seen the world so clearly. I had nourished my interest in the arts too, something which had been neglected for too long. I bought old books and records in town, and delighted in their magnificence. How far we had come from the days of our ancient ancestors; how eloquently one could express the symphony that a note on a keyboard roused within him. From past experience, I know the arts to be a powerful analgesic. It is Mozart's fortieth symphony that masks the frenzied jarring that can be heard trailing down a corridor, Woolf's ceaseless stream of consciousness that replaces my own; things that, when I am engrossed in them, obliterate all that other inconsequential matter in the mind.

Nonetheless, there are some things which cannot be so easily ignored. The institutional smell hangs around, like it used to at school – it comes from constantly purging everything, as if mental illness were contagious. And there will always be that unremitting talk of suicide somewhere in close proximity; but the most unavoidable, ineluctable thing is the gloom that eclipses this place like a starless night.

Yet I was not inconsolable – rather the opposite, for I had never been so easily consoled by the simplest things in all my life. Suddenly, I was recovering. I felt there was something within me that needed to recover, that would not let me die here, since everything I held dear had been vehemently taken from me, when I had been thrown into this place. It could have been worse, I knew that. It always could have been worse; this was something I had been preaching to myself ever since I could talk.

However, this place was certainly not what I had in mind when the words 'psychiatric institution' were uttered to me in the past. I had, of course, always imagined the worst: a detestable Panopticon, where guards lurked like sharks in dark corners, waiting to drag patients into a dingy lift that led down and further down, into to an ill-lit basement laboratory, where inconceivable horrors were performed. It was the stuff of nightmares, and whilst I never truly believed in it, the fundamental aspects of the Panopticon cannot be denied to linger in these halls. First, there is the continual sense of being watched; then the powerlessness, and finally the degradation that takes place in the questionable name of treatment. This is where two worlds fuse, where science meets fear, and healing meets imprisonment somewhere in the middle; but, I kept telling myself, it could be far worse.

On weekends we are allowed out in groups, accompanied by a member of staff. We may visit shops, parks, cafés – wherever we wish to go – and I use this as an opportunity to spend what little money I have on books and records. It really is the small pleasures which make the unbearable bearable – obvious, but true. We also try to make it bearable for each other; ultimately, you can only depend on yourself, but in times of adversity people tend to stop ignoring each other so much. You learn each other's limits, and your ties are close, but never too close. I soon learnt that my worst preconceptions about the patients proved as hyperbolic and misguided as the ones I had of the institution. It was if I couldn't quite believe that they were not completely insane. The patients I was yet to meet already occupied a space in my imagination, as tropes of caterwauling, garbling lunatics to whom I could never relate. I had learnt so little about the nature of these places. They were but a distant, inaccessible, and most importantly, irrelevant realm, where people either went to recover or remain – and yet somehow it had always felt too possible that I would end up here.

In my fellow patients I found a degree of happiness – yes, happiness – for in our shared misery there grew empathy; we all knew what marginalisation felt like. Each of us had our eccentricities, of course – that was why we were there – but in each other we saw right through them, even in the most sociopathic of individuals. It was the nurses whose sanity suffered the most, as they were still clinging to it.

Naturally, I have become familiarised with many psychiatric disorders; for instance, I now know that Amelia is no symptom of a split personality, which I instead see in a fellow patient called Frida. At unpredictable moments, Frida will burst into a Southern American drawl and believe herself to be an outlaw in the Wild West. It is distressing to see, but she is also alarmingly intelligent, and there is something in the unfathomable darkness of her eyes which suggests she knows everything. There is, however, something abstruse in her speech, most likely a reflection of her complex thought processes. In her bouts of lucidity, she collineates, "Factual knowledge with the innate kind, abandoning all else; it is the only way I can be certain that I am not deluded."

"Shut up, Descartes, I'm watching the news – you know they've just lowered the voting age to eighteen."

"How old are you, anyway, Florence?" asked Mary, another patient in the ward whose constant presence antagonised Florence, a profound sociopath of an individual.

"Nineteen."

"God help us."

"Save it, Mary," Florence retorted. "I can't vote anyway; I've got a criminal record," she added with an air of dignified defiance.

"What for?"

"I killed and ate my neighbour's cat; roasted him with rosemary and thyme – little Oscar was delicious, actually – tasted like a fine bit of rabbit with the juices and all." Everyone's eyes were on her, for we couldn't tell whether or not she was joking. "Oh, that was priceless!" she said, registering the look of horror on our faces, and bursting into laughter.

There is a true miscellany of individuals here, and in some ways it reminds me of boarding school; one arrives, shares a room, makes their friends, breaks the rules, and finally leaves. I do not know how I will feel when I leave this place; I had finished my school days in a cloud of chaos, with a confused vision that I would somehow start all over again, as if everything that had preceded that moment was somehow obsolete, because my days had become hellish. That was doomed to failure: Amelia will follow me for as long as I live. No pills, no mode of thought, nothing, could make her disappear. I often question the true nature of my illness, and wonder how it can ever really be treated, for delusions and hallucinations are quite real to the person having them; they say the experience of hearing a disembodied voice is as vivid as hearing an actual one – how can one's perception that something is happening possibly be doubted? It is true that what we perceive may be imagined and false, but how can one doubt that they are perceiving those things? How, I ask, for the answer eludes me, can even the mere memory of such an experience be treated, without damaging the brain entirely? Those with persistent and severe depression will ask the same question, and countless attempts to expunge the gloom have been made – drugs, analyses, electric shocks – but these do not remove the qualitative experience of a situation, or a thought, that was once felt. Once certain areas of the mind have been glimpsed at – both the illumined and the darkest, most recondite parts – one cannot regress to what they only knew before; or if so, it is only in the Freudian sense, which causes deeper disturbance than there was before. It took me a long time to realise all of this, for I believed that if one spared no thought for something that was purely inner, then it would dissipate; but just as with any other problem, it is not solved by denial of its existence. I thus found myself a patient, tracking continuously and tirelessly over how I got here, my thoughts becoming so complex that it is hard to articulate them in simple terms.

It was shortly after my last argument with Clint that I began to lose grip of reason. I could almost feel it sliding from my consciousness, as an iceberg meanders from its brink, and both sides yearn after each other; yet sometimes separation is part of the natural course of things, for with each icescape it is inevitable that a part should break off and melt away. There is no use despairing over what is natural.

Eventually, about a month after the unbearable alienation ensued, I returned to England. America was starting to appear to me as the vast and terrifying place that it had always been. I realised then how alone I had become, how everyone was a stranger, and I did not belong. San Francisco had become a cliché, a target for so-called 'hippies' who were following a trend, and mocking the ideals they believed themselves to be the embodiment of.

When I returned, I rented a small house in Mortlake, Richmond upon Thames; being in the suburbs meant that I could avoid the loneliness that stems from both the seclusion of the deep countryside, and the estrangement of bustling city life. My journalism was still bringing in a reasonable income, but the music and culture of London differed greatly from that of San Francisco, and I had to adjust. It was younger, sharper, trendier, and there was something remarkably sordid about the whole ordeal. This was the hyper-cool, and it made great photographs that paid well: shots of Carnaby Street with Union Jacks overhanging the cars, mod girls in tight tops and tiny skirts, and the most exclusive underground gigs across the city. This filled me with hope. I visited all those whom I had recklessly left behind, and revived the ties between my family and I, which had, of course, dissolved a little in my absence.

Polly was one of the first to hear that I had moved back to England. As soon as she did, she invited me to her house in Kew, where she now lived with her husband and two children. I hadn't seen her in such a long time, that I hesitated on the doorstep for a moment, holding the gifts I had brought for my godchildren. *You'll have to ring the doorbell sooner or later.* I held my breath as I pressed the small, white bead of a button, dreading the consequences of my decision to return at all, wondering what I could possibly have to say to the girl with whom I once shared everything—

"Clarice!" Her gentle features lit up in delight as she saw me; she had barely changed. "Come in! I can't believe you're really here!"

She led me into a large kitchen at the end of the house, with French windows that looked out onto the patio, where her daughter, Lucy, played. It had just gone four-thirty, and the table was laid with a tea set, little iced cakes and dainty sandwiches on cut glass plates. "I thought we'd have a spot of afternoon tea, just like old times," she said, beckoning Lucy to come inside and say hello. Polly and I spoke as if it were ten years ago; we laughed over old memories of Willow Hill, seizing and relishing, before relinquishing the past. For the first time, I spoke openly to her about Jim, told her what I had done in San Francisco, what I had learnt.

Polly was now married to William, the man she had been with since I was at the Academy, who, on meeting me, seemed just as kindhearted as her. I knew that a lot of women must have envied Polly, but I did not. The things I had encountered, enjoyed and endured made it clear to me that I could not withstand a life as seemingly utopian as Polly's, but they more affirmed to me the impossibility of utopia in a grander sense. Or perhaps this was affirmed when I saw Hannah, whom, even after my years of absence, still retained that evasive veneer which I could not quite unravel. She now lived in Suffolk, alone with her daughter, after a messy divorce. Or in spite of this, maybe the impossibility was affirmed by the fact that, like a child at a fairground letting go of a balloon, I had let go of Bridget, as she had sailed into the distance, away into the insipid atmosphere.

It would never stop being painful, having no idea what had become of someone I had once been so close to.

Leaving Polly's sugar-coated domesticity, I made my way to my childhood home in the country. When my mother saw me at the doorstep her face brightened in elation, and I had never been so glad to see her.

"Clare!" she exclaimed, throwing her arms around me. I was so relieved to see her that I almost cried.

During my stay, however, I noticed that my mother had changed. There was a time when she would have eaten a pear with her fingers, but it now had to be dissected and tried on a fork. She had once been unafraid of sitting down to dinner in the same clothes in which she had cooked it, but now she insisted on bathing and dressing before it was served. She had acquired an air of grandeur, which seemed so unnatural to the woman who raised me, as if age had obliged her to become this way. Her mother had made much the same transition. When we are young, they say that our freethinking ways are only temporary; my bloodline seemed to suggest that it really does have an expiration date. I couldn't see it happening to myself, but I was part of a new generation who believed they had broken the mould, and it may be that we have. Father had softened with age, full of knowledge about the latest article he had read, sailing through the dawn of his later years; yet he remained rigid in his ways and beliefs, caring no less for a routine which allowed him to play golf or go shooting during the day, and eat supper no earlier than eight o'clock, before a nightly game of bridge.

The fact loomed that I had reneged what they had given me; in my eyes, freedom, in their eyes, happiness, and in everyone else's, a ticket to America which I had essentially torn up and thrown away. I was encumbered with a hulking sense of guilt, and I sometimes find myself wondering if I should have just carried on in the States for a few more weeks, and I might have found solace; more often, I try to convince myself that I made the right decision in coming back.

Within a fortnight of my homecoming, I was once again plagued by fog and confusion, followed shortly by the inescapable reappearance of the mirrored phantom. This time, I challenged her. I did not tell her to leave me alone, but asked her all that I wanted to know.

"Why are you doing this?"

It is less a question of what I am doing, and more a question of what you are doing.

Had I been in a clear state of mind, and not shrouded by the greyness which often comes over me at these times, I might have been able to see everything as it was, and reason her out of continuity; but that was out of the question. I was worsening with each episode, becoming less rational with each apparition, hoping that I would not descend into incoherence, and have public outbursts, and speak words that do not follow from one another. The hallucination was becoming more frequent, and I knew that one day, I would not be able to wake up and impersonate a lucid human being; but I had not yet lost my mind completely, so I responded.

"What I'm doing? I haven't done anything – you've tormented me for over a decade."

I saw her pale lips part in anticipation of what she had to say. She was finally going to reveal her true nature, her purpose, and possibly mine. She swayed, as she often does, before speaking with her uncanny voice; a voice which resounds off every surface, causing a discomfort that feels like being on the boundary of death.

I shall explain this to you only once: I have been your tormentor for as long as you have been breathing the air of this planet, for I came from, and shall always reside, in that dark recess you call your unconscious mind. You waited for me, and when the opportunity came to enliven me, you heedlessly clutched it. But you must be curious as to why it is you who suffers in this way… Her voice trailed off into the night, she vanished, and I was left distraught and desperate for an answer. Perhaps I was mistaken, but she seemed to have implied that I was the cause of my own hallucinations. She was certainly right that I was curious as to why I, of all people, had been subjected to them all this time. Their frequency continued to increase as the weeks passed, and I was often confronted with her presence in my darkest hours.

One bleak February night, she made another appearance; I had been dreading it at the bottom of my heart, but nonetheless, she still took me by surprise. She appeared as I stared vacantly into the mirror at an inglorious hour, the dull yellow light of the bathroom melding every object into one, but for her white face. I wondered when she would ever fail to send an almighty shudder down my spine, like the ones my mother used to tell me were people walking over my grave, and when she would fail to bring goosebumps to my skin, and fail to make my heart rap at its cage of bones.

There is a solution to this, Clarice. A slight smile played across her equivocating lips, *you can escape if you wish, from this nightmare which both ensnares and is perpetrated by you.*

As incredulous as I was, I couldn't shut my ears, as intrigue defeated me. *Clarice, I see so much of my former self in you; I remember – I was so afraid. I pined after freedom – first from my parents, and then from myself. But there is a way, Clarice.*

"I'm not an idiot," I responded. "I'm not killing myself."

Her eyes widened in apparent disbelief, as if I was expected to comply with her transparent plot. My judgement may have been askew, but I was not entirely foolish.

Die by your own hand? How dreadful a remedy to recommend to anyone in such pain, even the most despicable of mankind! You have entirely misinterpreted my intentions, which were of the highest benevolence. I want nothing more than for you to avoid the same end that I did not; I want to lead you out of the blackness and into the dawn of a new life. Winter is coming to an end; soon enough the bare branches of the trees shall be replenished with new leaves, and fruit and flowers, and the unpleasant air shall become milder. This is your chance to recover. Her words infuriated every inch of me, so that an exacerbating rage burned from within.

"You mean you want me to recover from the pain that you inflicted upon me?" I could sense that she pitied me; it was in her eyes, the downturned corners of her mouth, and the air itself.

Your scrutiny is so very flawed. You are both the torturer and his victim; to accept one role and not the other is to preserve both. Once you realise that I am merely the key to and from the chamber, you may be perfectly able to escape. I suggest a pragmatic solution which I am sure anyone else would endorse – I believe this to be the most superior assurance of your recovery there is. You must seek help from those around you; find others alike to yourself, so that you do not lose your mind among those who cannot see the world as you see it. Somewhere along this road, you will understand.

Her words had done no more than confuse me, for I didn't know hallucinations could be such reasonable figures, and yet she made perfect sense; this often made me doubt whether she was imaginary at all, but it left me with no alternative as to what she could be. I couldn't quite convince myself that she was a spectre, after all I had seen and done in this world; my scepticism had utterly annihilated this possibility.

She faded out of sight, leaving me with an abject reflection of myself. The circles under my eyes which are sometimes less prominent, but ever-present, were so deep that it looked as if someone had slashed two knives across my face, which itself was blemished, lined and tired. The bloom and delicacy of youth had long dissipated, and I was now dishevelled, ugly, even. And as I stared into that mirror, agonising over what I had become both physically and psychologically, I realised that there was nothing to lose in fixing myself. Although

I feared the thought of every second of it – the words that would overturn everyone's perception of who I was, filling myself with chemicals that altered the very workings of the brain, supposedly curing it, knowing that the memories would stay with me always – the thought of doing nothing was even worse.

An enormous flaw that pervades human consciousness is the belief that we can control nothing, whilst attempting to control everything. Sitting in the drawing room with my mother and father, I cowered under their possible responses to my speech – and I failed to see how that was out of my control. I however, was not; I had complete control over what I was to reveal, and I how I was to respond, over how I would interpret, and how I would witness the world before me; yet I felt, needlessly, so utterly powerless. It seemed so undeniable that I was destined to ruin, that it thoroughly blinded me to any other perspective. As I approached my childhood home, down the grey road that matched the stolid sky, lined with leaves that cleaved to it after the rain, past the colourless fields which roamed onwards for miles, and the old country houses with shingled roofs and small windows, a deluge of panic rose within and submerged me, until I could think of nothing but the consequences of what I was about to reveal, over and over again, until I was drenched in and choking on my thoughts. Sitting in the conservatory with my parents, I was beginning to regret disrupting their peace at all.

Knowing whereabouts to begin was the hardest part; I couldn't just sit there and say nothing, or pretend I had come for a different reason – but I could not simply start at the point and confuse them. Starting at the beginning seemed just as absurd, considering I didn't know where the beginning really was. I partially lied to my parents, attributing the hallucination to drug abuse, which, although brought a great deal of shame onto me, spared them the dismay of knowing that matters where not so simple. I then explained how at first, the visions were infrequent and manageable; but the distress they had caused me had made them worse, so severe that I couldn't function normally, and I wanted to be cured. My mother recognised that there was something to be done, and supported my decision to go to whatever lengths it would take to treat myself. My father was silent; he did not even look at me.

The doctors decided that my hallucinations were potentially dangerous, so I find myself here, institutionalised for a while. It is a remote place, easy to drive past, accessible only by a narrow road that on one side overlooks a sheer drop onto the railway line below. There is also an abandoned chapel, but that is all, before one escapes onto the main road again. Due to its seclusion, there are extensive grounds here, with grand cedar trees and heavy roses which exude a scent almost oppressive in its profusion, yet at other times can only be described as pleasant. They have a bizarre effect on me, the grounds. Some mornings I open my eyes and realise how fortunate I am to be so close to nature; on others, I am trapped in amongst wild thickets and unbounded isolation. The ward itself is just as changeable, and whilst the great windows cast soft shadows onto the walls in the sunlight, those same white corridors breathe a spectral sheen in the moonlight, which loiters on the old wooden floorboards. The lobby itself, with its marble floors and old oak panelling by the front desk, had impressed me when I first arrived, but I also became suddenly aware of the anguish that had certainly occurred here. No quality had ever weighed so heavily upon my apperception; this building was lonesome, dolorous, as if aching for its vibrant past, if it ever had one. It reeked of wasted ambitions, its own appetite diminished long ago by melancholia so resonant that it could deafen for a minute or two, and nothing will be heard but that acute ringing that causes the ears to throb.

Imaginably, the vacant chapel stirs unease within its visitors. The steeple can be seen emerging from the trees at a distance, as if God Himself watches over the place. It is in fact part of the premises, but has remained unused for over twenty years. Of course, we have all ventured in there to take a look around. It is beyond the power of any patient to repair it, so those who are religious worship elsewhere; but more often than not, most of us are without faith. The pews sit unoccupied, overlaid with a veil of cinereal dust. It is unnaturally silent once the bulky wooden door is closed upon the world; time intermits, so that one has an experience so disconcerting, the ward itself becomes the home to which she hopes to return. This former place of worship is strangely untouched by any blasphemous wall-writing from young, troubled patients; no one can recall a single suicide attempt, séance or act of extreme vandalism which has taken place there. It is as if the chapel is perpetually frozen in time, dead as the inhabitants of the graveyard, and entirely stripped of its holiness.

It was with sensations of restlessness that I began my days as a schizophrenic patient. I feared many things – the nurses, the nights, my equals – they all amalgamated into one grim perception of a living nightmare. Henceforth, I thought, this is how I shall exist. I truly believed that the remainder of my days would wane in misery and isolation, and I would fade from the planet like the embers of a fire. Yet these feelings were only initial, perhaps one last attempt at pretending that I was not the same as the others; that my hallucinations were not reducible to mere malfunctions of the senses; that my mind was not the demon who deceived me; but I soon learnt that no matter how enigmatic my condition was, I belonged here; I needed to recover. Once I had understood this, the fear divided itself into what could be known and thus no longer feared, my beliefs waned, the dread faded.

In the first week, I detached myself from others, and tended to grieve for hours over my condition. This, of course, only worsened the symptoms. Often she would simply appear, watch me, perhaps laugh in a way so haunting that the sound seemed to creep into my bones, and once I was utterly shaken, she would disappear. By the fifth day in the ward, I was already estranged from myself, as a sunken shipwreck is from its days of splendour; I had been somewhat abruptly dehumanised, so that I could no longer recognise any characteristics unique to myself, aside from the undeniable intuition that I was insane. But insane is not all a person can be – surely there were other aspects to this self; and it was strange, for I had never viewed myself as having only one dimension, but now I was beginning to think that that just might be the case. By this time, I had truly abandoned hope – it had happened the second I set foot on the ward, and crossed the boundary into this curious and abnormal world. It came as a surprise, then, when on my fifth day of grieving, my roommate entered with a jug of large red daisies, and placed it on my bedside table.

"I picked these in the hope that they might cheer you up," Nettie said cautiously. I smiled in acknowledgement of the gesture, but I couldn't bring myself to say anything, with the lump that had formed in my throat. "You can't stay silent forever, you know. Do you want to talk about it?"

Until then, I believed Nettie had given up on attempting to befriend me. For what felt like weeks, all I had known were the illusions which mocked my sight, and laughed in my ears; but here she was, real as the bed on which I sat, the jug of daisies on the table, the very room we were in. In all honesty, I was embarrassed by my inability to speak, which I had evidently acquired in isolation. I spent a moment considering her proposal, unsure of whether or not I did want to talk about it. Yes, I did – more than anything. I suddenly realised that in this dismal state, all I wanted was an attentive ear. I risked being misunderstood, but that was not important – desperation had clutched me in such a way that I couldn't refuse – rather, I told her the whole true story of how I got here – something which I had always distorted for others' ears.

As I spoke to Nettie, I realised just how liberating it felt to speak freely and honestly, uninhibited by what my listener might think. As I related to her the events of my past, she remained thoroughly still, as if something had been unlocked within her – a remembrance, perhaps, of her own history, still entirely unknown to me. Once I had explained to her more than I had ever explained to anyone, she did not say much; for a few moments, she sat noiselessly, as if in contemplation; yet no words were needed to express the barrier which had been broken.

"You've achieved so much," she responded. This surprised me infinitely, and rendered me speechless; but then I saw – I saw so clearly what had always eluded me before: the truth.

"I thought I was to achieve something in leaving school at sixteen," Nettie continued, now disclosing her story to me. "I thought finding myself a secretarial job, and marrying the man I worked for was a flawless plan. He was French, charming, incredibly handsome, and lived in this vast empire of wealth, so entirely different from anything I'd ever known. When he first laid his eyes upon me, I saw in him a way out – out of what, I don't know – but I was led into a world of luxury… swimming pools, champagne." She laughed, paused for a moment, and looked up to the ceiling, smiling. "It wasn't as if my upbringing had been anything less than comfortable; I always knew I was fortunate, but I had never lived like I did with Yves; I could have eaten caviar every day of my life if I'd wanted to. He bought me clothes made from the most expensive silks you could imagine; I had loads of these thin, delicate shirts which cost more than any dress I had ever owned, and the jewels – there were so many jewels.

It wasn't long into our marriage, though, when I began to lose control. The slightest trigger – most often a thought – could send my spirits plummeting to the ground, destroying them completely, and just the slightest hint of joy, laughter or even hope, could send me into this euphoric state of happiness. I couldn't control it; my erratic behaviour was confusing other people as much as it confused me. I didn't know what to do – I knew that if I sought some kind of help, Yves would divorce me as quickly as he had proposed. I was completely at a loss; I didn't know how I would be able to carry on – as much as I fought against it, I was controlled by these unpredictable, crazy mood swings. And I knew it was more serious than just a matter of self-discipline – when I thought about it, I thought rationally. I knew I had the strength to control my thoughts, but if I tried to do it when they took over, my whole being seemed to give up on me, and then I could just sit for hours doing nothing, thinking about the same thing, over and over again. The scariest thing was that this person – this insane person with absolutely no regard for others, who let emotion triumph incessantly over reason – was me. I wanted to seek help, but at the same time, I wasn't sure whether anything could really be done about my personality; it was just the way I seemed to be now. You can't make an introvert an extravert, a wise man a fool, and I knew just as well you can't make a crazy person sane. So over time it got worse, until I just wasn't thinking straight anymore.

One night, I ran a bath and filled it with bubbles which smelt of pine and lavender; I remember that smell like it was yesterday. It just sticks in my head. I don't know how long it had been – seconds, minutes, hours maybe – but Yves said he found me, lying unconscious in a pool of bloody water. When I awoke in the hospital, he told me he was sending me to a psychiatrist, didn't even ask me why I did it, didn't care. I was useless to him now – useless to any man at all now that I had these ugly gashes on my wrists; how on earth could I be shown off if I was covered in scratches, looking and feeling lethargic all the time? I had been reduced from a trophy to a scrap. It turns out I have an 'affective personality'. People can live normally with it, but they said that I was a danger to myself, and a short stay here would help me to think more clearly. They were right: I now see that I actually *want* to stay here – there's nothing for me out there. But you? If you take anything from what I've just said, take this: do whatever you can to cure yourself and get out of here, because I'm not convinced this is where you should be; you've let this disrupt your life for long enough."

▌▌

On the night before my twenty-ninth birthday, I had a dream so vivid that I can recall almost every detail now. I was in the bedroom of the apartment in San Francisco, first confronted with the empty, unmade bed. I called Clint's name, to which I received no response, only an eerie susurration of the wind which rolled down the street, rippled the curtains, made me shiver. As I began to inspect the room, I saw that it was a mess; clothes and records were carelessly strewn across the floor, dust smothered every surface. This was not how I remembered our apartment; this place looked as if its inhabitants had impulsively deserted it. Stepping out of the front door, I beheld the tragic emptiness of the street before me, antiquated and forlorn, like an archaic frontier town left in the vestige of its past. And then, for a brief moment, music began to blare loudly from one of the windows on the street, which flashed with light, laughter, dancing – all for a second, before falling dead silent again, and the people in the room vanished. I had the distinct feeling of being watched, so ominous and so imminent that I sensed the blood rushing throughout my body as I stood petrified in the street, which soon began to melt in an acidic dream all around me. I tried to scream, before awakening out of one hell and into another.

The clock read five fifty-nine. I sat up in bed in the coolness of the early morning, still, even after four months, unable to ascertain whether I loathed or quite liked being here. The dream was heavily imprinted on my mind, causing me to remember the past. Whilst each day spills into the next, and nothing seems to change, when we look back over our lives, we find that we have lived many, and they seem so unconnected with each other; yet they are indeed firmly connected by a stream of people, events and ideas. It was only in this consideration that I comprehended – as far as I could – the amount of change that had occurred throughout my lifetime; how I had broken from a cocoon of mediocrity, longing and sadness into a new age. Even now – even though the dream had collapsed before my eyes – I saw it as an achievement. When I was seventeen, nothing had seemed more painful to me than remaining in a situation I knew I could never endure; and that is what had compelled me to change my surroundings. I could easily have settled, like many of my peers, into a more convenient path, and lived a far simpler life. I have no idea what it was that set my perspective apart from theirs; I can only surmise that it was death. My drive to escape a place so filled with memories of death had been intensified by my personal proximity to them. It was no wonder that I wished to leave everything behind me; everything except for that one love I could never lose: music. We evolved together, thrived on each others' delectation and dolour, gave meaning to places and created memories which a single song could conjure again. I was endlessly mesmerised by the power which music holds over every being on this planet; so I pursued it, until I fell in love with a person; and there is not time or words enough to stress how it is the glory and fall of man, the making and destruction of nations, when we surrender to love.

I had drifted into a daydream of sorts, and it swallowed up time – until I was forced to slip into the day's routine, which I had grown too all comfortable in – wash, dress, breakfast, medication; the rest of the day is governed by meals and drugs, with little structure elsewhere, until we are consigned back to our rooms at night. The place operates on a continual cycle, each individual progressing as it repeats itself, but as the day of release draws nearer, they always grow increasingly hesitant. As my own day of deliverance impended, I became anxious; not anxious to leave or stay – just pure anxiety. Perhaps I wished to freeze time for a moment, to gather my thoughts, to think how far I had come, and of where I was to go next – and this was something I hadn't considered. I knew that I was due a more stable life – a home, a marriage, children – and then perhaps I could give something back to the world for once, for I had spent so much time with myself that I had forgotten what it was to be selfless. Yet the truth spoke back to me, and I knew that such a reality was beyond my grasp – what kind of man would ever love a woman like me? I am an outcast, a chaotic disarray of experiences that will forever haunt me, and I will never have a child, not that it upsets me; to raise a child that had an ounce of myself in them was a thought that repelled me. What I also knew was that, inherently, I wished for no such stability – I never would – and that these things were better left unplanned.

Aside from these considerations, the tedium of this place drove me insane at times; this would come out in intermittent episodes. I am often tranquil and surprisingly complacent, but this is at the expense of subsequent moments of distress, when my thoughts become so loud that I cannot concentrate on anything for more than a few moments. I was encountering one of these episodes at breakfast, when all of a sudden the clouds issued forth an omnipotent roll that boomed through the walls, the windows, the floor, as a mass of rain began to cascade from the sky, catching everyone's attention.

"*I hear thunder…*" Florence intoned. Linda, a patient of a nervous disposition, shifted in her seat; she does this whenever Florence speaks with the menacing timbre that cavorts on the edge of her words. Florence leaned back in her chair and lit a cigarette. "Happy birthday, Clarice," she said to me; "I bet you didn't think you would be spending it here." I wanted to ask her how she had known it was my birthday, but she frightened me too much, so I simply agreed, assuming that she knew everything – which she probably did.

"So tell me about San Francisco – I've always wanted to visit the States," she implored, as the whole room became attentive, with only the sound of the torrential downpour outside to be heard. The dreary dining room was ignited with a flash of lightning.

"Well," I began, considering what there was to say.

"Tell us the whole story," Florence urged.

"Okay, well, I was there from '62 to '68. I'd visited the city once before, and there was just something about it – it was this incredible place of creativity, acceptance, and, well – life. I'd never known anywhere like it. Obviously the whole country was lapsing out of one mess and into another – first it was Jim Crow, then Vietnam… but there was so much going on in that city; there were so many activists, dreamers, writers, artists and musicians that had built their own history, in a way. All the other stuff that was going on didn't seem to matter. Recently, it's become something different – that culture everyone now associates with it is just a commodity now; but me – and anyone who had the opportunity to go there before all that happened – we were the lucky ones." Florence seemed surprisingly interested by the sentiment, and as if deeply processing it, drew silently on her cigarette for a moment.

"That's the problem, isn't it?" she eventually said. "Commodification… alienation, reification, repressive desublimation masked as liberation," she lilted lyrically, as I experienced a distinct sense of *déjà vu*.

She raised her voice, "The whole world's going to shit. There's no fucking liberation happening; it's all an illusion, just like the idea that you can measure happiness in bank notes; the song's the same, they just changed the tune." Everyone sat uncomfortably in the silence. "Thought of the day," she added.

Despite her acrimonious cynicism, and a frightening absence of any visible emotion, there is something to be admired in Florence. Perhaps it is her unique honesty, or her remarkable way with words, but she holds an extraordinary power over everyone else in the ward, even the staff. Of all the patients, Florence is the most feared, for unlike the rest of us, she cannot feel the pangs of empathy. However, it appears that no one actually knows how she came to be here. I have heard that when asked, she stares blankly ahead and doesn't respond; if that is true, then I can only conclude that something unimaginably traumatic had happened to her in the past – for a girl so numbed against feeling does not show weakness without reason for it. She remains a mystery to all of us, like a code to which no one has a solution; she is utterly indecipherable.

A nurse entered the room, carrying a modest assemblage of envelopes and two or three parcels.

"These came in the post today," she said, placing them down in front of me. "There was so much for you, I thought I would deliver it personally."

I had received a few cards containing birthday wishes from friends and family who were clearly pitying me. One of the parcels was from my parents, containing a box of Turkish delight – a favourite of mine – and another box with a delicate silver bracelet inside. Polly had also sent me a pair of turquoise earrings, which she had bought on Carnaby Street. I then proceeded to open the last parcel. Whatever was inside had been carefully wrapped many times to protect it. Inside the parcel was an envelope with my name on it, and something I had not seen in what felt like decades. It was my copy of The Doors' *Strange Days* album, which I had owned in San Francisco – my most prized possession to date – but I had left that apartment in such a hurry, and with such contempt for everything in it, that I had managed to leave the record behind. As I held it in my hands, I felt the blood drain from my face to my heart, and I froze. I quickly snatched the envelope from the table, as if to stop anyone else from doing so, and retreated upstairs, leaving a confused group of patients in the dining room.

My heart beat rapidly as I struggled to contain my disordered – no – tempestuous, emotions. I collapsed onto the bed, prizing open the envelope which contained the entirety of my interest, the sole lines that I ached to read:

Dear Clare,

I hope this has reached you on your birthday, along with the Strange Days album, which I know was your favourite. I also know that you told me never to speak to you again, but when I heard what had happened, I could only see it as heartless to not write to you. In the mountain of things that you left at the apartment, I found a letter from Polly which had her phone number on it. After a seemingly endless month of emptiness, I called, just to find out if you were okay. Our relationship had ended so abruptly – I couldn't bear to think that you had done something reckless. Polly told me that you had no interest in talking to me, so I just left it there, knowing it would be completely futile trying to communicate with you from the other side of the world, if you had no interest in speaking to me.

More months passed, and although I had moved on, there were things which reminded me of you, and of my own incapacity to live as fully as I did when I was with you. I know most of the time we were stoned out of our minds, but you being there made it into this metaphysical thing, like we were doing something much grander; it felt almost spiritual.

I had adjusted back to being alone, when I received a letter from Polly about a month ago. She said that you often mentioned me on the phone, and explained how, before, she had just assumed that I was an egoistic drain – which I completely understand, given all that you were going through. She told me everything that had happened with you, and that she felt like she was the only connection between you and I. She included your address in her letter.

And so I write to you with the sole object of making an apology for the way I acted. Looking back, I can only recoil in disgust from the things I said. I should have been supportive and understanding, but instead I was selfish, caring more about what drugs I was taking than the fact that I was about to lose the person I loved. I never thought it would come to this, Clare, I really didn't. Often I can't help thinking what might have happened had I not been so stupid, but it's too painful. What's done is done. I am infinitely sorry.

I really hope you're okay. I don't expect you to forgive me – I was a horrible person, and I don't know why I couldn't see that. You always tried so hard to keep me in check – I understand that my thoughtless behaviour probably pushed you away, just as much as anything else did. I am truly sorry for everything. You don't have to write back; I only meant to write in sincere apology, hoping, at the back of my mind somewhere, that you might one day forgive me.

Clint.

The letter which lay in my hands seemed to me the most precious thing I had ever held. It afforded me relief of the most sublime kind; the monotony of this place had worn me down to feeling happiness at the even slightest thing, so this left me exhilarated. Around twenty minutes later, Nettie entered the room, carrying what I had left on the table downstairs, a look of concern overspreading her face. I then realised how erratic I must have looked, rapidly storming off with a record and a letter.

"Is that from Clint?" she asked, sitting down on her bed to face me.

"It's the first I've heard from him since I left. I didn't think I'd hear anything ever again."

"God, that's a shock," she responded.

"I know. It's an apology." I fought to maintain my composure; my feelings were manifold and heavy, like every key was being pressed down on the piano at once.

"I feel awful." I tried to prevent myself from saying these words, but out they spilled, like the rain falling onto the ground outside. The storm was still happening. The thunder roared overhead, as if to proclaim the fateful realisation which suddenly filled me: I loved him. I could not suppress it; I still loved Clint. I had blocked him from my thoughts, but his letter seemed to reinvigorate everything I really felt for him, and that was love. A host of possibilities exploded, but they left me essentially helpless.

If only I could have left right then and there for San Francisco, and resumed a life that had been snuffed out too soon. My rash decisions to leave the beginnings of entire lives behind me had been my ruin every time, and this seemed only to warn me to stay put in the ward – not that I had any control over it anyway. However, a responsibility had now been placed in my hands, and that was whether or not I would write back. Despite every reason there was not to write back, I could not rid myself of the overpowering desire to do so.

"Don't allow him to let you feel this way. Men are so manipulative."

At the time, overlooking a mere attempt at consolation, Nettie's comment enraged me; what right had she to judge a man she had never met? I didn't want to feel so defensive, yet at the same time I trembled with frustration. As much as I had disliked his drug habits, as much as I detested our arguments, no other relationship was adequate; yet what could possibly come of it now? As much as I fought against the truth, I knew that I would never make it back to San Francisco.

"I know," I replied, unwillingly resenting her, but perhaps Nettie was right. Maybe men were manipulative – they manipulated entire countries, after all. I quickly expelled this thought – Clint and I were not of that nature; there was no unequal power balance, and I knew it.

"Anyway, you've got to focus on surviving here first. For the time being, *this* is our life." Nettie appeared more to be reminding herself of this, as a disheartening and intensely forlorn smile forced itself across her face. All the compassion and inner beauty in the world could not obscure her pain; I fear she may never free herself from it.

"The Largactil's just making me feel terrible all the time," I said.

"Just wait until they give you electroshock therapy – they won't let you leave without having that experience."

"Well I've gone four months without having an outburst, and I've only two left, so they're going to have to search hard for a reason to subject me to *that*."

"Oh, they'll find one," she said darkly.

"What's it like?"

"Terrifying. You feel so helpless, because you are. You know that the electric current is going to wipe out some of your memory – that's the most unnerving thing. The memory loss is only short-term, but surely if they did it enough times, that's got to have some lasting damage. And then for about a week afterwards, you know you're only half-there; there's this persistent feeling that something's been taken from you. The shock itself is horrific too; feels exactly like you would expect – as if an unreasonably high voltage is overrunning your brain. And then comes the overwhelming exhaustion, because all your mental energy has been sucked out in the process."

Listening to her account, goosebumps had appeared on my skin. "But," she continued, "it helps with the depression, because it wipes out the entire train of thought that led you to feeling depressed in the first place. You forget how to think that way for a while, but it normally comes back; it's like re-reading a book after some time, and then remembering how it all goes again."

Imaginably, I did not like the sound of one bit of it, and hoped that I would be discharged before I met such a dire fate.

"Sorry, I'm not being very supportive," Nettie added. "It's this place – the negativity just bleeds into every crevice!" she suddenly exclaimed, standing up abruptly. She rushed to the window, and tightly gripped the bars in front of it, pressing her face against them for a moment and staring desperately at the lawn outside. This is where the difficulty lay; it was moments like these when I felt like a prisoner. This feeling cancelled out the comfort that the ward sometimes provided, and it was clearly affecting Nettie too.

"Don't you ever just want to go for a walk? We should go for a walk!" she cried, turning around. "I just can't stand it in here!" I had never seen her so anxious and impulsive. I presumed that being reminded of electroshock therapy had put her on edge.

"Okay," I responded, slightly nervously; but the fresh air would soon calm her down, and the rain had stopped.

Before going outside, we had to ask permission to walk

around the grounds, and sign out. The sun was beginning to peep through the clouds, so that it cast a golden light onto the trees, contrasting against the pale grey sky. We walked in silence for a while, before either of us spoke.

"I do want to get out of here a lot of the time," Nettie sighed, "but then, after I've calmed down, I realise that it's not so bad; I could stay here for a long time." It then occurred to me that it really was quite possible that nothing lay beyond these boundaries for Nettie, that she existed only within the limits of the institution. I shuddered at this thought.

We ventured out of the ward's sight, and down towards the wooded area, which lay about half a mile away at the opposite end. A small brook ran gently beside the path, which Nettie stopped by, crouched down and dipped her hands in.

"I have the whole world right here," she said, letting the water flow around her fingertips. There was something romantic and saddening about this gesture. She then lifted her hands towards the sky; "It's all here," she repeated, "it's all here."

"I know it might sound like I've confined myself to something so small," she continued, after a few moments of silence, "but it's easier to allow yourself to be happy when you can be sure of what will happen tomorrow, and the day after that, and all the days after that."

How different we were – it was such certainty that I constantly wished to avoid – it was precisely the unpredictability of life which retained its excitement for me. As we reached the iron fence which kept us within the grounds, we both stopped, held the bars like prisoners, and looked out at the wide open fields ahead of us.

"It's all here," Nettie repeated again; this time she murmured it low, under her breath, almost as if she were desperate to ingrain it in herself. The light wind brushed against our faces and over the grass in the fields. We both watched this expanse, moved by the breeze, as if it were a work of art.

"It's going to be okay," I heard myself say; it seemed not to be addressed to anyone in particular, but the words blended into the air, the trees, the sky, the view. Over those few moments, something had calmed us; a serenity passed over our senses, softening the edges of our thoughts, and we walked back as if in a dream, focusing only on the sunlight, the flowers – whatever was currently affecting us in each moment.

This indistinct feeling accompanied me for the rest of the day; the commotion of the morning had exhausted me already – I am so easily drained by the slightest jolts these days – and so I retired back upstairs, while Nettie went to the day room. Shutting the door behind me, I took the *Strange Days* album from my bed and put it on the record player, which I had bought at an old junk shop. I knew that being reminded of a better past would do me no good, but I could not resist. I lay motionless on the bed, listening to that album for as long as it would take me to forget who and where I was, to be able to separate myself from that doleful figure, lying torpid and numb. I closed my eyes for a moment, absorbed by the music, listening to each instrument, word and inflection. Each song had its own meaning to me, explaining more than I ever could, but I could not listen to a single one without images of San Francisco, acid trips, and Clint emerging from it. This album was permanently entwined with memories I could not shake, and it became painful to listen to. Yet, again, it was the type of pain that is taken pleasure in, and it only compelled me to keep listening.

I was distracted from this reverie by the entrance of Nettie and Florence, in high spirits.

"Look what we've got!" Florence pulled a small, transparent bag out of her pocket and shook it. It was like being back at school, had I been the rebellious teenager.

"Where did you get that?" I asked, genuinely surprised.

"I maintain my connections."

"That's just ordinary stuff, right?" Is it so wrong to admit that I didn't trust her? She looked at me as if I was completely incompetent.

"Yeah. You want to smoke it with us or not?" she asked with a hint of impatience.

I knew that it could do little harm; smoking or not, my hallucinations persisted, even on antipsychotics, which only reduced their frequency, and I did not care enough about this matter to refuse. Singing the lyrics to *Moonlight Drive*, the three of us retreated to the back of the chapel, vivacious and carefree, as if we were not psychiatric patients.

August arrived with the ever-growing anticipation of my leave. Time seemed to move faster, and in a month and a half I would be free; I was convinced that my condition had improved – it was now something I felt I could live with. Amelia was merely a passing vision, a background noise which I had learnt to ignore. I had received numerous sessions with a psychiatrist, Dr Yates, during my stay, who helped me to see her as no more than a symptom, just like any other. She still appeared in the moonlight, her pale, menacing eyes staring back into mine, but I knew she was powerless in the face of rationality.

"Has she ever told you to do anything?" Dr Yates asked in therapy.

"Yes."

"Can you give an example?"

"Well, she told me to admit myself here." I could see no point in withholding the truth, yet hearing myself speak, I sounded as insane as anyone else who saw things that were not there.

"I see… she's clearly concerned about your wellbeing," he smiled.

"She seems to want something from me... yes... she is somewhat concerned about me."

"What does she want from you?"

"I don't know. I don't care anymore. I try not to listen."

"Well that's good," he replied.

Dr Yates had a face of benevolence, humility; I cannot quite discern what exactly it was that gave me this impression, but the lines on his face had the distinct look of being gained from years of laughter.

"I want you to know that these hallucinations will probably never cease completely. You have told me about your use of LSD over the past few years, which I would advise you never to use again, if you hope to improve, but I am also aware that your hallucinations span far further back than your drug use. I remember you saying that no one in your family suffers from schizophrenia. Are you absolutely sure of that?" I had thought about it many times in the past, and yet I still could not bring to mind any family member who suffered from it.

"Not that I know of," I replied.

"There is a very strong genetic basis for this disorder – that's why I asked. Have any of your relatives ever shown symptoms which may imply psychosis – talking to themselves, irrational behaviour, paranoia?"

"No." I wanted to cooperate, but I was clueless as to the cause of my hallucinations.

"It is strange, to say the least. What you describe sounds almost like being haunted by a ghost. You're lucky to be alive in this day and age – a few hundred years ago, you would have been subjected to exorcisms; although, between you and I, the convulsions induced by electroshock therapy amount to much the same thing. I'll see to it that you don't receive that treatment – it's wholly unnecessary, in my opinion."

A sense relief filled me, for since Nettie had told me that it was inevitable, I had been dreading the moment when I was to be dragged down the corridor by cold faces in white coats and gloves.

"Thank you."

"Is there anything else you want to talk about?" For a moment I wondered whether I should mention the letter from Clint, but the last thing I wanted to do was create more problems.

"No, nothing else."

"Well then, your improvement has been one of the most rapid and remarkable I've seen in years, and I think you can thank yourself for that – it takes a strong mind to contend with such a thing as schizophrenia."

I left that room with an alarming optimism, which I couldn't trust. Everything seemed to be becoming clearer to me, now that I had grabbed the reins of control. What I did next was either excessively foolish or has done more good than harm; I gradually began to diminish my intake of antipsychotics, by hiding each tablet under my tongue or in the side of my mouth, until I had the opportunity to quickly dispose of it. The side effects of Largactil were not only physically but psychologically ruthless, and too many times had I heard it being described as a 'chemical lobotomy' – the accuracy of which I was beginning to discover. If there is one fear which brews within each patient here, it is the fear of losing the faculty of awareness. We are all familiar with tales of the past; psychosurgery may have died its long-awaited death for the majority of us – reserved only for the most dire necessities – but the terror endures. Few of us place our full trust in medication. I reasoned that if I could not trust a drug which altered the chemistry of the brain in one way, and caused me to hallucinate, then neither could I trust a drug which altered it in another way, and caused me not to hallucinate. But it is the half-living which scares me the most, and perhaps irrationally, for it is unlikely the brain could work sufficiently to even understand this state while in it. We need not read books when finding a case of *vegetablisation*, as Florence calls it. There are many talked about instances of it here, although one can never be quite sure as to the veracity of some of these tales; crazed doctors cutting away recklessly at the human brain to create hideous silence were the exaggerations of the disturbed. Nonetheless, with the surgery room still in place and the knives out of our own hands, there was certainly trepidation on the subject, cutting deep into our nerves – and it must not be forgotten that no one's head is in its right place here.

The slow reduction of my Largactil intake removed the fear of at least a chemical lobotomy, and any unwanted side effects; I also noticed a significant improvement in myself after a week of reducing my dosage down to nothing; I was more alive, in every imaginable sense, and only then was I made fully aware that a recovery was taking place. It was by no means complete, but I knew then that I would soon be out of here, healed – as far as one can be with a lifelong illness.

Inevitably, people arrive and depart here, and as I was preparing to depart, another patient arrived. I first encountered her in the corridor where the bedrooms are situated, ambling aimlessly, presumably lost.

"Forgive me," she began, as I was opening the door to my own room. "I only arrived here yesterday, and I am already lost in the halls of this maze-like building. Could you possibly tell me where I might find Dr Yates' office?" Slightly taken aback by her sudden question, and the elaborate way in which she had posed it, I sent her in the right direction, noticing only the bewildered look in her eyes, and not much else about her appearance.

I walked into the bedroom, where Nettie lay, reading an old issue of *Vogue*.

"There's actually something on Anna Karina in here, would you believe," she said, before noticing the puzzled expression on my face. "You okay?"

"Yeah," I said with a nod. "I just saw a new patient looking for Dr Yates on this floor."

"How odd… she must be really dishevelled."

"I know, I remember being like that."

"So do I – it's astonishing how quickly you get used to it, though." She paused, and stared blankly ahead of her for a moment.

"There was a time when I would read magazines like this and want to look like the people in them." She smiled fondly at the black and white print of Karina, her closed eyelashes brushing the tops of her cheeks, they were so long. "Being here makes you realise how pointless all of that is. Now my biggest desire is to get a good night's sleep. You learn what's important here."

Of all the things I have heard during my time in the ward, this statement seemed to me the most powerful, the most truthful. Indeed, this is no place for whiling away time with frivolity, that is, if one is not afraid to relinquish it. To cherish materialistic ideals in a place like this may connect one with the world outside, but those ideals do not apply here; in the ward, one is at war with herself, and those unable to free themselves from values which do not exist within these walls cannot hope for peace.

Being in a small institution, where the majority of patients are long-term, gossip tends to spread like wildfire. The arrival of this new patient was undoubtedly going to be the subject of everyone's conversation. When the news on television and in papers seemed so unreal and irrelevant to us, we were more often intrigued by minor adjustments within the ward. By dinner time, the news had circulated the entire building, and the dining room was simmering with talk.

"Apparently she's in room eleven," came an utterance from the table behind me.

"Is that the first time… since?" was the curious rejoinder.

"I think so."

"What happened in room eleven?" I asked my own company, slightly concerned.

"Oh, a woman hung herself there about a year ago. People have been half-hysterical about it ever since. I bet the new patient probably isn't even in there," said Mary, with the rational authority of a mother trying to undo the shadowy effects of ghost stories upon her child.

"I can't see her down here," said Nettie, scanning the room for new faces. "What does she look like, Clare?"

"I can't remember," I responded.

"What do you mean you can't remember?"

"I don't know, I just didn't really look at her."

"She's probably doing what Clare did in her first week and weeping a thousand tears in her chamber," Florence teased.

"Maybe we should go and talk to her," Nettie suggested.

"Yeah, I'm sure talking to you two will make her feel more at ease," Florence replied flatly.

"You can talk," Mary responded, sending her an unrelenting stare.

Florence ignored her for moment, and then, "Bitch."

"Psychopath."

"Sociopath, actually."

At that, Mary rose from her chair. "You make me sick," she said, before leaving the room.

"I am sick, baby!" Florence called after her, leaning back in her chair and chuckling to herself. "Looks like it's someone's time of the month."

A few minutes later we were joined by Frida, who looked whiter than usual and notably pensive as she sat down. She stared at her food for a moment with a look of mild disgust, before speaking. "It is only due to gnawing hunger that I can bear to eat anything tonight."

"That's the only reason anyone eats this sediment," Florence uttered under her breath.

"What's the matter?" asked Nettie. "Are you unwell?"

"I have just seen something entirely inhumane; there is more madness out there than there is in here." She pushed the overcooked tinned vegetables around on her plate, then looked up at me. "Perhaps you are safer in here."

"What happened?" I asked.

"They've found the body of a famous Hollywood actress in her home, brutally murdered, eight months into her pregnancy."

"Which actress?"

"What?"

"That's horrible!"

It was only these kinds of stories, the twisted helter skelters of violence and death, which captured people's attention in the ward; they were undeniably shocking, and especially fascinating for certain individuals. We soon forgot about the new patient, and discussed this current subject.

"It never fails to amaze me how evil people can be," Nettie remarked.

"Whoever did it probably isn't evil, just crazy," conjectured Florence.

"Can't they be both?"

"No, I don't think so. Being crazy means there's something wrong in the head – you can't distinguish between what's good and what's evil; you just do what the voices tell you," Florence said with a chuckle. We all looked uncomfortably at the table.

"Sorry – I overstepped a line," she said mechanically, with the utmost insincerity.

We finished our food in silence, grimacing at the lasting

image that now lay in our minds. After dinner Nettie and I went upstairs together, briefly stopping at room eleven to see whether it had a new inhabitant.

"She's not staying in here. God, rumours travel fast." Growing increasingly inquisitive, we made our way back to our room.

"I just hope she's okay," sighed Nettie as she got into bed, clearly agitated by the absence of this new patient.

"She'll be fine, I'm sure of it," I tried to reassure her.

I rolled over in my bed and stared at the wall, attempting to recall what I had noticed about her in the corridor. I was with an unshakable feeling that she was like myself; it lived in her eyes – the only detail to which I had paid any attention. Perhaps I have known these walls for too long, but I had begun to see it in others – the traces of my own illness. Those who are like me seem to carry a distinct quality within their eyes; they dart about too hastily, stay still for a fraction too long, open slightly wider than they should; yet it is not just these motions which characterise the eyes that see what others cannot. The essence of a distortion of the physical world seems to manifest itself within them, in ways that only those who have similar experiences can discern. Other than this minute detail, I could barely recollect anything distinct about her features, and only the mannerisms of one who is disoriented and dazed. Thinking about my initial days in the ward, I lapsed into an uneasy and restless sleep.

The next morning, Amelia appeared to me in the bathroom. The absence of any noise – aside from the humming of the pipes that ran across and up the walls and under the tiled floor – was interrupted by a voice coming from one of the mirrors. I had not seen her in a whole week, and her sudden presence had me completely startled.

Do you believe in ghosts? she asked, swinging softly in her nightdress, awaiting my response.

"Why?" I replied. Dr Yates had taught me the valuable method of questioning Amelia's ambiguous inquiries, so as to uncover and challenge their meaning.

I am merely curious, for I myself believe in ghosts, although only the ones that we create ourselves – "daggers of the mind, false creations, proceeding from the heat-oppressed brain…" is that not how it goes? She smiled, as if she had enlightened me, yet I remained more in darkness than ever when it came to understanding her; as far as I could comprehend, I had not created Amelia; she had ravaged everything within her reach.

"What exactly is your point?" I asked, frustrated, resting my hands on the edge of the sink to hold myself up. I had suddenly been overcome by an abnormal heaviness from within, and my breaths were becoming more drawn out, deeper; yet when I looked back up at the mirror, Amelia was gone; I was alone again in the cold bathroom. And still, something was peculiar; there was an irregularity in this moment, an unusual atmosphere. It took me a while to realise that it was the discomposing instinct that I was being watched. In my peripheral vision I saw a figure, tall and slender, delicate, feminine, with long, fair hair and pale skin. It could not be. I prayed that she was not there. It could not be her; but I had not even turned my head before my legs were weak and everything was plunged into darkness.

I awoke shortly, perhaps minutes after. My vision was blurred at first, and I thought for a moment that Amelia stood over me, her faded hair dangling and brushing against my cheeks. I closed my eyes and heard a voice that did not belong to her.

"Are you alright?"

I looked up again, desperately hoping that Amelia had gone – only to find that I had been mistaken the whole time; as I dared look into the face of the figure above me, I instantly recognised her as the new patient. She looked to be in her late twenties, and had a certain familiarity in her face, which I could not quite place at first; but then it occurred to me that I detected something of myself in her; in fact, we could have been sisters based on our facial similarities; each line, feature and blemish was almost identical, uncannily so. But in spite of this, we were entirely different in our complexion, with my dark hair and eyes, and her blue-eyed blondness which had caused me to conflate her with Amelia.

"You were fortunate that I was here to catch you. If you don't mind my asking, what happened?" she asked, her eyes full of concern.

"I'm not sure – that's never happened before," I lied, embarrassed by my illness, as if she herself were not ill too, in some way. The young woman gave me an odd look, scrutinising me for a long time.

"Ah, I met you in the corridor yesterday! I thought your face looked familiar," she finally said, after I had once again surveyed her own all-too-familiar face.

"Did you manage to find Dr Yates' office?" I asked inconsequentially, wishing only to hurry the conversation along. After what had just occurred, I was in no frame of mind to be talking to anyone.

"Yes – yes, I managed just fine, thank you. I've been placed in a room all by myself, and it is impossible to find my way around, you see. I have no friends here," she said, her big blue eyes rolling gravely to meet mine. The day before, I had wondered whether her strange manner of speaking was due to some kind of distress, but even now, she spoke in that same formal, nervous tone. I was becoming increasingly interested in her.

"Which room are you in? I'll visit you sometime," I offered.

"Oh, will you? Oh, thank you, kind – I'm dreadfully sorry, but I do not know your name." Intrigued as I was, our conversation was growing more disconcerting by the second;

principally, I sensed danger in her manic demeanour.

"Clare," I responded.

"Clare… like the saint. What a beautiful name – clear and bright, as the light of the moon on a cloudless night." She did not tell me her name, but I had taken her response as a cue to try to leave as quickly as possible.

"Thank you, it's short for Clarice, actually—"

"Oh—"

"But I've wasted enough of your time – I'll leave you to shower. Perhaps I'll see you later."

"A great pleasure to meet you, Clarice!"

I left the bathroom, dreading the remainder of my days here. I knew it would be unwise to allow any kind of rapport to form between this woman and myself.

At eight o'clock, I went downstairs and tongued my dose of Largactil.

"Still no sign of the new girl yet," noted Florence as I sat down.

"She was just about to have a shower when I came downstairs."

"Did you talk to her?"

"Briefly, but I'm almost certain she caught me having one of my hallucinations." I decided against giving any sort of description of her as neurotic; if anyone could notice that for themselves, it was Florence.

"Let's just hope she's as mad as you, then," she responded, but I knew that such hope would be unnecessary.

At times I wondered whether one day, the people who were not put away would see as I did. Of course, they could with the aid of certain substances, but I could not help mulling over the matter, entertaining the chance that madness could collide with sense on its own accord; yet I knew that by definition, that was impossible. There is no in-between, only an edge which is fiercely clung to before one hoists themselves back up again, or falls. I know from experience that I am capable of being both 'sane' and 'insane', but never simultaneously, and not necessarily by choice. Thus, I wondered whether people outside the ward – in cities, small towns, country dwellings – would ever be able to see as those in straitjackets and padded cells did.

"I will always hate you, Clare," Florence continued, completely to my surprise.

"What? Why?" I replied, genuinely perplexed.

"Because I'm envious of you." She was silent for a moment or two, then lowered her voice and looked earnestly into my eyes. "You've travelled; you know what it's like to speed down a Californian highway with the windows down and the salty air caressing your face. That's something I will only ever be able to imagine. Not to mention, you know what it's like to be loved. And successful. And liked by many, I'm sure. My whole life has been so dull in comparison. *Nothing happens, nobody comes, nobody goes, it's awful.* I'm not searching for pity. I'm just having a bad day, you know – one of those days where you're certain you'd blow your brains out the first chance you got – you just happen to be sitting right across from me. But nonetheless, I hate you. Now tell me how fucked up I am like everyone else does."

I knew that any response I gave would be futile. I felt my throat tighten as I thought about what she had said; there was no adequate response. A part of me could not believe that no one had ever loved her, but how should I know? I have been loved all my life.

"I'm sorry," I said. I was sorry for having no words to say, for being like an empty well, providing nothing but a caliginous hollow for her to fall even deeper into. I was sorry for being that person, the one who always had it better than everyone else, and for no just reason.

"Sorry for what?" she responded; "for having people care

about you? For at least trying to make something of your life? For not being a waste of flesh and bone? Why do you think I'm like this, Clare? I am *nothing*. This is the only place where people haven't treated me like it, and that's only because they're terrified I'll stab them in the night. You have no idea what it was like—" Her voice broke off. She had frozen mid-speech, eyes wide open, transfixed on the tray of food that had no taste in front of her.

"Leave me alone!" she yelled suddenly, as I helplessly left her at the table. I had never seen her in this state, so completely overwrought with distress. As I turned away, two nurses dashed over to Florence and said something in muffled voices.

"Don't touch me! Mind your own business!" she cried, as the nurses proceeded to grab her by both arms. They were beginning to tug her away, when she produced a scream so peaked with horror and protestation that it silenced the whole room.

"Just let me speak!" she shouted, as all eyes fell upon her.

At that moment, to any visiting stranger, she would merely have exemplified the deranged mental patient, her eyes wild, her whole body shaking with white-hot rage, her jaw locked in a contortion of resentment; but to us, she was something we had never seen before, like a rare flower that blooms in a field of wilted ones. She loosened herself from the nurses and spoke directly to them, so that the whole room could hear. "You call this treatment? For once I show that I too am a human being and you treat me like an animal for it?"

She was grabbed once again by the nurses and dragged away, but continued to shout down the corridor, until they sedated her.

IV

In 1961 I graduated from the Royal Academy of Music, washed up with the debris of my youth and elevated dreams of solace. Conscious of it or not, by this time I was seeking solace not only from my personal experiences, but from my position as a young woman. I had to prove myself worthy of existence – either by fostering another, or by doing something truly extraordinary with my own. My degree was practically worthless beside any man's, and I understood that in order to get anywhere, with or without it, something had to be done on my part. Although, I still somewhat believed that I was erroneous in this estimation, that I was a perversely and persistently dissatisfied individual who could not settle for mediocrity, when some would do anything to obtain a morsel of it. At times, I even questioned whether it was worthiness that I sought, or merely an advantage. The latter prospect frightened me, but I was and still am always confused in this respect, and I don't know where all the self-doubt comes from.

To escape all doubt, I abandoned the past as thoroughly as I could, and that is when the inevitability of change struck me like a wave of truth: Kennedy was shot, The Beatles converged, Martin Luther King emerged from the shards of a broken country; my hemline gradually raised, I met Clint, my hair grew longer. Everything was rearranged too quickly for me to process it with a full and deep understanding, and somewhere along the obscure road that is my existence, I was no longer the epitome of mediocrity; no – I was an outcast, a lunatic, a schizophrenic.

No one, as far as I could gather, had suspected a thing. It was only I who knew, from the first moment I saw her ghostly face in the mirror, that I was not like everybody else. But despite the difficulties which would inevitably line every path I walked down, there was an unanticipated victory in seeing more distinctly that nothing is solid. It must be similar to the sensation a child has when they first notice those kaleidoscopic patterns that dance on a white ceiling, the transparent orbs that float in the sky, and objects that subsequently appear in different places each time they blink. It was this sensation that oddly reassured me at times that perhaps the others were missing something.

It was a quarter to four in the afternoon, and I was restless. Flies buzzed outside, an aeroplane made its tracks somewhere above, I sat on a chair in my room, absentmindedly swinging my leg from side to side. The boredom was eating into my thoughts, and nothing I could think of would end it. At twenty-nine years, I have far more lines on my face than is natural, although there is nothing unusual about it; those who have had sleepless nights over crying children, oppressive workloads, and chronic stress, all share in these same lines. Nonetheless, I resented the toll that years of anxiety had taken on my appearance, and not a day would pass when I did not look tired and ill. I had lost a lot of colour where the sun used to create a glowing tan. In the ward, everyone else had suffered in the same way; a lustrous lock or smooth, clear skin was a rarity. Everyone had been eroded like rocks, only in reverse, so that our smooth surfaces gained jagged edges and deep clefts.

The door of the room opened slowly and Nettie's face appeared, her eyes big and green and sorrowful. She sighed and walked in, very much within her own sphere, setting herself down daintily upon the bed, as if flinging herself would rupture her entire frame. She too had many lines and shadows on her face, indelible as those that marked her memory.

"I hate it when she's like this. Just gone," Nettie murmured.

"Florence?"

She exhaled slowly and nodded. "This happened the last time she had shock therapy. She stayed in bed for days, and then when she came out, she would barely speak for a few more; then she was okay again, but it was so wrong in that gap of time. She just wasn't the same."

"She'll come around before you know it," I tried to reassure her.

"I know – I just have this fear that everyone will leave me behind – you're leaving, Florence isn't talking to anyone, and I want to stay. I want everything to be exactly as it was."

I could not help but pity her broken soul; she wished for no more than stability in her shaken condition.

"You can't fight change," I responded, mercilessly. At this she replied with indignation, almost despair.

"Why not?" I looked at her in silence, slightly puzzled by her remark. She raised her voice, "Why must there be change? Because where there is time, there is change? True, but here we can stop time – you see – each day is the same, practically indistinguishable from the next. We don't measure in hours, but in dosage. Here, you *can* fight time."

What Nettie had evidently missed was that where there is mortality, there is time; no matter how exhaustively she forced herself to forget the number of hours in a day, to forget how long it took to perform a task, to believe that she was the same person now that she would be in five years' time, each second that she breathed, a second would pass: a second for the rain to fall, for the eye to blink, for the phone to ring, until one day, too many seconds will have passed for Nettie to convince herself that time can be defeated.

I looked into her troubled eyes, knowing that there was no way of communicating this message to someone so deluded. I lamented my lack of a desperate urge to escape, even when staring into the nauseating face of irrationality. Avoiding either encouraging or condescending her, I nodded at her wild suggestion of eliminating the notion of time, and did not say a word.

There was a palpable dissemblance in the dining hall. It is true, Florence has such an unprecedented air about her that she can continually subjugate the attention of each patient, even in her absence. Is it possible that a room can be filled with both ease and unease? If so, then this is the concoction that immersed us all. As Nettie and I sat down with our food, we were approached by Andrea, a patient whom I had hardly spoken to before.

"Clare, you've seen the new patient, haven't you?" she asked, in a manner so fierce that it verged on threatening.

"I've seen her twice, but only briefly," I responded.

"What was she like?" she urged.

"Odd, to say the least," I replied, truthfully, for she would find that out sooner or later.

"Didn't you say she spoke unnaturally?" Nettie prompted me. At that, Andrea glared at her, hit the table hard with the palm of her hand and stormed off, catching the attention of one of the nurses. Nettie and I exchanged a private look, which said, *Someone's clearly not taken their meds.*

"I think you should find out which room this patient is staying in," said Nettie. "She's probably lonely, and you seem to be the only person she's spoken to. You know how people here form attachments – maybe she's attached to you."

"As uncomfortable as that sounds, you could be right," I

said, and then paused for a moment, considering whether or not I should continue, but I found myself speaking anyway. "What really unsettled me about our encounter was the resemblance between us. It was more in the face than in anything else, but it was like looking into a mirror, and seeing a parallel self in it – that is, if I had blonde hair and blue eyes and were far stranger."

"Like Amelia, then," Nettie suggested. There was indeed something inseparable between her and Amelia, although I could never quite identify it.

"I really am losing my mind, aren't I?" I said, and as these syllables wended their way across the table, something was ripped from my soul, something short-circuited in the brain, and suddenly I was inexplicably disoriented.

I couldn't help it, I began to panic, feeling an intense paranoia rise within like a relentless flood; I had never experienced anything quite like it. I had so little control over my words, for no apparent reason. I spoke hurriedly, as if there was no time to breathe.

"I need to go back on my Largactil – I'm going crazy – I'm going fucking crazy, I can feel it. Okay, I'm going back on my Largactil." I could sense Nettie staring at me in astonishment. "Stop looking at me! Everyone's looking at me, aren't they? They're always looking at me. Oh God, everyone thinks I'm crazy! I need to go back on my medication – do you think they can give me a dose now? You have no idea how much I need it – I need to – no, no – I need to – San Francisco – oh my! Everything is in San Francisco – the flowers, the flowers – what am I doing here? No, I'm here to get better. I need medication, therapy, psychoanalysis – she said I would get better—"

"Nurse!" Nettie cried.

"Please, please, please, please get me a dose of Largactil," I asked the nurse, gripping her hand.

"I can't administer anything to you right now – you'll have to wait, I'm afraid."

"Please,"

"I'm sorry. Why don't you go and have a rest?"

Realising that the madness of the ward had finally trickled into the very blood which ran through my veins, I sank back into my chair, disgusted. I sneered at the nurse, who continued to stare back at me, as if I were an unruly child. I knew that I was behaving inappropriately, but I was revelling in it. Saying nothing, the nurse pursed her thin lips together, turned on her heel and walked back to her station. After a few minutes of sitting in silence, I rose and left the room.

As I found my way into the cool corridor, the surge of madness subsided; the sudden quiet induced calm, yet still I continued walking aimlessly. Perhaps if I walked up and down each staircase, past every room and round every corner, I could be brought back to my senses, I thought; but my ambling was shortly interrupted by the sound of light footsteps running up behind me. I turned around and saw Nettie.

"Clare." She ran right up to me, until she was at a speaking distance. There were furrows in her brow, a trembling in her lower lip, a lustre in her eyes, which all informed me that her next words held the potential to send me back into hysteria. "The new patient – are you sure she was a patient?" I tried to deny the implication of her question, approaching it the only way I could – by using every drop of reason within me. Attempting to recall each detail of our brief conversation, it seemed clear that she could only have been a patient; she was there, in the bathroom, saying that she had been placed alone in a room and had no company, and most importantly, her entire demeanour suggested mental instability.

"She must have been," I said, as Nettie's face sank. After a long pause of the most excruciating kind, she confirmed what

I had suspected the moment she posed the question.

"It's just that, someone asked the nurse about her just now, and she said that there was no new patient on record – and you're the only person who's actually seen her." Cutting the conversation short, I left Nettie standing there as I began to walk rapidly to the lobby.

The lobby was a room that was permanently chilly from a lack of insulation and its cold marble floor. It appeared gloomy in the dim evening light, and looking up at the high ceiling, I staggered on the spot. Composing myself, I walked to the desk as coolly as I could, and asked whom the last person to be admitted to the ward was. When the receptionist began to ask questions, I replied that Nettie had tried to dispute the matter with me, and would not rest until it was proven either way. Most likely not believing a word of this poor fabrication, but nonetheless, wanting to put my mind at ease, she pulled out a thick red book, filled with loose documents and lists. She flicked to a page towards the back and scanned down it with her finger.

"Dorothy Rome, admitted on the twentieth of July." I knew who Dorothy was; she suffered with a severe form of schizophrenia – it had impaired her brain to the extent that she believed everyone around her to be a cat – but this new patient was not Dorothy.

"No one after that?" I asked, trying not to sound too frantic.

"No one after that."

I thanked the receptionist, stating that my belief had been verified – playing along with the lie – and bid her good evening.

As soon as I turned away from the desk, my face began to feel as if it could shatter; an accumulation of every irrational thought I had ever had seemed to rush back to me then. Walking faster than I could realise, I headed straight out of the lobby, down the corridor on the right, out of the side door, and onto the driveway – until I found myself facing the patient whose very existence was now called into doubt. In a hazardous attempt to avoid confrontation, I walked straight past her and headed for the woods.

Now running deeper into the obscure twilight, I wanted only to be as far away as I could get from the ward.

I ran alongside the brook which led to a lake. It was surrounded by long, thick grass and a host of birch trees. A vaporous mist skirted the periphery of the water, rising from its surface like phantoms among the trees. I stopped near the edge of the lake, hearing only the subdued sound of the wind, whistling quietly through the gaps between branches and blades of grass. The water's surface was tranquil, interrupted only by the occasional gust of wind, which sent slight ripples across it.

As I looked more closely, to my absolute terror, I glimpsed the reflection of the unlisted patient standing behind me, and to my left was Amelia. These were my own creations, and now was what felt like a finality, a chance to rid myself of them – as if that was ever a possibility.

It was then that the most inexplicable of phenomena occurred. Both figures stood beside me, although only as reflections on the water, and did not speak a word. I waited for a number of minutes, and still, neither spoke. Even as I began to talk, falling to the overgrown bed of grass about my feet, not a single sound passed from their lips.

"What am I being punished for?" I called out. "I've been denied the chance to live and think freely, and for what? Of what use am I now?"

I talk to myself like a maniac; I stand by the edge of a lightless lake, asking the air around me what I have done, as if there has to be a reason for everything. All I know is my past, which has persisted in eclipsing my future; how can I look ahead if I cannot see beyond these illusions, which dance before my eyes in horrific splendour? I can only review the contents of my years, and establish that I was not built for this world. Idealist or pessimist, I know that I cannot go on in a place which defines me as insane, but overlooks itself. We live in a globule of contradiction. Don't assume, they say, but don't ask stupid questions. Say the obvious and you are *clichéd*, say something original and you will find that it's not. Cultivate your mind in a world where looks matter more; preen yourself in a world where it's shallow to do so. It makes no difference. Have some humility, be ruthless; be a good Samaritan, but put yourself first. Have some empathy, but only sometimes. Don't be a prude, don't be a whore. Settle down before you get old but don't settle for just anyone. Be authentically false. Enjoy yourself with contrition. Hate yourself with love. Your misery is unwanted, and so are you, but don't be morbid about it. Be curious, don't ask questions. If people just *thought* about things, but not too much... make up your mind and stay open-minded. Plan, plan, plan, *carpe diem*. All you need is love and the credentials to say such a ridiculous thing. This is what I have learnt, and I am no longer fit to think coherently in an incomprehensible world. Like the yellowed keys of an antiquated piano, I am exhausted.

Now I lie, breathing in shivers, sinking slightly, on the surface of the lake. I have relinquished care, it is beyond reach now, gliding off into the wailing halls of the ward, the colourful streets of San Francisco. The drifting fragments of another revolution; they pass in a dazzling, prismatic show.

ACKNOWLEDGEMENTS

I would like to thank the following people for their ongoing encouragement and support in the production of this work: My dad, forced to read page after page of my unfinished manuscript and give valuable writing advice; my mother, for being endlessly supportive of my creative ambitions; Susannah Frieze; Petronella Phillips Devaney; Abi Worlock; Nicky Clarke; Dan Fenton; Nona Hencken-Spurling; Ashleigh Turner; 16 Howard Road ("nasty little titus bramble"); Florence Nolan; Sam Kohn; Hattie Upton-Dance; Liv Myers; and finally, my gratitude to Jeremy Thompson at The Book Guild, who made the decision to publish this novel.